Allies, Spies, and Conflicts

Provinces of Rome
Book 1

J. Clifton Slater

Provinces of Rome series and the associated books are the creation of J. Clifton Slater. Any use of *Allies, Spies, and Conflicts*, in part or in whole, requires express written consent. This is a work of fiction. Any resemblance to persons living or dead is purely coincidental. All rights reserved.

When I write, my mind becomes occupied with multiple stories, historical events, and the ancient environment. In short, it's a jumble of information, and much like pebbles in an avalanche, they tumble around without order. Thanks to Hollis Jones for guiding my wandering mind as I wrote this book. She kept me on the path, adjusted the structure, identified rough spots, and called my attention to overly long descriptions. Because of her, *Allies, Spies, and Conflicts* exists.

I'd also like to extend my appreciation to you. My readers are the reason I can spend my days doing research and writing stories. And so I say to you with a salute, *Euge*. Which translates from Latin to mean Bravo.

If you have comments, contact me:
GalacticCouncilRealm@gmail.com

For a list of books and series, or to sign up for my monthly newsletter and receive articles on ancient topics, go to my website:
www.JCliftonSlater.com

Allies, Spies, and Conflicts

Chapter 1 - Macedon, Macedon

Chapter 2 - Assault On The Beach

Chapter 3 - Chios Wine

Chapter 4 - The King Is Dead

Chapter 5 - Half My Fleet

Chapter 6 - A Common Danger

Chapter 7 - Take Charge

Chapter 8 - Mount Lycabettus

Chapter 9 - A Stoic of Athens

Chapter 10 - Har'ris To Ilion

Chapter 11 - East or West Direction

Chapter 12 - Provocative Assertion

Chapter 13 - As Good As Gone

Chapter 14 - The Boii Tribe

Chapter 15 - Three Gifts

Chapter 16 - Where He Emerged

Chapter 17 - Faded Horsehair Plume

Chapter 18 - Comedy or Tragedy

Chapter 19 - For This Mission

Chapter 20 - During Every Cruise

Chapter 21 - Marcus Lepidus

Chapter 22 - A Code Mark

Chapter 23 - Ruination of Attica

Chapter 24 - Enchanting Priestess

Chapter 25 - The Tall Tale

Chapter 26 - Let Me Judge

Chapter 27 - Never Without A Blade

Chapter 28 - City By The Strait

Chapter 29 - Insult The Goddess Oizys

Chapter 31 - A King's Compassion

The End

Coming Soon:

Provinces of Rome series book #2

Lies and Shadows

Author Notes:

Other books by J. Clifton Slater

Allies, Spies, and Conflicts

Allies, Spies, and Conflicts

Chapter 1 - Macedon, Macedon

To be the King of Macedonia required little more than walking two thousand four hundred steps. But if a man coveted the crown of Macedonia's famed King Philip II, and his son, Alexander the Great, he must begin by pleasing the masses, the shield bearers, the hoplites, the Navy, and the nobility. The path was as clearly defined as were the stringent requirements.

From the pier at Pella, drink un-watered wine all night, fight to dominate the feasting table, boast of prowess in war, and brag of your ingenuity in the treaty tent. Then at dawn, strut twelve hundred steps from the harbor of Pella to the agora. Once at the center square of the Macedonian capital, give an elegant and rousing speech. Exhaustion and over intoxication are conditions not allowed for any man who desired to be the King of Macedonia. Yet the agora was but half the distance and half the steps.

From the public gathering place, the would-be King must weave through the crowd of excited citizens. Complimenting women, even if ugly, blessing babies, no matter the volume of the tikes' screams, acknowledging veterans and wealthy merchants with the same fervor, and all the while, be mindful of daggers brandished by assassins and friends, alike.

Twelve hundred paces from the agora, uphill, through the crowd, the want-to-be king entered the palace and encountered his next set of challenges. Now high above the harbor, the city, and the throng, he would be handed a great goblet of strong wine. Sauntering to the edge of the patio, he'd raise his arms and demand cheers in the name of Macedonia.

"Macedon. Macedon…"

As the citizens chanted, the man who would be King drained every drop from the vessel.

And finally, drunk and fatigued, custom compelled him to select from among his wives and concubines a mate to bed. Only then could he leave the public venue to fulfill his duty to produce an heir. Yet even in private, his performance and endurance in bed would be judged by the palace staff, the wives and concubines he neglected, and the foreign spies. Before the sun reached its zenith in the sky, the entire city of Pella would know of their King's stamina.

The steps were well defined, the tasks known to many, but few men had traveled those two thousand four hundred steps. Philip the Fifth made the relatively short trip many times in his years as the King of Macedon.

Scanlan Saltare Romiliia Kasia, among other things, was a scribe to Philip V of Macedon. The position gave him an intimate insight into Philip the man and a unique slant on the era. The tale begins from just before Scanlan joined the royal staff. It ended when he grew weary of war, subterfuge, sneaking about at night, and avoiding discovery and torture. Only then, with his thirst for adventure sated, did Scanlan return to his home at Lake Maggiore in the Po River Valley.

Thus is presented, to the best of his ability as a witness and from the facts he gathered, a story of allies, spies, and conflicts. It's about a King, a handsome, capable, and clever man with an evil, vindictive temper. And his scribe, who happened to be a Roman spy.

Welcome to 201 B.C. and the 2nd Macedonian War

Chapter 2 - Assault On The Beach

As a precursor to a beautiful day, fingers of pink light beamed from over the horizon. Along the white beaches of Samos, Egyptian warships leaned on braces to support their deep keels. Still in shadows, and under the protection of the God Tutu, rowers and sailors from the Pharaoh's fleet rested in blankets of fine linen. Mats of reeds, picked from along the banks of the Nile River, separated sleeping men from the ground, providing comfort, and relief from the grit and the sand crabs. Unfortunately for the men of the Egyptian fleet, those assigned early morning guard duty lounged with their eyes closed. And sometime in the wee hours, the God Tutu, who guarded men while they slept, left the Island of Samos.

***

Three miles from the beached ships, a handful of five-banker warships glided off the dark Icarian Sea and silently entered the bay. Their decks crowded with hoplites, shield bearers, and cavalrymen without mounts, the hulls sat low in the water. It made no difference to the oarsmen. They stroked in a slow rhythm to keep the noise of splashing oars to a minimum.

Two men in armor stood on the foredeck of the lead five-banker. Both held helmets under their left arms. The headgear had horsehair crests, signifying they were staff officers.

"Philip. It's a beach full of sleeping Egyptians," General Chrysogonus advised. "Let your shield bearers and the hoplites handle this."

"By the age of thirty, Alexander had conquered the known world," Philip agued. "He marched his Companions and phalanxes through Persia and all the way to India."

"But King Philip, your name sake and Alexander's father, didn't unite Greece until his was forty-four," the General pushed back. "You've got time, my King."

Philip the Fifth of Macedonia smiled at his friend and favorite General.

"Chrysogonus. You do have a way of making everything tidy," Philip remarked. He removed his helmet from under his arm and ran his fingers along the steel bill at the front. The split at the chin of the helmet and the eyes holes made the helmet resemble a hard faced. Contrasting with the steel of the helmet, a long plume of blue and blond horsehair trailed from the back of the crest. After a moment of contemplation, Philip offered. "If I hear you right, I still have seven years to emulate King Philip II, unite Greece, and create a modern day League of Corinth of my own."

With a bow to his King, the General confirmed the summation. "Exactly, my lord. And I'll be your spearhead."

"Alas, Chrysogonus, you've contradicted your own argument," Philip stated while placing the helmet on his head. The King of Macedonia stared down the bay at the approaching beach but didn't add any details to his thought.

"How do you figure that, my Lord?" Chrysogonus inquired.

The bronze ram, which had lurked just below the surface, broke water as the keel of the warship traveled up the shallows. Behind the King and the General, men stirred while hoisting shields and spears.

"Because in all of his campaigns, Philip II commanded from the front. Don't be late, General," Philip urged as he pointed at the beach and hoisted his shield. After placing a foot on the rail, Philip V bellowed, "Companions, follow me."

The quiet of the morning was shattered by the King's order and the splash of ramps being dropped into the shallows. While the infantrymen lined up, preparing to rush down the boards, King Philip jumped over the side.

Landing on the sand, he drew his kopis, pointed the front-heavy short sword up the beach, and he shouted, "Surrender in the name of Macedonia. Or die by my sword."

Fifty hand-picked Companions dropped from the warship and landed around Philip. They echoed his words while following him up the beach.

"Surrender in the name of Macedonia. Or die by my sword."

***

The order, and rough language, snapped the dozing Egyptians to consciousness. Grabbing their short spears and shields, the Marines of the fleet hesitated for a moment to consider the threat.

Beyond the surf line, four warships rested sideways to the beach. Heavy infantry and armored light infantry stomped down the ramps and into the shallows. Still far from shore, the infantrymen didn't present an immediate threat. But one five-banker had nosed onto the beach and deposited a cluster of warriors. Being far ahead of the infantry, the Marines selected Philip's group for annihilation first. It was a costly mistake.

***

"Macedon, Macedon," the Companions growled as they closed ranks on either side of their King. Meeting the shields and spears of the Egyptian Marines, they continued to sing as blades rang and spears tapped on shields. "Macedon, Macedon."

Loudest among them, Philip V roared as he blocked spear thrusts, kicked shields, and dropped Egyptians to the sand.

The pushing, stabbing, and shoving left injured Marines and Companions underfoot. Several crawled out of the brawl. They bled as the fray moved up the beach then back down to the water's edge. A spear thrust caught Philip's left shoulder and sliced the skin and muscles.

"You'll have to do better than that," the King responded with an upward swing of his sword. The blade entered the Egyptian's belly and Philip ripped it upward, splitting the Marine's heart. While tossing bloody gore into the face of another Egyption, Philip challenged. "Much better than that."

But the Marines had formed lines several ranks thick, and the depth began taking a toll on the Companions. Ignoring his own blood and pain, the King of Macedonia held his position. By virtue of his presence, the Companions maintained their lines even as they were again forced towards the water's edge.

Before their combat sandals splashed into the bay, General Chrysogonus thundered, "Ranks, forward!"

During the assault, the ends of the Companion's lines had battled to keep the Egyptians from circling around. An instant after the command of General Chrysogonus, the Companions on the ends were rudely shoved inward by armored shoulders. A moment later, ranks of hoplites and shield bearers enveloped the Companions in a cocoon of armor. Shields, both big and medium in size, and spears protected the King and his chosen warriors.

Philip let his heavy infantry sweep the Egyptians up the beach in waves of hurt and sweat. As the rear rank of the hoplites moved forward, Chrysogonus appeared at Philip's side.

"You're bleeding, my lord," Chrysogonus observed. He grabbed a cloth from a Companion and pressed it against Philip's shoulder. "You should retire from the battle."

"Tie the cloth over the wound, my friend," Philip instructed. "We've much to do to pacify these Egyptians."

"Your Companions, shield bearers, and hoplites are fully capable of defeating the men of the Nile," Chrysogonus assured the King.

"I am confident in my victory," Philip agreed. He continued talking as the General bandaged his wound. "But I need to be at the front for the sake of my Macedonians. And to stop the killing before they leave no ranking Egyptians alive to deliver my message."

"What message is that, my King?"

Philip swung his left arm in a circle to loosen the muscle. The movement caused fresh blood to stain the bandage. Ignoring the bleeding and the pain, he drew his kopis and swung the short, front-heavy sword.

"Why, Chrysogonus, my demand for the Pharaoh to accept my terms of surrender for Egypt," Philip disclosed as he tested the weight of his shield against the injured shoulder, "and to open the harbor of Alexanderia to my fleet."

While the General processed the declaration, Philip and his Companions charged after the lines of hoplites and shield bearers.

"Macedon, Macedon," they shouted until the cry was picked up by the heavy and light infantrymen.

***

Near the end, the Egyptian oarsmen, by far the most numerous body of troops at the beach battle, ran inland. While the rowers fled, the Nile Marines, sailors, and ship's officers clustered in a shrinking circle.

"Hold," Philip demanded before his infantry closed the loop and massacred the remaining Egyptians. "Hold. I have use for them."

Displaying signs of his part in the fighting, Philip pushed his way through the ring of spears. Blood splattered his face, arms and armor, red ran down his arm from bleeding that escaped the bandage, and clumps of gore fell from the blade of his sword. To the Egyptians, he didn't appear to be very royal, but they had lost the fight. To the victors, Philip's appearance matched exactly the look of a Macedonian Warrior King.

"Who is your Admiral?" Philip inquired as if he'd stumbled upon the Pharoh's Naval force in a market. "Speak up, Admiral. My men are tired from the slaughter, in need of a dip in the sea to wash away the blood of your best, and they are thirsty for strong wine."

The last comment brought a cheer of "Philip! Philip!" along with laughter.

A tall, suntanned man wrapped in a luxurious robe stepped out of the circle of Egyptians.

"I am Anubis, commander of the Pharoh's Fleet of Anatolia."

Chrysogonus chuckled. Looking over his shoulder, Philip inquired, "Is something funny, General?"

"Anubis is the Egyptian God of Funerals," Chrysogonus replied. He glanced around at the bodies on the beach. "I'd say, my lord, he is aptly named."

"I am worth a large ransom," the Admiral boasted. "As are several of my ship Captains."

"Order your Marines and sailors to throw down their shields and spears," Philip instructed. "Then we'll talk."

Anubis snapped out the order but several Captains resisted. However, the Admiral insisted, and after a moment of browbeating, the Egyptians dropped their shields, swords, and spears.

"Herd them to the beach," Philip directed his infantrymen. "We'll talk while someone stitches up my shoulder."

***

Companions took a sturdy wooden table from the village of Soma and placed it at the top of the beach. Philip leaned against an edge with his heels resting on the sand. A servant removed the bandage and rinsed the shoulder wound with sea water. Philip's only visible reaction to the salt water in an open wound consisted of him digging his heels into the sand as he tensed. After threading a bronze needle with sheep gut thread, the servant began the first stitch.

"Ransom and captives are too messy, and to be truthful Admiral Anubis, too small a reward," Philip explained. He grimaced in pain as the next stitch was pulled tight. "The returns, you see, are too small for my plans."

Holding the spout above the hands of his medic, Philip squirted red wine over the fingers, thread, needle, and his wound. He flinched at the discomfort as the liquid penetrated the raw opening and ran down his arm. The following stitch pulled the skin and muscle together, closing the gash. His infantrymen stood witness to the fortitude of their King.

"If not a ransom, King of Macedon," Anubis questioned. "What do you desire?"

"I require only that you deliver a letter to your Pharoah," Philip answered between streams of wine. Then, with a twisted grin on his face, he added. "But if the concept is too cumbersome for a three-year-old ruler, give it to the Regent of Alexanderia."

"And that's all you require?" Anubis asked.

"Is that all I require?" Philip replied loud enough for his Companions and infantrymen to hear. "Paying homage to Egypt's rightful King should be enough for any ruler of Macedon."

"General Ptolemy I Soter founded a dynasty in Egypt," Anubis argued. "His successor, Ptolemy V Epiphanes is now Pharaoh. And a Pharaoh of Egypt does not owe allegiance to you or any Macedonian King."

"Ptolemy was but a subcommander under General Parmenion," Philip countered. "His elevation came after King Alexander had Parmenion killed for treason. Therefore as a lowly commander Ptolemy, and his successors, are subjects of Macedon."

Admiral Anubis tensed as he prepared to rebuke the insult directed at the ruling family of Egypt. Tremors of anticipation ran through the ranks of Companions, hoplites, and shield bearers. A useful Admiral or not, Anubis had started a new battle.

To match wits with a scholar was a time-honored tradition in the agora. To duel philosophically with a King was tempting the spinners of fates. While *Clotho* spun the threads, and *Lachesis* handled a specific human's thread, it was *Atropos* who cut the thread to end a life. Or in the present situation, if Anubis angered Philip, the King would draw his sword and end the Egyptian.

Of course, what happened next depended partially on what Anubis said. And partially on how deep into the wine Philip had become during the discussion.

Chapter 3 - Chios Wine

While most of the Macedonians waited for Admiral Anubis to speak and seal his fate, units of shield bearers beat the bush to flush out Egyptian rowers. Their actions resulted in a growing cluster of oarsmen farther down the beach.

"You are the ruler of Macedonia. As such, you are in possession of a mighty army, a massive Navy, a strong sword arm, and a sharp blade," Anubis emphasized with a regal bow. "It would be unseemly of me to challenge you on any level, King Philip."

"Pick your ship's officer, your sailors, and Marines for two warships," Philip directed.

"What of my oarsmen?" the Admiral inquired.

"I'll have the letter to you after I deal with your rowers," Philip told him. He stepped away from the table and strolled towards the group of captured rowers. "You can pick your rowers from those that are left."

Thinking Philip intended to punish the runaways, Anubis insisted, "King of Macedonia, I must protest the murder of defenseless oarsmen."

Ignoring the Admiral, Philip approached the oarsmen while digging into the coin purse attached to his hip.

"My Spartan associates are all wealthy," he beamed, while tossing a handful of coins in the air. Even as the fortune rained down on the rowers, he reached for another handful of silver. "And my Cilician associates are rich."

While most of the oarsmen bent and grabbed coins, a few remained standing.

"King of Macedon," one called out. He waved a muscular arm at those scrambling for the silver coins. "While your coins speak loudly, we are plain spoken rowers. Is there a point to your generosity?"

"The Spartans, the Cilicians, and other special associates, have charters from me, giving shelter to their ships in the harbors of Macedonia and my allies," Philip described. "And marketplaces for any goods they carry. No matter if the merchandise comes from Egyptian merchants, Rhodian shippers, or Athens or Pergamon merchantmen."

"You want us to be pirates for you?" another of the standing men blurted out.

"The word Pirate has such an awful meaning and bad implications," Philips suggested. "I prefer associates, or if you'd rather, wealthy businessmen. Men, shall we say, like you and your oarsmen. Is that plain enough?"

"And if we turn down your offer, King Philip?" the first speaker inquired.

"For those of you who aren't picked by Admiral Anubis, or don't join my fleet or my cause, you'll become residents of Samos. I hope you enjoy being humble, island fishermen."

Several oarsmen stepped away from the crowd, moving in the direction of the seaside village. Obviously, they were sick of being rowers on warships and wanted to be fishermen.

A large group, more than enough to power Admiral Anubis' two warships, shuffled towards the Egyptian officers. Some of them would be left behind, no matter their commitment to Egypt. After the division, most of the oarsmen expressed their resentment at rowing for the Egyptians by staying right where they stood.

"Give me a first officer," Philip requested. When a second in command of a Macedonian warship stepped forward, the King instructed. "Select the best to row for our fleet. For the rest, break them into crews and get them letters of safe passage."

"Yes, my King," the first officer acknowledged.

Proud of the accomplishment of turning the Egyptian oarsmen into pirates or drafting them into his fleet, Philip swaggered back to the worktable.

"There are your choices for oarsmen," he disclosed to Anubis. Then the King looked around for staff members to write the letters he'd promised. Most had specific skills, but few could read or write. Seeing no one with the qualifications, he called to Chrysogonus. "General. Find us people who know how to read and write. Have them draft the letters. You'll oversee the task. But at no point will you or I sit down and write them."

"Yes, my King," the General agreed.

While the letters to the Pharaoh and the Regent of Egypt were prepared, and several letters of authority for the pirates were drafted, the other rowers were divided among the five warships. The second officers would evaluate the Egyptian oarsmen for their skill levels and distribute them among the benches with their rowers.

***

The sun reached the top of the sky and Philip climbed to the steering deck of his warship. Admiral Anubis had just rowed his two messenger ships out of the bay. A pair of newly established pirate ships had put to sea to give the mixed crew of rowers a chance to learn unison. Those absorbed into the Macedonian fleet were seated below the decks in the five original warships.

"Captain Kyree. This local wine is souring my belly," Philip declared. "Let's take the squadron to Chios Town and secure some of that quality Chios Wine."

"As you command, my King," the ship's officer confirmed. Next, the Captain called forward. "First Officer Nickolai. Get us off this beach."

"Aye, Captain," the First Officer replied before calling to his least experienced oarsmen. "Bow rowers to the beach. Hustle up. Get us wet."

The forward oarsmen clustered around the ram and the fore section. They waited for everyone to get positioned. From above, Nickolai judged that everyone had hands on the hull and directed, "Push. Push like your daddy did on the farm during planting season."

"My father had an oxen for the plow," a rower remarked.

"So do I," Nickolai retorted. "They're called oarsmen. Now push."

The five-banker ground on the sand until the ram dropped as the keel slid through the shallows. Then, as the big warship floated free, Nickolai turned to an opening in the top deck.

"Deck managers, run them out and reverse stroke, reverse stroke," he called down. Oarsmen from the bow section scrambled up the sides of the warship and dropped over the rail. They scrambled down ladders to their stations on one of the four lower decks. The First Officer turned to the ship's drummer. "Set a slow pace until we circle around."

Now under way, but in reverse, the helmsmen shoved the rear oars to starboard and the big warship, much like a wagon with the team walking backward, angled around until the bow pointed down the bay.

"Hold water," Nickolai bellowed. On either side and on all five levels of rowers, the oar blades remained motionless, which stopped the warship from drifting. Once satisfied the ship sat idling, the First Officer ordered. "Stroke. Stroke. Stroke. Drummer, give them a steady beat."

Nickolai walked from rail to rail, watching the oars to be sure they were rowing together on each side and that the sides were in harmony. Only then did he march the forty yards to the steering deck.

"Captain, the ship is underway and all oars are responding," Nickolai reported.

"Very good, First Officer," Kyree acknowledged. "Once we're out of the bay, set the sail. We're making for Chios Town."

"Yes, sir," Nickolai acknowledged, accepting the directions.

He returned to looking over the sides and checking the movement of the oars.

Behind the flagship of King Philip, the other four five-bankers came about and rowed for open water.

***

During the voyage to Chios, the hills of Anatolia were visible off to their right. By late afternoon, the five-bankers angled away from the mainland. Farther along their trek, a massive island came into view.

"Do we lower the sail and row ashore, lord?" Captain Kyree asked.

The King lifted his eyes. On the sailcloth, the image of a youth riding a prancing-stallion proclaimed for all to see, the five-banker was the flagship of the Macedonian Navy.

"No. Take us up beyond my fleet, and sail back. I want my people to witness the flag of Philip," he directed.

Almost two hundred warships rested on the beach of Chios. The numbers were impressive. As were the hordes of sailors, rowers, weapons specialists, and infantrymen cheering as the flagship sailed by. Philip's Navy, however, had an issue. Only fifty-three were four-bankers or five-bankers. The capital warships sported artillery, slingers, bowmen, and assault troops, while providing the ability to sink an enemy ship with a single strike of the ram. The remaining ships of his fleet were open decks with one or two levels of oarsmen and no ram. Although he did have several squadrons of three-bankers with the bronze weapon.

The tour up the coast carried Philip beyond the Fort at Chios Town and back. Where the Macedonians had cheered, the defender of Chios jeered the passing of the Macedonian flagship.

"They don't appear happy, sir," Ambrose, the Captain of Marines, noted.

"Could your Marines scale those walls?" Philip inquired.

"The upper deck of this ship rides four yards above the water, Lord," Ambrose replied. "If you could park it on the beach next to the walls, and supply us four-meter ladders, my Marines could top the defenses. Other than that, sir, I have no idea how to breach those walls."

Philip studied the high, thick walls as his ship sailed back to the fleet.

"Captain Kyree. Lower the sail, out your oars," Philip instructed, "and row me to shore."

"To shore, my lord," the Captain acknowledged. "First Officer Nickolai, roll the sail and prepare to beach the ship."

While Philip showed the colors, the four warships accompanying him had cut half circles in the water and backed into the shallows. They left a space in the middled for the flagship.

Kyree's helmsmen adjusted the aft as the oarsmen revered rowed until the First Officer called to the rowers.

"Hold water," Nickolai directed. Then he addressed the pushers. "Bow, over the side, and on my count, get us dry."

***

On the beach and from a steady deck, the walls of Fort Chios came into focus. Stone and sundried bricks blanketed a thick embankment at least nine yards tall at the lowest spot.

"I don't see any Macedonian colors on those walls?" Philip mentioned.

"General Philokles only had two days to break the defenses," Captain Kyree said in defense of the Macedonian General.

"I understand," Philip remarked. "It's just disappointing."

Philip strolled down the ramp. General Chrysogonus, who departed from a different warship, met him on the sand.

"No sign of Philokles," Philip observed.

Chrysogonus ran his gaze up the high defensive walls of the fort.

"He's only had two days, my lord," he stated.

"I've been reminded of that," Philip asserted. Four Companions rushed to the King and placed their shields between Philip and the walls of the fort. He inquired. "Is that necessary?"

A ship's length from where the ruler of Macedonia stood, clusters of upright arrows appeared to spring from the ground. More filled the air, but like the earlier ones, the arrows fell far short of where Philip stood.

"I can't blame them for trying," the King commented. "Come, let us go and find General Philokles."

The entourage started inland. As they moved, twenty Champions ran to surround the two commanders of the Macedonian expedition.

"I don't think a Cretan archer could reach me from those walls with two war bows," Philip suggested.

20

"They couldn't, lord," Griffin of the Companions confirmed the pronouncement. "But Marines on the other ships told me they have bolt throwers from Syracuse. And those can punch through an armored man at three times the distance."

As if to prove the comment, a bolt, as long as the King's arm, slammed into the dirt far ahead of them.

"What can we do about that?" Philip inquired.

"Only one thing, lord," Captain Griffin answered. "Run!"

With a wall of shields blocking the view of Philip from the crews manning the bolt throwers on the wall, the party ran. Their destination was a length of wall that protected the Macedonian camp. Just as they reached safety, a bolt buried itself in the short defensive stone wall.

"Isn't our camp a little close to the artillery?" Philip questioned.

"Sir, you'll need to take that up with General Philokles," Chrysogonus suggested.

***

The tent of the general charged with taking the fort at Chios Town offered shelter from the sun, but not much else. Pieces of parchment with lines drawn at angles and circles of different circumferences littered the carpet. Wine glasses, clay mugs, and wooden cups had been haphazardly dropped on the furniture and on the floor. They gave the tent the look of a place that had recently hosted a drunken feast. But the lack of leftover food, gnawed bones, and dirty dishes dispelled the notion of a festive gala. Other than a pair of hoplites on guard duty, the interior of the messy tent sat empty.

"Where can I find General Philokles," Philip asked.

"My King, he's in the hole," one of the guards answered. He pointed farther into the camp with his shield.

"But sir, it's not safe," the other hoplite warned.

"Because of the bolt throwers?" Philip guessed.

"No, sir, the onagers," the Hoplite answered.

Chrysogonus bowed and said, "My King, I need to check on the fleet and the men. If you'll excuse me."

"Afraid of the catapults?" Philip teased.

"Sir, every commander is afraid of onagers," the General admitted. "Especially when camped in a fixed position."

"You're excused General," Philip said. "Apparently, I need to find a hole and my other General."

***

The hole wasn't a simple depression in the ground. Instead, it was an entrance to an underground cave, or more specifically, a tunnel. A series of timber frames resembling the ribs of a giant barracuda held up the roof and prevented the sides from falling inward. Captain Griffin went first to see if the way was safe.

"The hoplite was wrong," the Captain of Companions complained. "It's the unstable frames that are dangerous, not rocks from a catapult."

A bend in the tunnel ended the natural light. Candles along the walls gave the space a head a little illumination. They moved down the tunnel, bent over to avoid the low roof. Ahead, a loud thud reached them. A few grains of dirt fell from the ceiling.

"What was that?" Philip asked.

From the gloom, a voice answered.

"That, my King, is a large stone from an onager, seeking to destroy my tunnel before its time."

"General Philokles. Have you discovered silver or copper," Philip inquired. "If not, why the mine?"

Stooped forward, Philokles came out of the darkness.

"Because, my King, we are approaching the walls of the fort," the General described. "They can't located the tunnel. If they could, they'd drop bigger stones until it caved in."

"You're going to breach the walls by tunneling under the foundation," Philip suggested.

"My engineers say all we need is to drop part of the wall into the tunnel and the collapse will create a ramp into the fort," Philokles told him.

"You come far in two days," Philip remarked. "How much longer to reach the wall?"

Philokles bent down and scooped up a handful of grainy material. As it spilled from between his fingers, he revealed an issue.

"A month at least, my lord. We've reached a boulder or a barrier of stone, it's hard to tell from down here. In any case, it'll require us to chip away at the material to create a passageway."

"I'm not sure the Rhodians or the Pergamons will grant us the luxury of a month," Philip admitted.

"Are you on a tour to inspect your commanders?" Philokles questioned. "Or will you join me for a meal."

"Only if you have Chios Wine," Philip commented.

"The island is famous for the beverage," Philokles assured Philip. "We have wagons full."

"Good. Tonight we drink," Philip proposed. "Tomorrow you dig, while I inspect my Navy. But your tent, General, is untidy."

"We spent most of the day figuring out if we could charge ahead, circle around the obstruction, or change the angle of the tunnel," Philokles mentioned. "My tent should be cleaned by now. I've learned that planning a tunnel is harder than preparing for a battle."

"Why is that?" Philip inquired.

"With a tunnel, I'm not sure what I'll find three shovels from where my laborers start each afternoon," Philokles ventured. "For a battle, I have days to plan the order of march."

The observation of excavation problems aside, neither Philokles nor Philip noted that the Goddess Até had joined their group. They had no idea the Goddess of Mischief and Folly took exception to Philokles' boast of having days to prepare for a battle.

In the morning, as they lazed about with glasses drained to the last drop of excellent Chios Wine, the Goddess awoke. Before leaving for Mount Olympus, Até flicked her wrist and delivered her unwanted blessing on the men laying siege to the fort of Chios Town.

Chapter 4 - The King Is Dead

The sun had yet to break the horizon when General Philokles stretched and shifted his weight. On the adjacent couch, Philip reacted to the movement.

"Chios wine is excellent," the King offered.

"Breakfast, my lord?" Philokles asked, suggesting food to soak up the wine from the previous night.

Before Philip could reply, the sound of feet approaching the tent reached them. Based on past events, the threat of assassination hung over every ruler of Macedonia. Both the King and the General leaped to their feet, drew their swords, and braced to face the threat. Along with them, five Companions lowered their spears in one direction and another five turned to defend the rear of the tent. Philip and his handpicked fighters were also aware of Macedon's history.

A running shadow came out of the early dawn and raced directly towards the tent.

"My King, awful news," Chrysogonus shouted. He entered the tent, noted the pair of naked blades and five spear tips. He stopped and held up his hands to show they were empty of daggers. Next, General Chrysogonus offered. "The Pergamon fleet has launched from Dikili."

"The bulls are coming out to do battle," Philip stated while sheathing his blade. "That's good news."

"While the Pergamon fleet is coming from the north," Chrysogonus cautioned, "the Rhodians are sailing up from the south."

"If we remain at Chios Town, we'll be cut off from our supply route and any of the escape routes," Philokles advised.

Philip paced slowly from one side of the tent to the other. As if confused, he seemed unfocused and indecisive. The servants noticed, as did the Generals. After several laps, he stopped and pointed at Chrysogonus.

"Take your squadrons south and delay the Rhodians," Philip instructed. "Philokles and I will take the bulk of the fleet north. We'll sink the Bulls and shortly afterward, we'll hasten to your aid."

"But my lord, you'll need five-bankers," Chrysogonus warned. "The Rhodian warships are fast and deadly in pairs. But the Pergamon fleet has size and weight behind their rams."

"I'm depending on you to keep the Rhodians off my back," Philip revealed. "Do the math. They have two fleets and we have one. If they combine, we lose the sea battle. But our fleet is balanced between large and small warships. Their fleets are overweighted with one or the other. Our best hope is to overwhelm one fleet then join our forces to deal with the other."

"But our strongest against their weakest?" Philokles protested.

"In a phalanx, the hoplites tend to drift right as each man attempts to cover himself and his neighbor with his shield," Philip described. "That leaves the left side of the formation exposed and vulnerable. I'm simply duplicating an old tactic."

"But the Rhodians aren't weak," Chrysogonus remarked, "just smaller, more maneuverable, and deadly."

"Our capital warships are better suited to wounding their deck rowers, sailors, and ship's officers," Philip pointed out. "Our three-bankers and smaller vessels would be nothing except fish food for the sailors from the Island of Rhodes."

"I'll hold them until you arrive," Chrysogonus promised.

"Go divide the fleet, General," Philip commanded.

After bowing, Chrysogonus ran to alert the ship's Captains. Philokles cocked his head and squinted at his King.

"If you're throwing your strongest against their weakest," the General proposed. "That means you and I are rowing our weakest into Pergamon's strength."

"On one hand that is true," Philip explained. "But we aren't going to form a battle line and attack."

"If not a battle formation, my lord, than what?"

"Have you ever seen Greylag geese migrate?" Philip asked.

"Of course," Philokles assured him.

Philokles hesitated, expecting clarification. The King of Macedonia didn't offer any. He grabbed his helmet, gathered up his chest armor, and ran for the beach. Caught off guard, General Philokles left the tent several paces behind Philip V.

***

Not only were the four-bankers and five-bankers bigger, they were faster with better trained crews. When Philip reached the beach, all the massive warships, except one, were raising their sails and heading south.

"Orders, sir?" ship's officer Kyree asked from the top of the ramp.

Some of Philip's Companions stood on the beach while others waited on the top deck.

"Come walk with me Captain Kyree," Philip invited. "And you as well, Captain Griffin."

With the Captain of his flagship and the commander of his selected warriors in tow, Philip marched parallel with the sea. As they walked along the beach, he instructed Kyree of the changes to the battle formation. When Philip reached the squadrons of three-bankers, the King of Macedonia beckoned the officers and men from the smaller warships.

"I've often wondered what the secret to victory was for ancient fleets." He spoke while climbing to the foredeck of a three-banker. From his perch four yards above the beach, the King waited for all the crews to gather. As the farthest away reached the crowd, others filled them in on the words they missed. When he had all the rowers, Marines, sailors, and ships' officers, Philip repeated his quandary. "I've often wondered what the secret to victory was for ancient fleets. And I believe I've worked it out. Three-banker warships have been replaced on the attack line by bigger vessels with more rowers. And you've been given the thankless duty of being the fleet's messengers."

Grumblings of agreement to the plight of the smaller warships interrupted the King. He allowed the men to complain about their fate, before adding, "What I've worked out is your bronze rams are as solid as the rams heads on bigger war vessels. Your hulls and keels are sturdy enough to support those rams. Your shoulders are broad enough and backs thick enough to row swiftly. And your ships are agile enough to bear down at the perfect angle of attack to emerge victoriously in any duel. I believe I've found what the ancients knew about three-tiers of rowers."

Philip eyed the men from his triremes. Each gazed up expectedly at their King. He waited for a sea breeze to nudge the backs of his men.

"Did you feel that? The sea and battle call to me," he began again. He stooped and grabbed the rail as if to jump down. "I must go and take my five-banker flagship against the Pergamon fleet."

"What did the ancients say about three-tiers of rowers?" an oarsman inquired.

His Captain moved to discipline the man who dared question the King.

"Hold, Captain. Your oarsman is correct, I never divulged the lesson from the ancients," Philip admitted. He stood straight, peered around at the faces of the crews. Then, in a deep voice that touched the hearts of his crews, he stated. "Men on three-banker ships are to be feared as sharks. For they are, like the fish, killers risen from the sea."

At the compliment from the King of Macedonia, the crews began cheering. Philip V stood and absorbed the adoration. When the noise level dropped, he held out his arms for silence.

"Today, I row my flagship against the bulls of Pergamon," he told the crews. "And to prove my faith in my three-bankers, I've sent my fours and fives south to face another fleet. What I want to know, as I put my fate in your hands, will you fight beside your King? Will my sharks row with me?"

During the wild cheering, clapping, and shouting of confirmation, Philip V climbed from the deck of the warship to the beach and walked back towards his flagship.

"Macedon. Macedon. Macedon."

***

Resembling migrating Greylag geese, Philip's fleet rowed north in a vee formation. As with all Macedonian Kings, he stood on his flagship at the point. Angling outward and back, like a flight of geese, his three-bankers and their deadly rams kept pace with their King. Filling in between the wings of triremes were smaller, undecked ships. Even though they didn't have rams or keels capable of handling the weapon, each vessel carried slingers, archers, and javelin men.

"At first glance," Nickolai admitted to his Captain, "this flotilla appears as deadly as a fishing fleet."

"At first glance, First Officer?" Kyree probed.

"The three-bankers are staggered so any warship attempting to get between them will get rammed and their hulls gashed on two sides," Nickolai clarified. "And even when our fleet moves on, the ranged weapons on the small boats will prevent the Pergamon sailors from quickly repairing the damage."

"If we faced the Rhodians in their three-bankers, I'd have more confidence," Kyree divulged. He pointed down the main deck at a horizon filled with massive hulls. "Instead of those monsters."

As mushrooms would sprout after an early summer rain, the Pergamon fleet of King Attalus rose from the water in the distance. In a matter of heartbeats, the hulls became visible, and soon after, the tiers of oars.

"I can make out the facing bulls on their King's sail," Nickolai reported. "It's off to our starboard."

"First Officer Nickolai, get to your station and prepare for maneuvering," Kyree directed. "We need the vee and us pointed right at Attalus' flagship."

The helmsmen adjusted the rear oars. Nickolai staggered a little as the long warship changed direction.

"Drummer, stand by for a rapid rhythm," the First Officer alerted the musician when he reached the foredeck. Then he leaned down and shouted to the four decks below. "Just another pleasant excursion at sea and another day in paradise."

A voice called back from one of the decks, "It's never pleasant or paradise when you say that, First Officer."

"Would you rather I lie, like the recruiter who signed you up as a rower in the King's Navy?" Nickolai shouted back.

"At least he paid us a signing bonus, First Officer," another voice challenged.

"If we don't have a pleasant day and make this one paradise," Nickolai replied, "none of us will be around to collect our pay."

Nothing came back from below for a moment until several voices spoke at once. "Just another pleasant excursion at sea and another day in paradise."

Philip's flagship performed a sweeping turn so the smaller warships, creating the wings, could maintain the formation.

***

As if a doubled-edged dagger blade, the vee sliced into a narrow section of the Pergamon battle line. Before the big ships on the sides could come about and join the fight, Philip's flagship raced down the side of Attalus' warship. The prancing-stallion sail and the sail with the facing bulls passed each other. For several deadly heartbeats, the air between them filled with bolts, arrows, and rocks from slingers.

While Attalus' Captain and ship's officers concentrated on the enemy's flagship, a three-banker angled in and ripped hull boards from the warship. Although it wouldn't sink, the water in the bilge made the Pergamon flagship sluggish.

Two ships over from the victorious three-banker, another trireme died. A Pergamon five-banker circled around and when the three passed between a pair of surprised warships, the five caught the smaller warship on its big bronze ram. As if a dull ax chopping into a dried, rotten tree, the three-banker exploded in a shower of hull boards and rower benches. Along with huge pieces of the trireme came rowers, Marines, sailors, and officers. They were caught and launched into the sea on shattered oak boards and pine splinters.

***

Kyree directed the flagship to come about hard to port. He wanted another run by the flagship with the facing bulls sail.

"Captain," one of the helmsman called for his attention.

Kyree stood at the rail, searching among the dashing hulls and splashing oars for the enemy's flagship.

"Captain," the helmsman called again.

Spinning around, Captain Kyree demanded, "What?"

Removing an arm from the rear oar, the helmsman pointed to a damaged Pergamon warship. Although taking on water, the vessel was slowly rowing for the mainland. Four Macedonian three-bankers were attempting to prevent the escape.

"They have the ship under control," Kyree stated. "What's so important?"

"Not that," the other helmsman directed. He shifted his arm farther to port. "Their flagship and two others are going to render aid."

Kyree pivoted, stared for a moment at the battle to let the shapes untangle. When they did, the facing bulls jumped out of the fray. The flagship turned and rowed with a pair of fives. He didn't know what was on the damaged warship. But he understood it had value to King Attalus of Pergamon.

"King Philip," the ship's Captain bellowed. The Macedonian ruler stood with a bolt thrower team. He wanted them to be more selective on the next pass and kill everyone on the steering platform. But Kyree insisted. "Sir, if I could see you on the steering deck."

After another few words of encouragement, Philip raced to the helmsmen's position.

"King Attalus is rowing to help that crippled warship," Kyree offered. He pointed in the direction of the facing bulls. "If you want, we can pin them against the beach."

Philip looked down the deck at his Companions. He didn't have enough fighters on the flagship to win an infantry battle. Especially against the land assets of four Pergamon warships.

"I think there's an old saying about catching a lion by the tail," Philip said with disappointment in his voice. "Sure you've caught a lion. But what can you do with it and not get eaten."

"We have flagmen, my Lord, and plenty of Marines on the three-bankers and ranged weapons in the small boats."

"You're saying I have a floating army," Philip exclaimed. "Signal them. All of them to follow us to shore. If we can't beat the facing bulls at sea, we'll surely destroy them on land."

Flags flashed and were answered. In moments, boats of slingers and archers rowed for shore.

***

Too late, King Attalus realized he'd sailed into a trap of his own making. In a flash of flags from the flagship boasting the sail with the facing bulls, the four Pergamon ships adjusted course and rowed directly for the mainland.

King Philip watched as they nosed through the shallows and rammed into the dirt embankment. The Macedonian expected the Pergamon Marines to set up a defensive line. Instead, the King in his long robe, his bodyguards, Marines and sailors, and finally all the rowers ran inland. At no point did any of them stop to examine where they had landed for a place to set a defense.

Then two of the first three-bankers reversed and backed to the shoreline. Macedonian Marines jumped to the ground, started to give chase, but stopped. In a cluster, they converged on the warship with the sail displaying the facing bulls.

"What are they doing?" Philip demanded.

"They seem to be collecting silver and gold items from the flagship," Captain Griffin answered.

"The shrewd old man," Philip declared. "Rather than fight me and die, he left his treasure on his flagship to slow down my Marines. Clever."

Then, as he'd done earlier that morning, Philip became unfocused and paced across the steering platform. After four trips back and forth, he pointed at the enemy flagship.

"The King is dead," Philip stated.

"I believe he's just run off, my lord," Griffin corrected. "And he seemed to be very much alive, sir."

Philip placed a hand on Kyree's shoulder and said, "I want that ship. Intact with the sail up, and a body covered in a royal robe at midship. Who do we have who can control it?"

"First Officer Nickolai," Kyree shouted. "Come here."

Nickolai sprinted down the deck. "Yes, Captain."

"The Pergamon flagship is yours, if you can get it off the mud, find enough rowers to control her while I tow it," Kyree explained. "And make it appear that you're escorting a royal body."

"A royal body?" Nickolai remarked.

"Yes, Captain Nickolai," Philip announced. "Because the King is dead."

Chapter 5 - Half My Fleet

Resembling cats slow-walking through a brawl, the sea battle continued. Three-bankers scratched five-bankers as the larger warships sped out of harm's way. Giving chase, the threes angled, attempting to cut off the retreat and re-engage with the faster vessels. In other sectors of combat, five-bankers bore down on threes, intending to claw in the hulls and destroy the triremes. For all the energy of the rowers, the handling skills of the sailors, and expertise of the helmsmen, each warship moved in broad loops, attempting to bring their rams around and hit the enemy at the most destructive angle of attack.

Into the madness of the sea battle, two warships rowed through the frays. They traveled procession-like, moving slowly enough to attract adversarial rams. Yet no warship targeted either of the flagships. In fact, all the combatants stopped rowing to witness the passage of the prancing-stallion sail as it towed the Pergamon flagship with the facing bulls on its sail. To add weight to the occasion, a priest stood over a prone body wrapped in a robe of royal purple. At the rails, several Pergamon hoplites stood facing the body as if an honor guard.

After watching the body drift by, the battle ended. Pergamon warships collected survivors from the sea and rowed for their home port at Dikili. Macedonian ships fished out their own survivors before rowing after the funeral ship.

"It worked on the Pergamon fleet," Philip remarked. "Will it move the Rhodians?"

"You said it yourself," Captain Griffin suggested. "Neither Pergamon's fleet nor the fleet of Rhodes could defeat you alone. Now that you've won against one, the other will flee."

"I hear the men from the island of Rhodes possess a steadfast attitude," Philip mentioned.

"That's true, my King," Captain Kyree confirmed. "But they aren't suicidal. In short, sir, they will run."

The Captain of the Companions bowed to the ship's Captain and allowed, "You know the sea. And you know the men who fight above the depths. I pray that you are correct."

Philip turned to the Captain of his flagship. His eyebrows reflected a question.

"As soon as we arrive, my King," Kyree began to assure Philip. He stopped talking, looked back, and waved at the officer on the foredeck of the towed vessel. The man, chosen from officers off a three-banker, was unknown to Kyree. But the attentiveness of Captain Nickolai's First Officer gave Kyree heart. "The Rhodians, my King, will run from you. Or, we'll sink them with a funeral ship."

***

General Chrysogonus gripped the shaft and pointed with the other arm at the Rhodian flagship.

"On the next pass, I want a bolt in their Admiral's butt," Chrysogonus ordered while working the arrowhead out of his chest. The armor had blunted and slowed the flight of the arrow. Nevertheless, blood poured down his torso when he yanked the shaft free. Looking at the bloody tip, he spit and offered. "Two gold pieces for the bolt thrower team who pins the Rhodian Admiral to the deck."

He walked away, still holding the enemy arrow. Behind him, the crew from each torsion weapon checked the bands of hair, sinew, and hemp rope. They would wait to twist the torsion bands until their five-banker came about. When it did, the meter long bolts would be placed in the slots, the bands twisted, and the ranged weapon aimed at the flagship with the image of a rose on its sail.

General Chrysogonus marched to the steering deck, mounted the platform, and approached the Captain. Thrusting the shaft into the face of the warship's officer, he instructed. "I want to smell the beer on the breath of her oarsmen. Put us close enough for their Admiral to eat a bolt."

With a powerful fling, the Macedonian General threw the arrow over the side.

On the first pass by the vessels, where Chrysogonus caught the Rhodian arrow, the flagships passed starboard to port. Both ships avoided wrecking their keels and rams by veering off from a bronze on bronze impact.

The larger Macedonian warship carved a half circle in the water. Attempting to broadside the larger vessel, the ship from Rhodes cut across the circle.

"Port side, hold water," the First Officer shouted. "Starboard side, power ten."

Chrysogonus felt the warship almost stall in mid stroke. Twisting around, he noted the Rhodian three-banker racing directly at the five-banker. He wanted to shout orders and direct lines of hoplites. But there were no infantrymen to battle or targets for the spears of his heavy infantry. Simply a bronze ram, riding just below the water as if the snout of a monster from the deep.

"Port. Starboard. Power ten," the First officer roared.

Already swinging around on the momentum of the last order, the five-banker leaped forward. This time, the warships passed starboard to port, in the opposite positions, but much closer.

Snap sang the first bolt thrower. The meter long projectile flashed from the Macedonian warship to the steering deck of the ship from Rhodes. Catching the bolt in his hip, the Admiral flew to the deck. He landed bloody, limp, and dirty, as if a discarded armload of wool after a sheering session. The second bolt zipped by the fallen man and pinned itself to the deck beside a helmsman.

With their Admiral down, the Rhodian fleet angled off from every engagement and rowed away. General Chrysogonus pulled out two gold coins, and while displaying them overhead, walked to the first bolt thrower.

"A job well done," he announced, handing over the coins.

From the foredeck, the First Officer called out, "sails approaching from the north."

Fearing the Pergamon fleet had been victorious, Chrysogonus watched, trying to identify the warships.

Then, the Captain shouted, "sails coming from the south."

Seeing two sets of approaching sails, the General searched the far off shoreline for a landing spot. His part of the fleet had fours and fives. But they had lost so many and were in no condition to fight a combined enemy fleet.

"Rhodians," the Captain said, identifying the fleet approaching from the south.

"Are the Rhodians coming back?" Chrysogonus asked.

After a moment, the Captain explained, "No, General. The other had a rose on the sail of the flagship. This fleet has an image of the sun on its sail."

"First Officer. Report," Chrysogonus requested.

"I see the facing bulls," he stated, and every soul on the warship was crushed. But then the First Officer called out. "And I see the prancing-stallion. It's hard to tell at this distance."

"Orders, sir," the Captain questioned.

Ship handling and sailing tactics weren't part of the General's education. But he had experience with battle strategies and the placement of combat elements.

"Captain. Turn the fleet and face us south," Chrysogonus directed. "We can only fight one enemy at a time. It'll be impossible for the facing bulls to hit us with a battle line if we're intermixed with the Rhodians."

"Sound reasoning as always, General," the Captain agreed. "First Officer, turn us south and prepare for a fight."

***

Where the Macedonian fleet rowed into the melee, partially exhausted from the initial fighting, the new

Rhodian fleet had just come off sail power. The fresh arms and backs of the oarsmen made the difference. In a feeding frenzy of oar splashes, flashing bronze rams, and shattering hull boards, the Macedonia fleet lost thirty of their five-bankers to the more nimble ships. Those wrecks joined the earlier losses. Then the momentum shifted, and the Rhodians began losing warships to the better of the Macedonian crews.

During the churning of oars, shouting by rowing officers, and the power rowing to get the best angles of attack, two five-bankers rowed to the edge of the sea battle. As they approached, General Chrysogonus searched for the two sails. From the Rhodian flagship, their Admiral also studied the prancing-stallion on one and the facing bulls on the other sail. They had good reasons for staring as one would bring assets while the other an overwhelming force.

"Those are our triremes," the Captain told Chrysogonus.

The Macedonian Captain wasn't the only one to reach that decision. Around the battle zone, Rhodian warships broke away and rowed for safer waters.

"Should we pursue them, General?" the Captain inquired.

Chrysogonus slowly spun around, surveying the damage to his part of the Macedonian fleet. Pieces of four and five-bankers floated on the surface. Men clung to some, but most of the wreckage bobbed in the waves, being simple driftwood. All total, there weren't enough of the bigger ships left to continue the battle.

"We'll let King Philip decide," the General replied.

***

On the Macedonian flagship, Philip stood beside Captain Kyree. He also looked over the devastation.

"I've lost over half my fleet," Philip observed. Hooking a thumb over his shoulder, indicating the Pergamon warship behind him, he confessed. "If not for King Attalus' cowardly retreat, we would have lost these battles."

"Or for your cleverness, my Lord," Kyree suggested. "Any other tactic would have us dead and fish food by now. Or swimming until we drowned."

"Signal the fleet to make for land," Philip directed. "In the morning, after prayers and sacrifices for our dead, we'll row for Pella. The fighting is over for this year."

"Yes, my King," Kyree agreed.

The signalmen flashed the retreat messages. Survivors of the battles of Chios and Lade relaxed as their warships rowed for the beach. Unlike the oarsmen, the King of Macedonia didn't unwind.

Philip had failed in his quest to conquer new lands and grow his kingdom. Next spring, he would change his tactics. Then, he'd march his victorious army over Rhodes, across Pergamon, down the Nile of Egypt, and take Anatolia from the Seleucid upstart. For now, he looked forward to wintering in the capital with his wives and some strong Macedonian wine.

Chapter 6 - A Common Danger

Two days after the battle at Chios, a three-banker raced from Dikili. Without the weight of extra soldiers and artillery, the Pergamon ship traveled south at a rapid clip.

"Three hundred miles to the Island of Rhodes, Ambassador," Captain Petridis reported. "We should reach the port in three, or maybe four days."

"Rhodes is but the first stop on my journey," Ambassador Malis Aeson cautioned. "But it's possibly the most important."

"Sir, according to command, every stop you make," Petridis told him, "is important for the survival of Pergamon."

"Based on our history of competition with Rhodes," Aeson reflected, "the island nation might prove to be a challenge."

"Then we'll sail to another port," the Captain suggested.

"We've few friends in the eastern Mediterranean," Aeson warned. "If we fail at Rhodes, Paragon might end up alone in the world."

"The crew and I have faith in you, Ambassador. Anywhere you need to be, we'll transport you. If nothing else, sir, you can count on us."

"That's very comforting, Captain Petridis. In a universe with enemies over every horizon, having friends close by is heartening."

Hugging the mainland, the warship sailed close to shore to avoid Macedonian patrols and Cilician pirates.

***

Two days after Ambassador Aeson left Pergamon, At Rhodes in a villa situated in the hills overlooking Mandraki Harbor, a man cried out before going silent forever. His injured body relaxed and peace descended over the corpse. Above his bed, a tapestry woven with a rose hung on the wall.

"Admiral Theophiliscus of the Rose fleet has passed," a Magistrate of the Council declared. "The city mourns the passing of a fine commander and a hero to the people of Rhodes."

"Had I known he was going after the Macedonian fleet alone," Admiral Cleonaeus whispered, "I would have rushed my journey. We could have attacked together."

"No one knew when the Sun Fleet would return," the magistrate assured him. "Theophiliscus wanted to lead the assault and decided not to wait. In the end, he wouldn't have had it any other way."

"I realize that, Magistrate," Cleonaeus stated. "But to lose the King of Pergamon, and my friend Theophiliscus, in the same battle is hard to grasp."

"If anyone is to blame, it's that monster Philip of Macedon," the Magistrate spit out. "Had he remained in the western Aegean and held a tighter rein on his pirates, our fleets wouldn't have fought."

Admiral Cleonaeus of the Sun Fleet shivered with emotion as he spoke. "But he didn't and we did. Mark my words, on the next occasion Philip ventures into Rhodian waters, no matter the odds, a funeral ship won't make me retreat."

"Of that Admiral, I have no doubt," the Magistrate told him. "Now, if you'll excuse me, I must prepare the Council for the funeral games."

"Tell me one thing before you go," Admiral Cleonaeus requested. "Did he finish his report on the battle before he collapsed?"

"Ever the dedicated professional, Admiral Theophiliscus stood unassisted before the Council and delivered his final report."

"As is befitting a leading citizen of Rhodes," Cleonaeus maintained.

***

By late afternoon on day four, Admiral Aeson's warship rowed into Mandraki Harbor and navigated around massive piles and lines of rock. Finally, on the side of the docks and deep harbor, the Pergamon vessel backed onto a clear spot of beach.

"That is the resting-God Helios," a man from the island told him. He pointed at the lines of carved boulders in the shallows. He had a sack slung over his back, but it was too small to be a load of fish. "Twenty-five years ago, the God Poseidon, jealous of the Sun God Helios, shook the earth and toppled the Colossus of Rhodes. The stones have been laying here since that fateful day."

"Aren't you fearful of speaking so plainly about the Gods?" the Ambassador from Pergamon inquired.

His tone revealed the offhanded remarks troubled Malis Aeson.

"By day, I row out and cast my net, like any other fisherman," the man answered. "By night, I build and tend the cremation fires. As the flames lick the stars and consume the physical bodies, I pray and offer the custom up as a sacrifice. The job puts me, Elias the Fire Tender, in good stead with the Gods."

Two bodyguards of his six rushed from the warship and flanked the Ambassador.

"I can tell you're a person of significance with important business in Rhodes," Elias commented. He creased his eyebrows, then squinted in thought. Neither facial expression disrupted his straight nose with the slight hook at the end. After a moment, he told Aeson, "But it won't do you any good today."

"Why is that?" Aeson inquired.

Nimbly, the man climbed out of the sand and mounted a high section of the harbor wall.

"Come up," Elias urged. "See for yourself."

Aeson and his bodyguards scrambled from the beach and onto the wall. Moments later, the three stood next to Elias, peering at the city of Rhodes.

"Give me a coin," Elias suggested. "A token, if you will, as a sacrifice. I'll add you to the prayers I'll offer during the cremation tonight."

Aeson and his bodyguards dug into coin purses and pulled out coins. Only a few bronze and a couple of silver were deposited in Elias' palm.

"The offerings are a little meager, but I'm sure the Gods will accept your sacrifices," the Fire Tender mentioned. After dropping the coins into his purse, Elias pointed towards the building and streets. "There is the grand city of Rhodes."

The view appeared as if they were in the orchestra pit of a massive amphitheater. Spread out before them and rising in even steps, the streets of Rhodes resembled tiers of seating in a theater.

"Businesses and government buildings are closed today. Look close and you'll see a large funeral procession as mourners snake through streets," the fisherman instructed. "At the front, musicians, singers, and poets perform sad songs of grieving. Later today, they'll compete to see who can touch the hearts and minds of the audience with their talents. In the center of the procession, robed figures hold up a platform with a statue of the Sun God, Helios. On that platform, unlike in the harbor, he is upright. Behind the God, other mourners support a coffin sized warship. Inside the wooden frame, Admiral Theophiliscus takes one last ride in a vessel of Rhodes. Later tonight, far from the eyes of Helios, Theophiliscus will be cremated, in the style of Athens. By tomorrow, when the ashes cool, I'll place his remains in an urn. The council will present it to the Admiral's widow for transport to the family mausoleum. By then, I'll be on the sea fishing. At the rear of the procession, athletes are walking solemnly, saving their strength for the afternoon games to honor the deceased, Admiral Theophiliscus."

"Is nothing open?" inquired Ambassador Aeson.

"Let me think." The man shifted the sack and offered. "Two departments in Rhodes are always open."

"And they are?" Aeson inquired.

The fisherman jumped off the wall and landed in the city. He turned and called up to the Ambassador.

"Two departments are always active," he repeated. "And you'll meet both in a moment."

"Meet who?" Aeson demanded.

"The Harbor Manager, he collects the taxes, and harbor security, they enforce the payments," the Fire Tender replied just prior to vanishing behind a building.

From the beach, to the rear of the Ambassador and his bodyguards, a gruff voice warned. "Do not even think about leaving the harbor before seeing me. Now get down off that wall and identify yourself. And that other man."

The Harbor Master stood apart from a group of soldiers. Four armed and armored men and a military officer stood off to the side.

"Do you want us to go after him?" the Lieutenant questioned.

"No. We have these three and their crew to contend with," the Harbor Master advised. Then to Aeson, he expressed. "Avoiding taxes and smuggling goods into Rhodes will not be tolerated. Come down off that wall and don't even consider running."

"Harbor Manager," Aeson assured the man. He handed the Harbor Master a scroll and stated. "I have no intention of fleeing. Or of going into the city, until I have an invitation from the Council of Rhodes. Elias the Fire Tender was simply explaining about the funeral procession and his prayers while he cremated the bodies."

"Elias who?" the Harbor Master inquired.

"That's what the smuggler we've been chasing calls himself," The Lieutenant explained.

***

Ambassador Malis Aeson spent another uncomfortable night on a beach with the ship's officers, sailors, rowers, and his bodyguards. At dawn, stiff, sore, and hungry, he sat up to find a Magistrate of Rhodes and an escort marching down the beach.

"Good morning, Ambassador Aeson," the man in a richly embroidered robe proposed. "Come, the Council is eager to hear of the transfer of power in Pergamum."

"Transfer of power?" Aeson repeated. "Why would there be a transfer of power?"

"Because King Attalus I was killed at Chios," the Magistrate answered. "The entire Island of Rhodes extends our condolences."

"King Attalus is very much alive," Aeson insisted. "His ship ran aground during the battle and he had to flee. But the ruler of Pergamon is very much in command."

"What a relief to hear," the Magistrate gushed, holding his hands shoulder high with both palms up. "Surely a blessing from the Fates. I am Xydis. But we must hurry, the Council will want to hear the good news."

The Ambassador and the Magistrate strolled along the beach. Just before reaching the walkway leading into Rhodes, Aeson mentioned a quandary.

"Our two nations have never been friends. We compete for the same ports-of-call and compete for the same shipping contracts. Although we speak the same languages, our nations have never been exactly friendly. Yet, you're escorting me to your Council and seem delighted about the survival of my King."

They reached the pavers and turned towards the city before Magistrate Xydis commented, "In the writings of Aristotle, he proposed that a common danger united even the bitterest enemies."

"Philip V of Macedon is certainly a common enemy," Aeson agreed.

***

After a brief meeting with the Council of Rhodes, the Ambassador was dismissed from the assembly. The Magistrate guided him to a patio where a table had been set.

The marble table held pita bread, thin slices of lamb, grapes, olives, asparagus, and artichoke thistles. For beverages, the Council provided watered wine, Egyptian beer, and spring water. Aeson scanned the table before walking to a patio. From the terrace, he watched sunlight twinkle off the waters of the bay.

"You Rhodians eat well for breakfast," he remarked to the Magistrate.

"Not every day nor very often," Xydis admitted. "But today we celebrate you. And your mission."

"From the reception, I didn't think anyone was convinced," Aeson admitted.

"They didn't need to be convinced," the Magistrate told him. "The Council just needed to sort out who would be joining you."

"They agreed that easily?" the Ambassador from Pergamon inquired. "The Council barely asked me any questions."

"Two reasons, your story about the Goddess Cybele and the Dying Gau," Xydis explained. "The third being King Attalus' reaction to Philip V's actions."

"You mean abandoning his flagship?" Aeson asked with more than a little suspicion in his voice. The Ambassador at his core didn't trust the Rhodians.

"Not that action," Magistrate Xydis advised. "The action of sending you, an Ambassador."

Their discussion ended when the Council of Rhodes walked out from the building and sat at the table.

"Come, Ambassador and break your fast with us," the President of the Council urged. "Sub-Commander Katsaros will be along."

"Sub-Commander Katsaros?" Aeson whispered, still facing the city.

"Theo Katsaros is a sector commander of the island's defenses," Xydis answered. "He's a good man in a fight. Or in a treaty tent."

"Thank you," Aeson said as he turned.

Bending over and placing a pot on the table was the man from the beach. His profile displayed the straight nose ending in a slight hook.

"Elias? What are you doing here?" Aeson demanded.

Elias dropped the pot. He spun from the table and raced for a set of steps on the side of the patio.

In a flash, the suspicion Aeson held for the Rhodians blossomed into an understanding of the situation.

"Don't eat from that pot," the Ambassador from Pergamon shouted.

The men of the Council raised their arms to demonstrate that no one was reaching for the ladle. Although spicy aromas drifted from under the lid.

***

From below eye level, farther down the steps, Elias complained, "Let me go." His speech grew more frantic the second time he pleaded. "Let me go. I haven't done anything."

Below the level of the patio, a gravelly voice noted, "Every time one of my spearmen says that, he's guilty of something. Let's go see what you've been up to."

"Sure, no worries," Elias assured the raspy voice. "You'll see."

Almost as if experiencing a theater performance with the lights out, only their voices and sounds relayed what happened down the staircase.

A sharp slap, the sound of thin steel landing on a marble step, and a meaty punch to a melon came from below.

"I live every day with the threat of an assassin's blade," the rough voice exclaimed. "Did you think a wharf rat could stab me."

***

The man was bronze, toned as deeply as the chest piece of his armor. Although not pretty in the least, he had the even-features of a handsome man. Except for the scars from knife fights, mangled ears from wrestling, and a nose that had been broken on several occasions. Tucked under one arm hung a limp Elias. In the other hand, the warrior held a sharp knife.

"Does anyone lay claim to this sea urchin?" the man demanded.

"Captain Katsaros," the President of the Council answered, "Ambassador Aeson appears to know him."

Katsaros strutted to Aeson, threw Elis down on the stone of the patio and placed a foot on the man's neck. Then he extended the knife.

"Does this belong to you?" the Captain inquired softly.

"Neither the man nor the knife are mine," Aeson assured Katsaros. "I met him on the beach yesterday. He told me a tale about being the fire tender for the city's cremations. Based on that, I was surprised to see him serving the Council."

"What was he serving?" Katsaros inquired.

Magistrate Xydis walked to the table and lifted the lid. Spicey scents rose in a cloud of steam.

"Lemon and vinegar, and way too much garlic," Katsaros announced after sniffing the air. "Let's see if this pile of dung has an opinion about the dish. Bring me a ladle of it. And be sure to stir the pot."

A moment after beginning, Xydis reported, "It's a sheep's head stew."

After lifting out a scoop of broth, onions, and bits of meat, the Magistrate carried it to Katsaros. The Sub-Commander grabbed Elias by the hair and yanked him to his feet.

"Here have a taste," Katsaros urged. "It smells delicious, don't you think?"

Elias twisted and attempted to kick Katsaros. A punch to the man's ribs settled him. Hanging with only the tips of his toes on the patio, Elias twisted, trying to move his mouth away from the ladle. His entire body rotated, pulling his hair tighter, but he seemed to prefer the pain to eating the stew. Another punch to his other side drove the fight from Elias.

"Eat it," Katsaros whispered. "Or I'll cut your throat and pour it down your neck. Eat!"

With tears in his eyes, Elias attempted to make a bargain.

"I'll tell you everything," he pleaded. "Who sent me and what my mission is."

"That's the first interesting thing you've done since trying to cut me," Katsaros suggested. "All right, I'll bite, who sent you?"

"King Philip of Macedonia," Elias blurred out.

"Not interesting," Katsaros snapped. "I figured that out from the aroma. A Pergamon assassin would have used Aleppo pepper instead of garlic. Now you take a bite."

Aeson flinched at the suggestion that an assassin from his nation would try to poison the Council of Rhodes. His thoughts were interrupted by Elias.

"But I," he attempted to say.

Katsaros leaned the man back and used the knife to prop open his mouth.

"Give our friend a bite of stew," the Sub-Commander insisted.

Xydis dumped the ladle of stew into Elias' mouth. When the man attempted to cough it out, Katsaros jerked his head back, then slammed it forward. The motion cause Elias to swallow.

The Sub-Commander dropped him. Elias immediately rolled over and shoved two fingers down his throat. As the man retched and puked, Katsaros faced the table.

"I wasn't sure until now," the Sub-Commander of Rhodes' defense addressed the Council. "But as you can see, this man is guilty of attempted murder. If I caught him in any other establishment, I'd execute him. Spies and assassins have no value as hostages for ransom or information."

"We'll pass judgement for you," the President declared after getting approval from other the Councilmen. "Death by crucifixion."

Katsaros stepped to the edge of the patio and shouted down, "Lieutenant. Send up a couple of hoplites to take charge of a prisoner. Then assign a Lochias to crucify him. By order of the Council of Rhodes."

A muffled reply came from below.

"Yes, all one hundred of the men," Katsaros responded to an unheard question. "Tell the Sergeant to be sure all the spearmen are there to witness what happens to assassins and murderers."

A moment later, two heavy infantrymen appeared on the side steps. Each took an arm. They carried Elias down and out of sight.

"Council of Rhodes," Katsaros pondered. "I'm sure you didn't bring me here to investigate a possible poisoning. Did you have another reason?"

"Ambassador Malis Aeson from Pergamon is on a mission and you Sub-Commander Katsaros have been assigned to represent Rhodes," the President of the Council replied.

"Pergamon," Katsaros sneered.

Finally, Aeson thought, someone in Rhodes who mistrusts Pergamon as much as I mistrust Rhodes. Aristotle was correct though, a common danger would serve to unite the bitterest of enemies.

Chapter 7 - Take Charge

A few days after the affair on the patio, Malis Aeson and Theo Katsaros stood on the beach in the muted light of dawn. Hulls of warships on each side created a darkened alleyway.

"But Egypt is also a victim of Macedonian aggression," Aeson pointed out. "They should be part of this."

"That may be true," Katsaros seemed to agree, "but the boy Pharoah and his advisers have their hands full with the Seleucid Empire. Antiochus III is gnawing away at Egyptian territory. They won't be of a mind to help us with Philip."

"In that case, we're off to Athens," Aeson suggested. "Unless, of course, you have a different destination in mind?"

"The Athenians may be snobs and overly proud," Katsaros offered. "But, Macedonia is just as much a danger to them as it is to our nations. They should be next."

Aeson thought of Socrates and the philosopher's idea that people often criticize others for faults they themselves possess. The Rhodian Sub-Commander's opinion of Athenians as arrogant proved the theory. The Ambassador didn't reveal his thoughts. He simply confirmed their goal. "Then Athens is our next destination."

"Ships' Captains," Katsaros called to both warships, "get your boats wet and set your headings for Athens."

Aeson and Katsaros parted. Each took a ramp up to the top deck of their vessel.

"Ambassador Aeson," Captain Petridis of the Pergamon warship admitted, "it's good to have two ships for protection. But I'm uneasy about being so near a Rhodian ram."

"It's a long journey across the Aegean Sea," Malis Aeson pointed out. "Few pirates will attack a pair of warships. But to my mind, it won't hurt to keep our eyes on the ship from Rhodes."

"Yes, sir," Petridis allowed. Then he ordered. "Get us off the beach, First Officer."

Moments later, rowers from the Bow section pushed and the Pergamon warship ground on the beach before floating free in the shallows. While the Bow rowers were still climbing over the sides, the First Officer shouted to the oarsmen in the Stroke and Engine sections. "Stroke. Stroke. All together stroke."

Between the power and the smooth dips and pulls of the experienced rowers, the ship moved rapidly through the harbor of Rhodes. Ahead of them, the Rhodian trihemiolia rowed out of the harbor and angled to port on a northwest heading.

The warships were forty-four yards long and sported three rows of oarsmen. But, where both three-bankers had about the same number of rowers on the top and bottom tiers, the Rhodian vessel was wider in the center. Meaning on the middle level, the trihemiolia was able to accommodate more oarsmen. One hundred and ninety-six rowers gave the Rhodian an advantage in starting speed and speed over distance. By comparison, the one hundred and eighty rowers from Pergamon left the trireme a little under powered. For that reason, the Rhodian was the faster of the two. And as feared by Ambassador Malis Aeson, it proved that Katsaros was as arrogant as he feared.

Shortly after leaving the harbor and rounding a tip of the island, the ships withdrew their oars and unrolled their sails. As the sun emerged fully over the eastern horizon, the warships sailed away from the Island of Rhodes.

***

The journey to Athens could take as few as four days' sailing provided they sailed into no storms, neither ship was sunk, or captured, by one of Philip's pirate crews, and the winds didn't peak before midafternoon. Although the prevailing wind blew from the north, the Island of Kos, their first stop, and the mainland of Anatolia, caught the wind and changed its direction. Now in currents flowing westward, the swirling air filled the sails.

Even in the relative calm of the southeastern corner of the Aegean Sea, the Captains divided their attention between the fullness of the sails, the wind on their faces, and the horizons around them. On the first day, between the sun's apex and sundown, the God Boreas sent gusts from the north. The winds whipped around the islands and skimmed along the coast of Anatolia.

"Oars out," Captain Petridis instructed. "The God doesn't want to help us. Oarsmen, make the sacrifice."

From the forward section, the First Officer called cadence for the oarsmen and the musician.

"Stroke. Stroke. Slow and steady," he directed. "We're helping the sail not running a race. Slow and steady."

His words didn't carry to the other warship. If they had, it wouldn't have made a difference. The Rhodian surged ahead as their rowers dipped oars at a quicker rate. Responding to the strength of the extra oarsmen, the trihemiolia shot ahead of the trireme.

***

From the steering deck, Malis Aeson observed the Rhodian vessel pulling farther and farther ahead.

"It's not a race, Ambassador," Captain Petridis said, sounding as if he was apologizing for his crew.

"You and I know it's not a race," Aeson suggested. "Someone forgot to tell the Rhodians. They seem to have a problem with the details of a joint venture."

"They'll understand it tomorrow," Petridis offered. "Any rowing crew that works that hard will be sore and sluggish in the morning."

As if he heard but disagreed, Sub-Commander Theo Katsaros on the steering deck of the Rhodian vessel turned and looked aft. Although a small figure in the distance by then, his laugh was obvious, as was the dismissive wave of his arm.

***

Near sundown, the Pergamon vessel rounded the western tip of Kos Island. On the beach, the warship from Rhodes sat high and dry. The crew, sitting around campfires, laughed as the slower trireme pointed its ram out to sea, before backing to the shallows.

"Welcome to Agios Theologos Beach," Sub-Commander Katsaros called. "If you'd been any later, we'd have launched a raft with a stack of lit firewood to guide you to the beach."

With a whisper, Aeson told his Captain, "It's not a race."

"You and I know that, Ambassador," Petridis repeated the observation, "I don't believe the Rhodians know it."

***

At daybreak the next morning, the Captain ordered the launch of the Pergamon warship. Petridis had monetary control over his hired oarsmen. The rowers from Rhodes, despite being better oarsmen, were also citizens of the island and claimed agency over harsh treatment. Thus, Ambassador Malis Aeson stood on the steering platform watching Katsaros eat a leisurely breakfast. The Sub-Commander's crew slept in, frolicked in the surf, or cast fishing nets.

"It's not a race this morning," Aeson noted.

"I'm sure they'll catch up," Petridis proposed.

The Pergamon vessel rowed away from the beach, unrolled its sail, and caught a current of air deflected off the island of Kos. Aeson stood looking back, waiting for the Rhodian ship to catch up. Yet, by midday, Ambassador Aeson hadn't seen the mast or sail of the warship from Rhodes.

***

All predators had favorite hunting grounds. Lions preferred tall grass on flat land for stalking and quick runs for the takedown of a meal. Eagles soared over lakes and rivers, watching for fish that lurked just below the surface. A downward swoop, a parting of the water, and a grab with strong talons preceded the flapping of mighty wings. An instant after the sudden attack, the bird-of-prey would fly away with its treasure. And on the rocky island of Megalo Livadi, two boat crews of humans, raiders protected by Philip of Macedon, loitered.

A plateau of arid, brush covered land, shaped much like linen body armor, the island only rose four yards in two spots above rocky beaches. In appearance, and for amenities such as water and shade, it offered nothing. Except, the island of Megalo Livadi sat halfway between the big island of Amorgos and the small island of Kinaros. Merchant ships crossing the southern Aegean Sea would pass through the channels between the three islands. That explained the preferred hunting ground of the two predatory vessels and why their lookouts noticed the lone three-banker coming from the east.

***

"A pair of two-bankers, Ambassador," Petridis alerted Malis Aeson.

"Fishermen?" Aeson offered, hoping for the best. He stood and inquired. "Where?"

"Coming off that small island," the Captain pointed out. "And they aren't fishermen, not with that many spears and shields."

"Can we out pace them?" Aeson asked.

"If we had the wind at our back, maybe," Petridis answered. "But they're lighter vessels with over a hundred rowers on each bireme. And when they tie up with a prize vessel, their oarsmen double as fighters."

"What then, Captain Petridis, is our strategy?"

"We're going to sink one and hope the other boat stops to save their comrades," Petridis described. "Or it's going to be a hard day of fighting before we die."

"Would they take a ransom?" Aeson inquired. "I hear that Cilicians pirates can be bribed."

"Unfortunately, Ambassador, based on the repairs done to the hulls of those two pirate ships, you're standing on the only ransom that lot will accept."

"An Ambassador of Pergamon mustn't be taken alive," Aeson declared. He patted the coin pouches under his robe and stared at the water. "Do you suppose drowning is painful? I've never been particularly brave except with words."

"We're not done yet, sir," the Captain assured him. Then to the Ambassador's bodyguards, Petridis instructed. "They'll throw grappling hooks. I'll pull a few oarsmen to help, but you've got to cut those lines or we'll be hauled in like a net full of herrings."

With men assigned to cutting grappling lines positioned around the deck, Petridis ordered the sail rolled and the oars extended.

"Wouldn't the sail give us speed?" Aeson asked.

"Ramming another vessel is not about speed, Ambassador," the Captain explained. "It's about rower muscle, control, agility, and the angle of attack."

Malis Aeson bowed to his Captain in respect and backed away. Around a negotiation table, the Ambassador could sling ideas, strike with cutting logic, and wrap up his opponents in endless loops of rational arguments. On the deck of a warship, he was as useless as the sea birds that rested on top of the sail between flights to land.

The small island in his vision grew until he noted the bushes, rocks, and sand. "Such an inauspicious landmark for my grave," he thought.

Next, straightening his back, Aeson picked up a knife from the pile of iron cutting tools, and marched to an empty spot on the deck. One of his bodyguards began to shift to his position, but the Ambassador waved him back.

"We cut lines and live," he told the hoplite. "Or we fail and the Fates cut our strings. Stay at your post."

"Yes, Ambassador," the soldier replied.

Only then did Aeson examine the two biremes rowing out to meet the trireme. One rowed towards their right and the other to the left. He could tell by the wake of disturbed water behind the vessels that they were rowing hard and moving fast.

***

"We'll take the one off our port side," Petridis told his rear oarsmen. "Give me a little movement to starboard."

The navigators pulled left on the twin oars and the prow of the trireme angled to the right.

Seeing his victim heading away made the pirate Captain overconfident. He angled in, going for a close pass to give his men on the grappling hooks a better chance to capture the warship.

Petridis allowed his ship to drift to starboard. By then, the raider on the right side had rounded his approach to come in from the side and avoid the ram. But the one on the port side rowed directly towards the trireme.

"First Officer, give me thunder and lighting," Captain Petridis shouted as if to relay the idea of a storm to his rowers and the musician. As the beats increased in tempo and volume, on the power of big strokes, strung close together, the trireme surged ahead. Then Petridis turned and faced his rear oarsmen. "Gentlemen, to port. Find me the angle and gut that pirate."

Riding just below the surface, the ram threw up twin rooster tails of water. But it wasn't the sight of the arches of sea water, or the ship-killing bronze blades riding below the surface that brought a chill to the Captain of the pirate ship. It was the sudden turn that aimed the ram at the side of his bireme.

Petridis stepped to the port rail, and although he couldn't hear the raider Captain, he recognized the panicked wave of the man's arms and the open mouth that screamed, "to starboard, to starboard."

The port side oars withdrew into the trireme. Some of the momentum bled off when the bronze blades shattered hull boards and crushed beams of the lateral structure. As the ribs of the raider vessel snapped, the two-banker gave way to the flooding and rolled on its side. As quick as the destruction began, it ended when the bronze ram swung free at midship and the port oars were runout.

"Stroke, stroke," the First Officer bellowed. "Stroke."

But the warship hesitated as if towing another vessel. Looking across the deck of his warship, Petridis understood exactly what happened.

The raider ship on the starboard side had slung and hung enough hooks to draw the two-banker in. On that side, the raider hull snarled the Stroke section and half the oars of his Engine rowers. The three-banker wallowed as pirates swarmed up the side.

Although his oarsmen rushed to the upper deck, they lacked the spears, swords, and shields of the raiders. Petridis grabbed a long curved knife from the pile of weapons and looked over his shoulder. His navigators had rested the rear oars on the deck and drawn their own blades.

"We got one of them," he boasted.

"That we did, Captain," the pair of rear oarsmen confirmed.

"Ambassador, please join me on the steering platform," Petridis invited Aeson.

Malis Aeson shuffled to the rear deck. Blood dripped from one hand. Petridis couldn't tell if it was an amputated finger from a sword slash or a slice from an errant spear thrust.

"You're bleeding Ambassador," the Captain pointed out.

"Indeed I am," Aeson stated with more confidence than he'd displayed when the pirates first appeared. "I'm bleeding, yes. My assailant, however, is swimming with the fish."

"I'm afraid, we'll be joining him soon," Petridis warned as more raiders crawled over the rail and joined the fight. They pushed back the defenders and one of Aeson's bodyguards dropped to his knees. Before any of the others could save him, pirates swarmed the hoplite, pulled off his helmet, and hacked him to pieces. He was dead before his lacerated head hit the deck boards. Petridis offered. "I'll go over the side with you, Ambassador. You should have enough gold to take us both to the bottom."

"It'll be good to have company in my final moments."

"Captain," one of the rear oarsmen shouted. "The Rhodians are coming."

***

Standing on the foredeck of the trihemiolia, Sub-Commander Katsaros crouched like a mountain cat. Although his face was hidden under the helmet, his drawn blade quivered as if an asp seeking a victim. His arms and legs taut, the Rhodian appeared ready to spring across the distance and join the fight.

None of the raiders noticed the arrival until the sound of their wooden boat being ground into kindling reached them. The bronze ram, chewing through the raider vessel, preceded the arrival of an embarrassed Sub-Commander. He jumped to the two-banker and fought his way across the pirate ship. Moments later, Theo Katsaros took charge of defending the Pergamon three-banker.

Chapter 8 - Mount Lycabettus

Shields with the image of a sun embossed on the face shoved the pirates aside. As if pushing through a dense crowd on a festival day, the soldiers and armed oarsmen from Rhodes opened a path and formed a new battle line between the exhausted Pergamon hoplites and rowers and Philip's chosen raiders. Then, while wielding their short spears like swords, they slashed the forward ranks of raiders. Leading and anchoring the center of the fighting, Sub-Commander Katsaros roared challenges.

"Attack a friend of Rhodes, you mangy cur," he bellowed, "is to rain down death and ruin on your souls."

Although hard to make out his words from inside his helmet, if they even were supposed to be comprehensible, Katsaros' vicious thrusts and larger-than-life presence encouraged the oarsmen from Pergamon and Rhodes.

"Cut the trash loose," Theo Katsaros ordered when the raiders broke contact and hopped from the trireme to their flooded two-banker.

Relieved at the outcome, the oarsmen, hoplites, sailors, and soldiers cut the grappling lines, freeing the pirate ship. Without the tension of the lines, the raider vessel rolled over and dumped the pirates into the sea.

"There's an island just over there," Katsaros instructed the men in the water. "It doesn't look like much. But it's high ground and free of sharks. Have a nice swim."

Sub-Commander Katsaros marched to the steering platform, saluted, and bowed.

"Because of my pride, I almost lost the Ambassador from Pergamon, a worthy crew, and a sturdy warship," Katsaros stated. "Can you sail on or do we locate a beach for the rest of today and tonight?"

"We have some wounds to bandage and slashes to sew," Captain Petridis reported. He looked at Malis Aeson with questioning eyes. "The ship is intact and my rowers able. Ambassador?"

"There's your answer, Sub-Commander," Aeson declared. He held up the hand with the bloody bandage and pointed to the northwest. "We sail onward. Tonight, we'll cremate our dead."

Sailers shoved a ramp across the top deck, creating a bridge to the warship from Rhodes. As if on a drill field, Katsaros marched over the plank to his three-banker.

As the two ships parted to allow room for their oars, Captain Petridis remarked. "He didn't apologize."

"His type never does," Aeson informed his Captain. "He did save us."

"In Plato's Crito, he portrays Socrates arguing that it is not merely about escaping punishment for wrongdoing," Petridis commented. "It's about avoiding the greater evil of doing wrong in the first place."

"How would you chastise a man like the Sub-Commander?" Aeson inquired.

The Captain smiled and pointed at the injured hand.

"Every time he sees your wound, he'll be reminded of his negligence," Petridis described. "It'll affect him more than a shouting match or several bouts in Apollo's sport."

"I'm no match for him in a boxing contest," the Ambassador suggested. "Perhaps I should keep the bloody bandage on my hand."

"It'll work better than a flogging or a beating, to stress the fault in the Sub-Commander's constitution," the Captain assured him.

***

Over the next three days, the two ships beached and launched together from the islands of Naxos and Serifos, and finally from Thimari Beach on the tip of the mainland. After leaving before dawn, by midday, they sailed to the entrance, rolled their cloth, and rowed into the harbor of Piraeus.

Along the shorelines, old warehouses, crumbling, leaning and forlorn, displayed the past glory of Athens. Adding to the decay of the once mighty seagoing city, the ribs of derelict half sunken ships and boats poked out of the shallows.

"First Officer, watch for underwater obstacles," Captain Petridis warned.

"The center channel appears clear," the ship's officer called from the foredeck.

At a slow rate, the oarsmen powered the Pergamon warship through the harbor while Petridis eyed the land on either side of the harbor. He, and the Captain of the Rhodian ship behind him, searched for a safe place to beach their three-bankers. Near the end of the harbor, a few lengths of new piers serviced a couple of merchant ships.

"Port side of the dock," the First Officer alerted the Captain. "The bottom looks clean and the beach is pebbled."

To his navigators and First Officer, Petridis instructed, "Turn us around and get us dry."

As the Pergamon warship angled around and began backing towards shore, the Rhodian ship mirrored the turn. Both keels touched harbor bottom and inexperienced rowers dropped into the shallows. They pushed the boats out of the water and onto the beach.

***

When the warship came to rest, Ambassador Malis Aeson studied the rough new piers and thought that the old tales about Athens being a sea power in a bygone age might be exaggerated. Next, he raised his eyes to a massive wall that circled the harbor. Set in the wall to the north were two gateways.

"Those gates," he mentioned to Petridis. "They seem very close together."

"Because, Ambassador, the left gate opens to the rest of Attica. It's a long walk to a side gate back into Athens," the Captain described. "The right gate puts you on a road between two defensive walls that sit about two hundred paces apart. It ends at the city of Athens."

"Both gates look ceremonial?" Aeson inquired.

"And defensible, sir. Over a hundred and twenty years ago, when King Alexander died, and the Macedonian threat ended, they rebuilt the walls," Petridis described. "Now after having rebuilt the long walls, another King of Macedonia threatens their sovereignty."

"But two ornate gates at this wreck of a harbor?" Aeson inquired.

"A nod, I believe, to the amount of cargo once shipped to and from Athens and the countryside. Perhaps two gates were preparation for a prosperous future," the Captain proposed. "And you are correct, sir, from the looks of Piraeus Harbor, it doesn't appear they're handling enough volume these days for one gate."

Theo Katsaros called up from the pebbles of the beach, "Ambassador Aeson. Athens awaits us."

Malis Aeson regarded the ramp being lowered to the beach. His five remaining bodyguards were lined up in war gear, preparing to escort him into Athens.

"This is a diplomatic mission, hoplites, not an invasion," Aeson sighed. "I'll take one of you, but not in armor with a spear and a shield. A sword, a knife, and a robe should suffice."

Malis Aeson waited for one bodyguard to unbuckle and drop his armor. Once in a robe, and while tying on his sword belt, the hoplite raced to the top of the ramp. He stood rigid, waiting for the Ambassador.

"Now that's more political," Aeson boasted to Petridis while brushing his robe with his hands.

The Ambassador had chosen a robe with fine embroidery and a shoulder clasp of fired clay. He left the ostentaticus one with silver threads and the gold clasp in his cedar chest.

"Yes, sir," the Captain agreed. "You and your bodyguard are the essence of diplomacy."

"Petridis, you keep talking like that, and before you know it, you'll be the Ambassador," Aeson teased. He strolled across the deck and nodded to his bodyguard to proceed him. But when the Ambassador reached the top of the ramp, he halted and slapped a hand over his mouth.

Curious why he stopped, Captain Petridis moved quickly to Aeson's side.

"Ambassador, we are wasting the day," Theo Katsaros warned. He stood on the pebbles of the beach. His polished steel armor was edged in silver trim and the torso sported gold leafing in the shape of the sun. Rich red and pure white sections of the horsehair plume on his helmet sparkled in the midday sunlight.

"I see, Sub-Commander, that you are prepared to do battle with Athens," Aeson observed.

"If that's what it takes," Katsaros replied. "So be it."

He rested his hand on the hilt of his sword.

For all Ambassador Aeson's caution about downgrading his and his bodyguard's wardrobe to appear more diplomatic, the Sub-Commander had gone full military splendor. The incongruity between the representative from Pergamon and the one from Rhodes caught Petridis as funny. The Captain placed his palm against his chin to hide the smile, turned, and walked back to the steering deck as if deep in thought.

***

"We are on a mission," Sub-Commander Katsaros announced as they approached the gates.

"Destination?" the guard Captain inquired.

"We're here to address the Assembly of Athens on Pnyx Hill," Katsaros snapped. "Allow us to pass, your Archon awaits us."

The Athenian officer looked at the Sub-Commander's parade ground worthy gear, smiled and indicated the left gate.

"Yes, sir," he instructed. "Through the left gate and head northeast. It's a brisk walk of four and a half miles."

"Very well," Katsaros said, accepting the hike.

Aeson stopped the Sub-Commander with a hand on his shoulder while addressing the guard officer, "And how far is it, Captain, through the right gate?"

After taking in the subdued robe and the pleasant smile, the Captain admitted, "It's under four miles, sir. And there are horses to rent at the stable."

"Very well, I believe we should take the right gate, don't you agree Sub-Commander?" Aeson inquired.

"Yes, of course, we'll take the right gate," Theo Katsaros declared.

Without waiting for the Ambassador from Pergamon, he marched towards the portal.

"Thank you again, Captain," Aeson said.

"We have a lot of officers like that," the guard Captain remarked. "Good luck with that one."

Aeson noticed his bodyguard saluting the guard Captain as they walked by.

***

The wall towered over nine yards from the surface of the road. And once through the first gate, the high stone works created a dark canyon, or a death trap if one attempted to invade Athens. When they passed through the interior gate, a road stretched out before them. Massive stone walls paralleled the road, and in the distance, the trek appeared to merge into a point.

"From here it looks like a spear shaft," a stableman remarked. "You can walk it. But it's a hot day and a lengthy hike between the long walls of Athens. Or you can rent a wagon and a driver for a few coins. He'll get you to your destination. But to really enjoy the city blessed by the Goddess Athena, you'll want to rent three horses."

"We'll rent horses," Katsaros told the stableman.

"Have you been to Athens before?" Aeson inquired.

"No, I haven't," Katsaros admitted. "But it's not that big."

"I've never visited Athens either," Aeson divulged. "I've read, however, that the Acropolis is the tallest point in the city."

"If I might, sir," the stableman interrupted, "Mount Lycabettus is the highest point in the city."

"What's your point Ambassador?" Katsaros uttered.

"My point, Sub-Commander, is you can't see the Acropolis or Mount Lycabettus from here," Aeson presented. "If that's the case, how would you know the size of the city or where to go once we reach it."

"But a wagon would be undignified," Katsaros protested.

"I'll tell you what," the Ambassador promised. "If you don't tell anyone that we were hauled around Athens like so many sacks of grain, neither will I."

"A wagon and a driver for you gentlemen?" the stableman inquired.

"A wagon and a driver," Sub-Commander Katsaros ordered. "And be sure, the driver knows his way around Athens."

"For sure, sir, his name is Har'ris," the stableman told him. "My son knows every corner of Athens. You'll be in good hands."

Chapter 9 - A Stoic of Athens

The horse clopped along the stone road, guided by a switch that Har'ris barely employed. It was obvious the creature knew the way, which wasn't giving much credit to the mare because it was an enclosed roadway.

"Ambassador, if I might comment?" the bodyguard requested. He wiped sweat from his forehead.

"Speak freely," Aeson granted. He as well felt the heat of the day, but in his cheeks and not on his brow. "It's a long ride without much scenery."

One hundred paces to either side of the road, massive defensive walls climbed to the sky. At regular intervals, guard towers sat atop the walls at small gates. The height of the walls limited a person's view to granite blocks, grass, dirt patches, a few carts coming from Athens, and the flat stones of the thoroughfare.

"The hinges on the gates at both ends of the portal were encased with dirt," the Hoplite reported. "As were those on the gate we just passed."

"Why is that worth mentioning?" Aeson inquired.

"Sir, Athens hasn't closed those gates in years," the bodyguard ventured. "If attacked, the guards would need a day to oil and work those hinges free before they could swing the gates closed."

"An excellent observation," Sub-Commander Katsaros complimented the hoplite. "Few men have a head for military intelligence."

"I hardly think Pergamon or Rhodes will be attacking Athens," Ambassador Aeson ventured. "If anything, we're here to elicit aid from their council."

The four-wheeled cart rolled to the end of the long walls and entered the ancient city. Low structures of stone, two and three story apartments of wood, and a rare granite building boarded narrow streets off the wide avenue. Continuing straight into the city, Har'ris indicated a series of tall mounds in the distance.

"You can just make out the tops of Kilios Hill and Pnyx Hill up ahead," the teamster pointed out. "Behind them is the Acropolis and the Temple of Athena. As the ground rises and we get closer to Pnyx, you'll see a little of Mount Lycabettus."

The three passengers twisted around in the bed of the wagon and studied the cityscape. It felt older than Rhodes, which was ancient, and for sure Pergamon the newest of the three. Athens had blocks high on building walls that revealed they had been repurposed from older foundations. As with most cities, the residents recycled materials from demolitions to rebuild after fires, earthquakes, or large projects by wealthy citizens, the government, or religious orders. Natural disruptors in a municipality always required change. Yet, despite the latest arrangement of blocks and a few fresh boards, Athens showed its age in the streets. Barely wide enough for a wagon, the dirt had been stomped flat and hardened by centuries of foot traffic. As if receding gums in an old man's mouth, the streets sat low, revealing a layer of foundation stones.

Har'ris guided the mare and wagon around several plots of high ground. Some had villas on top, while others hosted groves of trees.

"The Goddess Athena watches over the city from her temple," he described. "Sects of other deities have preserves around Athens. You'll notice the well-ordered trees of sanctuaries on a few of those hills."

***

The deeper into Athens they traveled, the higher the elevation climbed. Buildings became sparse as a foothill forced the boulevard to drift right. The first knoll began a series of ever rising mounds.

"If you're feeling poorly," Har'ris advised, while pointing to openings in the hillside. "The healing God Asclepius has a sanctuary in those caves. Plus there's a sacred spring with healing waters."

"We're fine," Katsaros answered for the Ambassador. "Keep going."

As the wagon passed the entrance to the reserve of the healing God, Malis Aeson glanced down at his hand. While the bandage appeared clean on the outside, underneath where the cloth rested on his wound, the skin festered and oozed. Not wanting to delay the trip for a minor injury, he allowed the Sub-Commander to direct the mission.

"Hold on," Har'ris warned. The wagon tilted when the wheels left the boulevard and rolled onto a rutted dirt road. "Up on the right is Pnyx Hill. Now that the heat of the day is gone, the Council of Athens will be holding its afternoon session."

The mare dug in her hooves and pulled the wagon up a steep trail. As they moved under trees, branches blocked the afternoon sun, giving relief from the heat. Everyone enjoyed the shade except for Aeson. He shivered.

After a long climb, Har'ris eased the horse to the side of the trail.

"To your right and uphill a little is the meeting place," he instructed. "I'll be here when you're done."

Malis Aeson and his bodyguard shimmied to the rear of the wagon and stepped to the ground. The Ambassador wobbled, but a hand from the hoplite steadied him. It took longer for Theo Katsaros in his heavy armor to scoot off the rear.

"Undignified," he whined, brushing off his legs. "Now, where do we find the Council?"

***

Although the hillside above the rocky plateau was steep, the trees and lush growth held the soil in place. Where the rock emerged from the soil, it formed a natural bench. Almost as if a reverse amphitheater, the audience seating was the narrowest part. Lower down, where the Council of Athens met, the rock flattened and widened. Below there, the surface dropped off quickly and dangerously, before vanishing into more trees.

"Pnyx Hill isn't much to look at," Katsaros declared as they approached the hill. But next, after examining the height above the city and a view of the long walls, he revised his thinking. "But it does limit access to the council to healthy men with ambition to make the climb."

Ambassador Aeson missed the declaration of the Sub-Commander. Sounds of *Tink-Tink-Tink* drew his attention. A new stone and rail fence across the rock before the drop-off caught his eyes. Only two posts of what would be a safety barrier had been constructed, and each had a perfect ball of granite balanced on top of the post. Higher up from the dangerous fall, a stone mason worked on another sphere of granite, *Tink-Tink-Tink* went his chisel and hammer. To one side of the craftsman sat finished rounds. On his other side were blocks of rough stone. What puzzled Ambassador Aeson, the workman had set up his chisels, hammers, blocks, and work materials in the center of the Council's meeting area.

Tink-Tink-Tink

"There's a scribe making a list of people wanting to petition the council this afternoon," Katsaros told Aeson. "I've put our names on the list. I argued for better placement, but the stubborn man wouldn't listen."

"We'll be fine, Sub-Commander," the Ambassador assured him. "They seem to have experienced a problem with the lower portion of the rock. I should go and talk with the stone mason."

"You have an odd sense of what's important, Malis Aeson. Let's try and focus on what's important and why we're here."

"Fair enough," the Ambassador relented. "Where do we wait?"

Katsaros indicated a small crowd higher up on the plateau at the natural bench. The Ambassador, his bodyguard, and the Sub-Commander strolled to the group and introduced themselves.

Tink-Tink-Tink

***

The sun sank towards the horizon as farmers asked about prices for their grain, herders questioned the availability of grazing land, merchants argued for tax relief, and men in dispute came to have it adjudicated. Eventually, as the citizens either stormed off Pnyx Hill or joined the spectators, the Archon of Athens looked at the crowd.

"Negotiation means no one walks away happy with the deal," Zervas, the elected ruler of Athens, announced. "But everyone leaves with something that addresses their wants. It's the way of compromise in a Democracy."

Tink-Tink-Tink

During the arguments and discussions, the stone mason continued to chip away at the block of granite, fashioning a sphere from a coarse block.

"I guess now is the time for something different," Archon Zervas told the Council. "Let us hear from Ambassador Aeson of Pergamon and Subcommander Katsaros of Rhodes. Gentlemen step forward and address the Council of Athens."

Aeson and Katsaros hesitated. It felt odd speaking to the ruler and his court from above them. In both of their countries, they stood below or level with their leaders when addressing the King or Chief Magistrate.

Zervas seemed to understand and spoke to the issue. "Here in Athens, every man is equal with every other. From up there, you are easier to understand. So state your request and we of the Council of Athens will vote on the issue."

Malis Aeson took a step forward and raised both arms.

"Men of Athens, we have come to ask for the weight of your city in our quest," he proclaimed. "Our two states have given us a mission to bring about the downfall of Philip V of Macedonia." He paused, as if slightly confused.

Tink-Tink-Tink

Irritated by the sound, Theo Katsaros stepped up and barked, "Can you not hold the petty work while an envoy finishes his discourse?"

Tink-Tink-Tink

"Your anger is unwarranted Sub-Commander. I was collecting my thoughts," Aeson pleaded, while placing a hand on the armored shoulder. Immediately, he withdrew the wounded hand. "Friends, Athenians, Philip has attacked both our navies, our shipping, and our colonies. Something must be done with the lout."

"How does that effect Athens?" Zervas inquired.

"Once he controls the Aegean Sea and the Port of Alexandria Egypt," Katsaros threatened, "he's sure to turn his attention to Athens and the rest of Greece."

"And what would you have us do?" Archon Zervas questioned. "Build a navy, raise an army, or send a delegation of poets to Pella to charm Philip V of Macedon?"

Tink-Tink-Tink

"Can you just stop that incessant noise?" Sub-Commander Katsaros roared at the stonemason.

Tink-Tink…Crack

With a vicious strike to the top of the carved sphere, the stone mason cleaved the granite in two. One side crumbled, and the other fell away in a half orb.

Aeson studied the man's face to judge how angry he was. Obviously, his ire at the Sub-Commander caused him to ruin an intended work of art. The Ambassador envisioned the entire mission failing because of Katsaros' impatience. Seeing as no one was looking at the stonemason, and hadn't reacted to the damage, Aeson decided to talk fast and get to the point.

"If I might make a comment," Aeson begged.

"Please Ambassador," Zervas said, just as calmly as when he first invited Aeson to speak.

"Thank you, Archon and Council of Athens," Aeson began. "We are on a mission to Rome to ask their Senate for assistance in reining in Philip V of Macedon and stop his conquests. Rome's ships trade with Egypt and Athens, Pergamon, Rhodes, and the rest of the eastern region. It is in their best interest to give us aid. But truthfully, because Athens is the leader of the Hellenistic region, we need you with us."

"Tsolak of Fyli, what do you have to say?" Zervas asked.

Malis Aeson studied the faces of the council members, trying to identify Tsolak of Fyli. When none of them moved, Aeson looked at Zervas, then followed the ruler of Athens' eyes to the craftsman.

The man sat holding the broken sphere, peered at the sky, and watched a bird fly overhead.

"Virtue is the only good," he proposed, leveling his eyes at the Archon of Athens. "Health, wealth, and pleasure, are not good or bad in themselves. They are but material items for a virtuous man to interact with."

"Then answer this question, Tsolak of Fyli," Zervas urged. "Will you interact with the mission proposed by Pergamon and Rhodes?"

"If nominated, I will not serve," Tsolak of Fyli divulged. "If ordered, I will not go."

Both Theo Katsaros and Malis Aeson physically deflated. To come so far, only to have an apparently mad craftsman dash their hopes, left them defeated. They could go on to Rome, but without the weight of influence from either Egypt or Athens, their chance of success rested more with luck than with diplomacy.

"Well, Ambassador," Zervas inquired.

"I guess we have our answer," Aeson stated.

He took a step towards the trail to the wagon when words from the craftsman stopped him.

"He isn't as smart as I'd hoped," Tsolak of Fyli mentioned.

Aeson turned. He stared at the sculptor whose only artistry, as far as he knew, was chiseling orbs from blocks of granite.

"My home is rustic compared to historic Athens," Aeson uttered. "But in Pergamon, we treat guests with kindness and compassion. And I would hope to never insult anyone at the first meeting."

Tsolak of Fyli rubbed his forehead, leaving streaks of granite dust on his brow.

"Archon Zervas," Tsolak pleaded, as if his patience had been spent on a petulant child.

"Ambassador Aeson, before you storm off, think on this for a moment," Zervas proposed. "If a man cannot be forced by an obligation, nor compelled into an action, what path is left?"

"Cannot be forced by an obligation, nor compelled by an order," Aeson whispered, lifting his eyes to the sky. After several heartbeats, he said. "The only path remaining is to ask him to act."

"Well?" Archon Zervas probed.

"Tsolak of Fyli," Aeson questioned. "Will you accompany us to Rome and plead the case for Athens?"

"If I wasn't a philosopher from the school of stoicism," Tsolak explained, "I'd say it would be my pleasure. But seeing as that goes against my teaching, I'll simply say yes."

Zervas raised his arms and inquired, "Is there anything else?"

"Will Tsolak of Fyli have a ship of his own?" Aeson asked.

"Why would he?" Ambassador Aeson remarked. "It was you who invited a stoic of Athens to go on the journey."

Chapter 10 - Har'ris To Ilion

After a restless night at an inn, the Ambassador and his bodyguard found Har'ris waiting with the wagon. Moments later, the Rhodian Sub-Commander emerged.

"I asked about breakfast establishments," he explained. "There are a few restaurants nearby."

"Young man," Aeson addressed Har'ris, "let's begin the day with a meal."

"Aren't you going to wait for Tsolak?" Har'ris asked.

Aeson glanced at the entrance to the inn and inquired, "Did he sleep late?"

"No, sir," the teamster reported. "The Philosopher went to get food. According to him, we must not waste the day lounging about."

"I was worried about the man," Katsaros declared. "But I like his attitude. I don't like to waste my days either."

Tsolak of Fyli came strolling around a corner. He had a sack in his hand. At the wagon, he opened the bag, revealing pieces of bread and chunks of cheese.

"Grab some," he instructed. "You can eat on the way."

With a piece of cheese wrapped in a pocket of bread, Har'ris started the horse moving down the street.

"Hold, hold," Tsolak directed. "You are moving in the wrong direction."

"But the harbor is that way," Katsaros protested.

"No voyage can start without a ritual," Tsolak stated. "And that requires us to take the Dipylon Gate."

"Which way is that?" Aeson questioned.

Tsolak bowed his head towards Har'ris.

The youth pointed over his shoulder and disclosed, "It's a northwest gate."

"Then let's go," Aeson declared. "The sooner we complete the ritual, the sooner we can get to underway."

The horse and wagon turned around at the intersection and the group headed away from the long walls and the harbor.

***

A few streets from the inn, Aeson asked Tsolak, "Why did Zervas call on you for this mission?"

"The Goddess Athena protects Athens," the Stoic replied.

"I understand that," Aeson debated. "But why you?"

"Athena is the Goddess of wisdom, war, and crafts," Tsolak stipulated. "The Archon observed you, and the Sub-Commander, and sought to honor the Goddess."

"I'm the warrior," Katsaros boasted. "You are the craftsman, and Ambassador Aeson must be the wisdom."

"Socrates pondered love," Tsolak lectured. "Love derives from an unattainable object. Philosophers strive to have the wisdom not to lack anything. A sage, on the other hand, does not love or seek wisdom, for he already possesses everything he needs."

"I don't understand," the Sub-Commander admitted.

"That's a start," Tsolak of Fyli stated.

"And neither do I," Aeson added. "Can you be more specific?"

"Socrates examined the two types of people who do not partake in the ideals of philosophy," Tsolak related. "The two categories of people who do not partake in philosophy are Gods and sages, because they are wise. And senseless people, because they think they are wise."

"I never said I was wise," Aeson emphasized.

"Of course not, Ambassador," Tsolak agreed. "But you are superb at discourse. One might say a craftsman of elocution. You possess the skill of clear and expressive speech."

"Then you are the wise one," Katsaros grunted as if challenging the stoic.

"Alas, there were no Gods or sages available for this journey," Tsolak revealed. "Zervas chose the next best thing. He picked a stoic philosopher."

They rode in silence until the road straightened and a tower appeared in the distance.

"The Dipylon Gate," Har'ris announced. He pointed to the massive structure. "That's where the procession for the Panathenaic Games begins. The games honor the Goddess Athena and people come from all over the world to compete. It's said the Dipylon Gate is the tallest gate in the world."

No one questioned the claim. They simply leaned back while watching the top of the gate loom high overhead. The closer they got, the more they craned their necks to maintain sight of the crown over the portal.

"I bet the Colossus of Rhodes is taller," Katsaros bragged.

"Perhaps we should measure them," Tsolak suggested.

The Sub-Commander's face sagged, and he admitted, "The statue fell years ago."

"We have, in that case, nothing to compare the gate with," Tsolak stated.

Like the gate at the harbor, the Dipylon gateway had two gates, one at the opening and another on the far side of the portal. They rode through the first and the hoplite bodyguard jumped off the wagon and marched beside it.

"This is a kill zone," he explained, eyeing the tall inner walls and the archer platforms at the top of the stonework. "Assaulting this gate would be suicide."

When they emerged outside the city's defenses, the land opened to a couple of farm hovels and pastureland. Farther from Athens, the road vanished between trees as it ventured into a thick forest.

"How were the hinges?" Aeson teased when his bodyguard remounted the wagon. He expected to hear the ceremonial gates were well maintained.

"Caked in dried mud, Ambassador," the hoplite reported. "It'll take two days to free up those hinges and close gates of that size."

Malis Aeson looked to the rear and marveled at the majestic stonework of the walls and the impressive height of the Dipylon Gate. Then, with a cynical eye, he studied the gateway and the wide open portal that negated the advantage of a strong defensive barrier.

***

In the woods, the trail began to rise for a few hundred paces before dipping sharply to the bank of a river. Har'ris guided the horse up a stone abutment and onto a wooden span. Tsolak of Fyli leaned over one side of the wagon, then shifted and studied the other side.

"Is something wrong?" Aeson inquired.

"Even though it's late in the fall, the waters of the Cephissus flow well," Tsolak responded. "And the bridge at Sepolia stands sturdy."

"And if it wasn't in good repair?" questioned Katsaros.

"Nothing," the Stoic replied.

"What kind of answer is nothing?" the Sub-Commander demanded.

"I'm neither a master bridge builder able to make repairs, nor a fisherman seeking river fish, nor a farmer in need of the bridge to reach my market," Tsolak expounded. "Thusly, I have no emotional connection to the river or the bridge. Well, other than a mild curiosity."

"Don't you care about anything?" Sub-Commander Katsaros inquired.

"Virtue," Tsolak the Stoic stated.

Theo Katsaros huffed, crossed his arms, and sat back against the side of the wagon. Under him, the wheels rolled over the log span as they crossed the Cephissus River. On the far side, the land rose, and the forest thinned.

***

Between two hills, the trail entered a wetland. Tall weeds jutted from blue-green scum that covered the surface. On one side, the land climbed to pastureland. Sheep dotted the slope.

"Stop," Tsolak directed. "We aren't too late."

"Too late?" Aeson inquired.

"Later in the year, the water will evaporate," Tsolak replied. "And later today, all signs of the Goddess Achlys will vanish."

At the mention of the Goddess of the mist of death, the other occupants wanted to flee the swamp. But the stoic had stepped down and waded into the standing water. Har'ris held the horse still.

A trace of morning fog hovered near the far edge of the wetland. Tsolak splashed towards the mist with his arms extended. His voice, although incomprehensible, drifted back to the wagon. After long moments of walking in circles, grasping at the fog, Tsolak straightened his path and splashed back to the trail and the wagon.

"Was that part of the travel ritual?" Malis Aeson asked.

"Whenever I pass this way, I try to meet the Goddess Achlys," the stoic told the Ambassador. "A conversation with her would be enlightening. But when I attempt to hug her and her mist, she eludes me."

"Drive on," Katsaros instructed Har'ris. His voice revealed a touch of impatience.

At the edge of the swamp, they passed a stone arch inscribed with the name of the Goddess and a warning about the dangers to travelers of lingering in the mist.

***

The road climbed from the lowland to a high ridge. Along the crest, iron sculptures of Gods and heroes sat on top of blocks of granite. The Stoic touched Har'ris before the wagon reached the apex. Pulling on the reins, the teamster halted the transport.

"Are we here so you can chip away at a granite block and create a sphere?" Katsaros dared.

"An interesting idea but the orb would be too large to be useful," Tsolak remarked. "But this is a good spot for you to start your stroll and reflect on the real purpose of your mission."

Katsaros bristled at the suggestion. Then he noticed the warriors depicted in the sculptures and nodded. While climbing off the wagon, he inquired, "Where will you be while I'm praying to Hephaestus?"

"We'll wait for you in the smithing village," Tsolak answered. Then to the driver, he said. "Har'ris onward."

***

Once over the ridge, a village came into view. Several forges were prominently displayed. If the smithing forges wasn't connection enough to Hephaestus, the God of metalworking, craftsmen, and sculpture, a stone temple dominated the village of metalworkers.

Late in the morning, Sub-Commander Katsaros came over the ridge and made directly for the temple.

"He appears to have more energy in his steps," Aeson commented.

The Ambassador from Pergamon and Tsolak of Fyli sat under a shade tree.

"Warriors face a difficult challenge," Tsolak offered. "Most Gods and Goddesses represent virtuous acts, progress, or affairs of the heart."

"In a broad sense, I can see that," the Ambassador commented. "If I accept your premise, how does that create difficulty for warriors."

"For the most, they have Ares the God of War to worship. Ares, however, is a cautionary tale," the Stoic explained. "In Sparta, if you can stand the irony, they keep their statue of Ares in chains. Should he be released, along with his blessing of bravery comes pain, injury, death, destruction, famine, and every war evil imaginable."

"I never thought of Ares in that context," Aeson admitted.

"The Sub-Commander's walk among the artworks of Hephaestus, other than weapons of war, may quiet his heart," Tsolak described. "Or not, it's his choice."

When Theo Katsaros returned to the wagon, he climbed in without saying anything.

"Har'ris, to the grove of Priapus," Tsolak ordered. Turning to face Aeson, he informed the Ambassador. "The grove is our next to last stop."

***

The horse easily pulled the wagon downhill and into a forest. A few turns later, the trail started up a gentle slope. Before they reached the top, the chaos of the forest gave way to neat rows of fruit trees.

"Stop the wagon," the Stoic instructed.

He leaped to the ground, beckoned the others to follow, and guided them between the rows of fruit trees.

"Smell the best of man," he exclaimed.

"In what sense?" Aeson inquired.

"Who could imagine the separation between the disorder of nature and the order of man other than on muddy streets, sour body odors, and the dung heaps of a city. Yet here, in the Grove of Priapus, the God of Fruit, we are blessed with sweet and earthly delights for our officiary senses."

Tsolak held up his hands as if feeling for something in the dark. After turning right and left several times, he settled on a row of trees. Then, as if pointed in a specific direction by an invisible hand, he marched to one tree, reached up, and plucked a fat pear from a branch.

"As the great Homer described in The Odyssey," the Stoic declared while holding up the pear, "this is a gift from the Gods."

***

On the downhill slope, the wagon rolled by a wooden temple dedicated to the God Priapus.

"Aren't we going to stop and pray?" Aeson asked.

"The sun is high in the sky," Tsolak observed while admiring the skin of his pear. "We have far to travel to reach the harbor and your ships. But first, we'll have lunch."

Katsaros peered around at the rustic huts of the priest, who tended the grove. And scanned the polished, carved wood of the temple built for the God Priapus.

"Hold on," the Sub-Commander muttered, "I thought this was a travel ritual. So far, you've chased mist and plucked a pear. I strolled among a host of heroes. What about something for Ambassador Aeson?"

"There is nothing for Ambassador Aeson," the Tsolak admitted. "Now we'll have lunch."

"We came all this way so you could have a pear?" Aeson questioned.

"And lunch. What did you expect, I'm a stoic, not a priest," Tsolak of Fyli explained. Then to the driver, he directed. "Har'ris, take us to Ilion."

Chapter 11 - East or West Direction

At daybreak, the Rhodian and the Pergamon ships rowed from the harbor at Athens. Outside Piraeus, the Captains lowered their sails, angled southwest and cruised down the Saronic Gulf. The day on the beach at Athens allowed their crews to caulk the hull boards, mend benches, replace rope lines, and sew the edges of their sailcloth. Both three-bankers were ship-shape and prepared for the long journey to the city of Rome.

By midday, they reached the Island of Idra and steered their ships westward. As the barren coast of the island drifted by, Malis Aeson swayed, staggered, and fell off the steering platform. Although his fall was only from hip high, the representative from Pergamon laid on the deck, unmoving.

"Ambassador," Captain Petridis exclaimed. He raced across the deck, hopped down, and squatted beside Aeson. Running a hand behind the unconscious man's head, he searched for a wound or a bump. "Sir, can you hear me?"

"Is he bleeding?" Tsolak inquired.

The Stoic sat on the edge of the steering deck with his legs crossed.

"There's no sign of blood or a cut," Petridis reported.

"Is there no sign of any wound?" Tsolak questioned.

"Other than the bandage on his hand and on his arm," Petridis uttered, then stopped. After a moment of reflection, he informed the Stoic. "He was only wounded on his hand."

The five hoplite bodyguards crowded around to better see their Principal.

"Place him on the platform and wrap him in blankets," Tsolak directed.

Two hoplites took Aeson's feet and two more lifted his shoulders. The fifth held the Ambassador's head level.

"We should do something," the Captain urged. "Maybe he was bitten by a snake or stung by a spider."

"Place him on the platform and wrap him in blankets," Tsolak repeated, before adding. "Your Ambassador was indeed poisoned. But not by a reptile or an arachnid. He was infected by pride and vanity."

The bodyguards carried Aeson to the side of the steering platform and gently lowered him to the deck. Petridis kneeled down and cradled the Ambassador against his chest. From that pose, he demanded, "What are you saying?"

Tsolak advised, "Take the bandage off his arm."

After unwinding the cloth, Petridis exposed Aeson's forearm above the wounded hand. Bloated and stretched taut, the skin on the limb resembled the outside of a cooked sausage. Besides the swelling, several veins, running black, traced up the arm before vanishing below the shoulder.

"What can we do?" Petridis begged.

"Wrap him in blankets and give him water," the Stoic stipulated. "Had he admitted to the rot earlier, a physician might have saved his life by amputating the hand. As it stands, he will soon pierce the veil of death and face the judges of Hades."

"We can't let him die," the Captain protested. "He's our Ambassador."

"Death is a natural, inevitable part of life," Tsolak lectured. "It's not something to fear. But a reminder to live a virtuous life of meaning while alive."

"You spray philosophy like a mule spits globs of saliva," Petridis accused him. "It spatters everywhere and no matter how thoroughly you clean, days later, you'll find another spot of goo."

Tsolak of Fyli stared at the Captain until Petridis squirmed.

Aeson stirred and inquired, "What happened?" His lips were dry and cracked.

"I'll get you water and a blanket," Petridis told the Ambassador.

"I feel weak and chilled to the bone," Aeson whispered.

***

For the first legs of the trip, the two warships sailed from one body of land to another. Sometimes they passed islands and at other places, they cruised by peninsulas of the mainland. As they traveled west, rarely did the ships lose sight of land. One benefit for Petridis, his rear oarsmen could handle the navigation, freeing him to sit with Malis Aeson and Tsolak of Fyli.

"When you reach Rome, Ambassador," the Stoic inquired, "what will you say to the Senate to move them to aid Pergamon."

"They have a granite sculpture of the Dying Gaul in Rome," Aeson replied. The short speech caused him to stop and try to catch his breath. While patting his chest as if he could beat air into his lungs, the Ambassador indicated for the Captain to finish the story.

"During the age when our King, Attalus I Soter, came to the throne of Pergamon," Petridis told the story, "the land was ravished by Celtic Gauls from Thrace. They raided at will, demanded tributes from larger villages, and carried off our harvest. They had been torturing, starving, and abusing the people of Anatolia for so long, the Celts assumed it was their right. But then, King Attalus came to rule Pergamon and refused to pay them tribute. He gathered warriors and met the Gauls at the Caecus River."

Aeson lifted his hand to stop the Captain.

"Warlord Attalus, sick of seeing the citizens of Pergamon treated like slaves, gathered an army," the Ambassador corrected his Captain's narrative. "At the river Caecus, he directed the tribes of Pergamon to strike the Gauls from the front. And at the same time, to perform a flanking attack from the side. After cutting the Gaul's force in two, he led attacks on both. From reports, the Gauls kept fighting, aroused by their belief that they couldn't lose to their subjects. By the end of the day, the Gauls were dead. The land freed. And Pergamon had a King."

Aeson physically wilted, as if the telling the tale had drained him. The Stoic looked from the sick man to the ship's Captain.

"How does that story concern Rome?" he questioned.

"The King commissioned a bronze statue of a collapsed Gaul with a wound in his side," Petridis described. "The Dying Gaul statue rests in the King's garden for all citizens to adore and our enemies to fear. An artist liked the images so much, he sketched it on Pergamon parchment, went to Rome, and carved a copy out of granite. The Dying Gaul is on display in a place called Capitoline Hill."

Aeson revived enough to say, "The Senate has to see that the strength and vigor of our people is worth saving from the Macedonian threat."

Tsolak of Fyli leaned over and pulled the blanket up and over Aeson's shoulders. Dropping his hand into his lap, he stated, "I see."

"See what?" Petridis inquired.

"Why the Ambassador didn't alert anyone to the rot on his hand," the Stoic Philosopher replied. "He believed a representative of Pergamon had to show strength. Perhaps he will survive."

"Will he?" Petridis asked.

"No," the Stoic disclosed.

***

They beached at the end of the day. The bodyguards began an overnight vigil over Aeson. Before anyone could settle, Sub-Commander Theo Katsaros marched over from his three-banker.

"How is the Ambassador?" he demanded.

"He's no better," Petridis insisted, "but he's no worse."

"You should turn back to Pergamon," Katsaros declared. "He's too sick to be of any use. As always, Rhodes will carry the load for Greece."

The Captain glanced at the Stoic, expecting the man to dispute the assumption. Almost as if he wasn't sitting next to Aeson, Tsolak continued to stare into the flames of the cookfire.

"In the morning, turn back," the Sub-Commander ordered.

He spun in the sand, and one of his sandals threw grit into the air. It rained down on the Stoic's lap. Ignoring the insult to the representative from Athens, the Rhodian strutted away.

"Why did you let him slight you like that?" Petridis asked.

Tsolak stirred the ash to allow air to reach a smothered log. Flames burst from the embers and began consuming the wood. Behind the Stoic and Ambassador Aeson, the bodyguards tensed, feeling anger about the interaction with the Sub-Commander.

"Young Alexander, the King of Macedonia, had just put down rebellious city-states," Tsolak began. "Once he'd established the treaties and enforced the accords they signed with his father, the King set up court at Corinth. When he began audiences with petitioners, a servant informed Alexander that Diogenes of Sinope, a famed stoic philosopher, was also visiting Corinth. Excited about the news, the King sent a messenger asking the stoic to come and dine at the palace."

"You're talking about Alexander the Great?" Petridis gushed.

"In Athens, we do not honor butchers like Alexander, or his father, Philip II of Macedonia," Tsolak chided the

Captain. "They terrorized my city. It was only after Alexander's death that we were able to rebuild the long walls. But yes, I am talking about King Alexander known as the Great, and also, about Diogenes of Sinope."

"A stoic like you," Petridis suggested.

The five hoplites had gathered around to hear the story. Above the fire, a fish roasted on a stick. The Stoic turned the stick in order to cook the other side of the fish.

"It would be un-stoic of me to compare myself with the prodigious teacher Diogenes," Tsolak offered in response. He poked the burning wood and watched smoke detach from the flames and drift into the sky. After lowering his chin, he resumed the story. "The messenger returned in the afternoon. He informed the most powerful ruler in all of Greece that Diogenes had refused to attend the King."

"Because he was a stoic," the Pergamon Captain ventured.

"As a matter of fact, Captain Petridis, it was indeed because he was a stoic," Tsolak agreed. Continuing, he said. "The next day, Alexander finished his morning meetings and rode out with his bodyguards. They located the stoic in a quiet neighborhood and the warhorses promptly ruined the harmony of the area. The arrival of so many people and horses disturbed the stoic's morning sunning and meditations. Attempting to ignore the commotion, Diogenes dropped an arm across his eyes. Due to his victories and his ascension to the throne, Alexander had been courted and flattered by all manner of rulers, magistrates, and warlords. He expected an impoverished philosopher to hail the conqueror of Greece. Instead, Diogenes remained motionless, as if nothing unusual was occurring around him."

Tsolak of Fyli stretched out an arm, pulled a piece of flesh from the fish, and sat chewing.

"What happened next?" Petridis demanded. The five hoplites nodded their heads in agreement.

"Oh, that," Tsolak said as he licked fish oil from his fingers. "Irritated by the dismissal, Alexander stepped in front of the philosopher. I am Alexander the King of Greece, Ruler of Macedon, and soon to be Monarch of Persia. What do you desire, stoic? Name it and I'll bring it to you. Diogenes of Sinope lifted his arm, gazed on the man, who would in a few years conquer the world, and said…"

The Stoic took his little finger and worked a fish bone from between his teeth. After admiring the delicate structure of the bone, he flipped it into the fire.

"Stoic," Petridis urged when Tsolak gazed at the sea for too long. "What did Diogenes say to King Alexander?"

"He said move a little to the left, you're blocking my light," Tsolak revealed. "Angry at the rude comment to their King, Alexander's bodyguards began to draw their swords to punish the stoic. Hold, the King ordered. Then he told them, if I wasn't Alexander of Macedonia, I'd be Diogenes of Sinope."

"The great King was a stoic?" Petridis guessed.

"From what I've read, his thirst for land and challenges and wine, might conflict with your assessment," Tsolak proposed. "But in his heart, I believe he wanted to be a stoic but lacked the discipline."

***

Ambassador Aeson revived slightly in the morning. With the aid of a bodyguard, he walked up the ramp to the ship and stood by the navigators as the ship launched.

"Where to Ambassador," Petridis inquired from the other side of the steering platform, "to Rome or to home?"

"Where to indeed, Captain," Aeson commented. "Our mission already dictates that. To Rome. But where to next is an excellent question."

"We should make Kithira Island late this afternoon, Ambassador," Petridis answered. "It's not much, but the Mani Peninsula is only a half day straight west. If the weather is bad, we'll need to cross to the mainland and cruise the shoreline of the bay. That will require a couple of days."

"Then let us pray for good weather," Aeson declared. "I'm feeling a little dizzy."

Two hoplites lowered the Ambassador to the deck, and the Stoic brought him a blanket. Petridis crossed the platform to see how Aeson was doing.

"Tell me Ambassador, what else will you say to the Romans?" Tsolak inquired.

"I will point out that at the height of their troubles with the Carthaginian, Hannibal Barca," Aeson began, but his voice gave out. "Captain Petridis, if you will tell him about the Goddess Cybele?"

"Of course, Ambassador," Petridis agreed. "The Romans arrived in a state of distress. Their lands were being ravished by a Carthaginian army. And signs of displeasure from the Gods began appearing. Snakes in temples, stars falling from the sky, and famine caused by rot even in protected grain houses were just a few. Fearing total defeat, they consulted their Oracle books and the Oracle of Delphi. Following the guidance of the Seers, the Romans arrived in Pergamon, seeking a Mother Goddess to protect their city."

Ambassador Aeson waved his good arm and picked up the story. "King Attalus listened to the Latians, consulted advisors and holy men, then recommended the Goddess Cybele. Her being as fierce as a Lioness protecting her cubs, the priests of the Cybele reflected her protective nature and wild abandon. Her priests and a black sky stone to represent the Goddess were loaded onto their warship and launched. Based on the survival of Rome, we believe the gift of Cybele gives the Latians a reason to save Pergamon from Phillip."

"We hear the Latians built a large temple for Cybele," Petridis added. "That's a sign of their admiration for what we gave them."

"One would think that sharing a Goddess," Tsolak proposed, "would draw two cities closer together. Or would it?"

"What do you mean Stoic?" Petridis inquired.

"If the Goddess is in Rome, how can she be in Pergamon?" Tsolak questioned. "And if the Latians have built a temple for her, bigger than the one constructed by King Attalus, would Cybele prefer Rome to another city?"

The ship's Captain settled against the rail and stared at the sky. As he watched the blue drift by as if the heavens moved and not the warship, Malis Aeson uttered a small cry, a loud sigh, and then died.

"The Ambassador has passed beyond our world," Tsolak stated. "What will you do?"

Petridis looked from the Stoic to the five bodyguards bending over the body of the Ambassador.

"We'll beach at Kithira Island for the night," Petridis described. "Seeing as the ground is rocky and not suitable for digging, we'll collect large stones. Tomorrow, Ambassador Aeson will be buried at sea."

Under his breath and unheard by the bodyguards or the Captain, Tsolak whispered, "But in what direction, Captain Petridis, easterly to home or westerly to Rome?"

Chapter 12 - Provocative Assertion

Around the northern tip of Kithira Island, the Pergamon warship cut a sharp circle in the water and backstroked to a small beach. Just behind, the three-banker from Rhodes also backed to the shallows. Both ships came to rest high and dry. While the crews prepared for a night on the beach, the five bodyguards carried a board supporting Aeson's corpse down a ramp. Seeing the deceased, Sub-Commander Theo Katsaros marched over and saluted.

"He was an honest, well-spoken man," the representative from Rhodes declared. Then, turning to the Stoic, he recommended. "Grab what baggage you have, Tsolak of Fyli, and load them on my ship. You can finish the journey with me."

Ignoring the advice, Tsolak walked to the bodyguards and directed them to a spot of flat land. A moment later, sailors arrived with poles and drapes. While Captain Petridis finished checking on his ship and rowers, the sailors constructed a tent. The afternoon breeze made the material flow in and out as if the pavilion over the dead man was a living and breathing entity.

The hoplites drifted away, searching the ground for rocks to weigh the body down in the morning. Although the crews would spend a leisurely night ashore, Katsaros snapped his fingers as if impatient. He jerked a thumb at his three-banker, indicating the trihemiolia.

"Wouldn't it be a courtesy to my host if Captain Petridis were here before you started issuing orders?" Tsolak mentioned.

"I didn't think stoics cared about such things," the Sub-Commander challenged.

"Have you not heard about the sphere of choice?" Tsolak questioned. He strolled to the death pavilion, sat down, and rested his back against a corner pole. Picking up a smooth, round stone, he circled it with his hands. "Everyone has the power to choose their response to external events. It's like being inside this rock. Even when events unfold outside your control, you can choose to react with wisdom, courage, temperance, and justice. The sphere of choice teaches us to nurture inner peace and flexibility by acknowledging what we can control, instead of responding to stimuli we cannot. Like what happens outside our sphere, such as you being rude."

"Who is being rude?" Captain Petridis asked as he approached the pavilion.

"We're having a discussion," Tsolak told him. "It's about qualifications."

"We are? It is?" the Sub-Commander blurted out.

"Qualifications for what?" Petridis questioned.

The five bodyguards returned and stacked their rocks beside the pavilion.

"The prerequisite to be a diplomat, let's say," the Stoic mentioned. "Should he be a negotiator or a mediator? But wait, what if he's a military commander?"

"Just a second," Katsaros grunted. "Are you questioning my right to represent Rhodes in Rome?"

"Not at all Sub-Commander," the Stoic remarked. "What I was asking is what right does a philosopher of stoicism, a man who lives inside a sphere of choice, have to deliver a message for an ancient city like Athens."

"Hold up," the Sub-Commander ventured. "You're building to something. Why don't you just say it?"

"If I was a priest, I'd point out that Athena is the Goddess of war, crafts, and wisdom," Tsolak listed. "We began this journey with a trilogy infused with her blessings."

"Her blessings have been apparent. The weather has been good for this season," Petridis offered. "Although we did have that pirate raid."

"It hasn't been that easy a trip," Katsaros pointed out. "You lost your Ambassador."

"Did we? What are the qualifications for an Ambassador? Must he know the stories to be told in Rome," the Stoic inquired. Lifting both hands, he indicated the five hoplites. "Should he have a fine robe with a gold clasp. Should he be guarded by five loyal sons of Pergamon?"

The five hoplites moved to flank and protect Petridis.

"You should row home, Captain," Katsaros suggested. "This is an important mission. And not one for amateurs."

"But not important enough to honor the Goddess Athena?" Tsolak inquired.

"You ask too many questions," Sub-Commander Katsaros proclaimed. "How can a man find solutions when all you do is ask questions and not give straight answers."

"Allow me to ask one more question before we dine," the Stoic proposed. He looked at the Pergamon Captain and inquired. "Ambassador Petridis, will you allow me to ride with you to Rome?"

Petridis hesitated before nodding and saying, "Tsolak, Philosopher of Athens, Pergamon will be honored if you'd accompany us to Rome."

***

In the morning, the pair of three-bankers rowed into deep water. Once stable in the waves, the body of Malis Aeson, swaddled in white linen and weighed down by rocks, was lowered over the side. Once in the water, they allowed him to slip below the surface.

"First Officer," Ambassador Petridis instructed, "set a course west towards the Roman Republic."

In short order, the two warships and three representatives sailed from the watery grave.

***

Eight hundred miles farther on, the ships reached the Roman port of Ostia. From the shore, the three representatives and the five bodyguards disembarked, hiked to the stables, and secured horses.

Once mounted, Petridis asked, "What kind of reception will we receive?"

Tsolak of Fyli rubbed the round stone he brought from the island but didn't speak. For once, the Stoic didn't have a question or an answer.

With apprehension, they headed northwest on the road to Rome. The three, however, shouldn't have worried, for they were the answer to the prayers of Consul-elect Sulpicius Galba. Even if the Senator didn't know it yet.

***

Senator Cotta remarked, "The Boii Tribe is raiding way beyond their borders."

"Are you complaining, Aurelius, or is that wishful thinking?" Senator Sulpicius Galba inquired.

"Perhaps a little of both," Cotta reflected. "The General who brings the Boii Tribe under control could earn a victory parade."

"You can keep the tribes of the Po River," Galba commented. "I want Greece. That's the future."

"May the Goddess Fortūna grant you that festering latrine of stinging flies," Senator Cotta scoffed. Then he asked. "How did you keep straight who are your friends, allies, enemies, and those who will turn with the wind?"

"You have a low opinion of our Greek city-state neighbors," Galba submitted.

"And your opinion of the Hellenists is inflated," Cotta countered.

Before next year's Consuls could speak further, Consul Gnaeus Lentulus banged on the lectern.

"The Senate of Rome will come to order," Lentulus announced. "Before I hand the meeting over to the President of the Senate, I want to ask for your prayers and sacrifices. My Co-consul Aelius Paetus has marched his Legions to the Po River. As most of you know, the Boii Tribe has broken their treaties with local Latin towns and their Gaelic neighbors."

"Is he going to end those troublemakers, this time?" an older Senator demanded. "Or will he be settling for another treaty the Boii won't honor?"

Calls for eliminating the Po River tribe came from a few Senators. But most remained calm and silent, showing their distaste for war by their lack of enthusiasm.

Sulpicius Galba noted the popular opinion of the peace party.

"That's not good," he whined.

"Missing Greece already?" Cotta asked.

"I haven't given up," Galba pushed back. "I was just thinking it's an uphill battle."

"Sacrifice and pray," Cotta recommended. "Perhaps the God Mars will bring you a gift on the Ides of March."

As the two talked, the President of the Senate took the lectern and called for new business.

***

Late in the afternoon, Sulpicius Galba left the Senate and returned to his villa. While awaiting guests to arrive for a feast, he sat in his study examining maps of Greece. Another man looked over his shoulder at the disjointed land masses and city-states.

"Sparta is as far south as Syracuse," Scipio Africanus observed.

"Have you ever been to Greece?" Galba asked.

"No. My fighting was mostly done in Iberia and on the coast of Africa," Cornelius replied.

"Where you finally fought Hannibal," Galba quipped. "If you'd delayed any longer, I'd have rowed there and handed the Carthaginian his first defeat myself."

Scipio Africanus leaned over and stabbed the map with a finger.

"Don't give me that," Cornelius corrected. "You had your hand's full with Philip of Macedonia."

The finger circled a wide plain with a large bay on the eastern edge. Around the north and west, high mountains were clearly marked as difficult terrain.

"I never reached Macedonia or Philip's Capital, Pella," Galba told Cornelius. The finger touched a mark on the eastern section of the bay designated Pella. "Philip came to the treaty table at Phoenice and signed a treaty before the Legions pushed him back to his homeland."

Galba rapped on the map at a spot just south of the Gulf of Patres.

"The peace of Phoenice ended Macedonia's support to Hannibal, you are welcome for the assistance, Africanus," Galba told Cornelius. "But we left Philip on his throne, and I don't trust him."

"Perhaps you'll get another chance at Macedonia," Cornelius proposed.

"It's unlikely, considering the mood of the Senate. But I have been praying…"

A knock on the door caused Sulpicius Galba to look out the window. Light poured in, letting him know the evening was a long way off. None of the guests should be arriving that early.

"So soon," he questioned before calling. "Come in."

The door opened, and a servant stood in the frame.

"Senator, they aren't on the guest list," the domestic informed him.

"Who is not on the guest list?" Galba asked.

"Representative Petridis from the land of Pergamon, Sub-Commander Katsaros from the Island of Rhodes, and a man from Athens, sir," the servant reported. Then he insisted. "But Senator, they aren't on the guest list."

"Did you order three Greeks as entertainment?" Scipio Africanus teased.

"If I had, I'd never have chosen those exact city-states," Galba responded. "They're our primary trading partners in the Aegean Sea. I wonder what they want?"

"Probably a trade delegation, seeking a tax break for the Aegean region," Cornelius suggested. "You could invite them to the feast and find out."

"And upset my wife's carefully balance social event," Galba declined. He pointed to the servant and instructed. "Tell them to come by the Seante at daybreak and I'll speck with them there."

"Very good sir, as they aren't on the list," the domestic repeated while closing the door.

"Now where were we?" Galba asked. After a moment to recall, he told Cornelius. "That's right, I've been making sacrifices to Janus asking for a gateway to Greece. A chance to bring Macedonia to her knees and Philip to justice. But so far, there haven't been any signs."

***

The Senate of Rome began each day at dawn with sacrifices to a group of Gods and Goddesses.

"Please accept these offerings of spices, incense, and flowers," the President of the Senate exclaimed. "Jupiter, Juno, Neptune, Minerva, Mars, Venus, Apollo, and Diana, protect our Republic and bless our citizens."

All the Senators added their voices to beseeching the Thunder God, Goddess of Mothers, God of the Sea, Goddess of Wisdom, God of War, Goddess of Fertility, God of Healing, and the Goddess of the Hunt. Except for Senator Galba, who included a prayer to Janus.

"Before we begin," the President told the chamber. "Take this opportunity to consult with your supporters and collect consensus on your proposals."

The Senators gathered in groups and spoke of which issues they would bring before the Senate of Rome. Sulpicius Galba moved to a sector to voice his views. A moment after joining a cluster, a hand tapped him on the shoulder. Galba turned to find one of his aids pointing to the exit door.

"There are three representatives here asking for you, Senator," the young man told him.

"What do you think of them?" Galba asked, expecting his aid to be dismissive. "Is it worth me meeting with a trade delegation?"

"One was sent by the King of Pergamon, another by the Council of Rhodes, and the third came with a scroll from the Archon of Athens," the young man reported. "Senator, they aren't a trade delegation. All three are Ambassadors from allies of Rome in the Aegean Sea."

Sulpicius Galba tensed and waited. As he paused, he restated his prayer to the God of Gates and New Beginnings.

"God Janus, forgive me for ignoring your signs," he prayed. Then, grabbing the tunic of his aid, he urged. "Take me to them."

On the way up the tiers of seating, Galba reeled in Senator Cotta and his aide. The four Romans hurried to the exit and the porch where the Greeks waited.

***

As they pushed through the doors, Sulpicius Galba announced, "I'm Senator Galba and this is Senator Cotta."

Upon seeing two men in togas with purple stripes, and two men in tunics, Katsaros braced.

"Sub-Commander Katsaros, representing the Island of Rhodes," Katsaros introduced himself. He added a crisp salute.

Ambassador Petridis strolled over from where he gazed at the temples around the Forum and the ones on Capitoline Hill.

"It's a beautiful city," he remarked when he reached the Romans. "If our purpose was different, I'd enjoy touring Rome."

"Keep a civil tongue in your mouth, Petridis," Katsaros snapped. "Speak only when you are spoken too."

Petridis bristled, and declared, "Ambassador Petridis from the Kingdom of Pergamon."

Sulpicius Galba stared at the two men from separate city-states. They obviously didn't get along.

"Weren't there three of you?" he inquired.

Petridis and Katsaros turned and pointed at the steps. Sitting with his legs stretched down three risers, Tsolak had twisted sideways to take in the sunrise.

"And you are?" Galba inquired.

"Tsolak of Fyli," the Stoic responded with a wave of his arm.

"Who do you represent, Tsolak of Fyli?"

Not turning to face the Senator, the Stoic divulged. "From Athens. My feuding fellow Greeks have prepared statements. If you don't find the answer in their testimony, I'll be available."

"You might be the strangest Ambassador I've ever met," Galba remarked. "Most beg for an audience with a Senator of Rome."

"He's a Philosopher of Stoicism," Petridis answered.

"I see," Galba moaned. Next, with more enthusiasm, he announced. "Let's hear from Pergamon first."

The sea Captain slouched and shuffled his sandals on the porch, hesitating. Katsaros coughed as if offering to step in and go first. But the man from Pergamon straightened his back, lifted his head, and scanned Rome.

"While waiting, I marveled at the types of buildings in your city," Petridis described. "From huts constructed of scraps of lumber to brick structures four stories high. It is quite the range. But it occurred to me that you Romans have reserved the best for the gifts from Pergamon."

"Gifts from Pergamon? Please explain your statement," Galba urged.

"Up there, on the hill you call Capitoline, in a grand marble temple, you have on display a gesture of respect to my King, Attalus I Soter. It is an honor for the people of Pergamon."

"What gesture to your King?" Cotta asked.

"The marble statue of the Dying Gaul," Petridis informed the Senator. "Such a place of respect for a sculpture inspired by my land surely acknowledges the bindings between our peoples. And so my King requests help with protecting Pergamon, a friend of Rome, from Philip V of Macedonia."

"It's thin," Cotta remarked. "But there is an opening for you, Sulpicius."

"You said gifts," Galba said, addressing the Ambassador. "What's another gift from Pergamon?"

"In another grand temple, I'm told, but not just as a display, but as the reason for the marble palace, is the Goddess Cybele. A deity carried from Pergamon with the express purpose of saving Rome during its darkest period." Petridis illustrated his next point by waving an arm at the city. "Again, I look upon the unmolested buildings and busy citizens and I marvel at the success of the joint venture between Rome and Pergamon. We share a protective Mother Goddess and so trust in Rome to come to the aid of Pergamon, during our darkest period."

"Your road to Greece, General Galba, is firming up," Cotta proposed.

"But Pergamon is a Kingdom," Galba reasoned. "I'm not sure the Senate of Rome will rush to the aid of a King."

"Rhodes isn't a Kingdom," Cotta advised. "If my Greek teachers are to be believed, the Island is a Democracy with a ruling council and magistrate elected to run the government."

"You don't have much faith in your Greek tutors," Galba suggested.

"They weren't very good teachers," Cotta responded. "They spent most of the time complaining about the weather and the food in Rome."

Sulpicius Galba looked at Theo Katsaros and asked, "Is the Island of Rhodes a Democracy?"

"It is, Senator Galba," the Sub-Commander confirmed. "But the government of my island is less important than the Rhodian Navy."

"For both our causes," Sulpicius Galba urged, "give me something to further my argument."

"If you don't stop Philip V of Macedonia," Katsaros stated, "Rome, Egypt, and every Greek city-state will be paying tariffs to Philip by this season next year."

"Now there's a provocative assertion," Cotta conceded. "Tell Senator Galba and me about your Navy's part in this."

Chapter 13 - As Good As Gone

"Most sailors and merchants know about the Sea Laws of Rhodes," Katsaros explained. "It's as simple as when cargo gets thrown overboard to save a ship. The expenses for the loss of the goods are shared between the shipowners, cargo owners, and the passengers. But Rhodes contributes much more to the movement of merchandise than the sea laws."

"If you say so," Cotta remarked, seemingly unimpressed by the legal stuff.

"How about you tell us," Galba encouraged, "how else Rhodes contributes."

The Sub-Commander thrust out his chest, gave a curt nod, and replied.

"All the descendants of King Alexander's Generals have attempted to take control of my island," Katsaros answered. "From Antigonus' Macedon to Philip V's Macedon, to Egypt, and the Seleucid Empire, they have challenged us. Because we have no army of any size, what kept us free is our island. Beyond that, Rhodes maintains a strong Navy. Unlike other city-states, our warships have few Marines for boarding. Rather, we build fast-attack vessels. Through patrolling the Aegean, we keep the pirates under control. But recently, the number of pirates, because of Philip's support, have increased. And with Philip taking key ports and islands the situation is deteriorating. If the

Macedonian's expansion continues, no merchant will be safe sending goods through the Aegean. The evil will overwhelm commerce and by this season next year, Rome, Egypt, Pergamon, and every Greek city-state will be paying tariffs to Philip V of Macedon."

"He's a financial threat in addition to endangering a friend of Rome," Cotta summed up. "That, General Galba, may be enough to get you Legions for Greece."

"Or not," Sulpicius Galba concluded. "Let's go make a speech and a proposal to the Senate of Rome."

"You speak," Cotta urged. "I'll support you."

"After the session, a servant will take you to my villa," Galba told the three Ambassadors. "We may need to speak again and I don't want to have to track you down for more information."

"Yes, sir," two of the representatives responded. Tsolak waved an arm over his head. When he realized everyone was waiting for him, the Stoic stood and followed the others into the Senate chamber.

Once inside, Galba and Cotta left the three Greeks at the observation gallery and returned to their seats. They were about to introduce a new agenda for the day and needed their supporters to be aware.

***

At the center of the chamber, Gnaeus Lentulus bowed to the President of the Senate. Next, as if cupping handfuls of a substance, he extended his arms and allowed them to sag.

"Imagine the weight of earth, silt, pebbles, and rushing water," the Consul encouraged. He tossed the invisible concoction at an unseen wall. Fanning his hands outward, he brought them together, touched his fingertips, and formed a circle. "Floods last spring washed down mud which partially clogged the channel under the Ponte Mallio. When the Burano River floods this year, we will have water, branches, pebbles, and silt washing over the bridge. The Via Flaminia, an important artery of commerce, could become covered in mud at Cagli. But that's the least of our concern. At the worst, the flood could dislodge stones and we'd lose the bridge completely."

"Isn't road surfacing and bridge maintenance up to the Provinces?" a Senior Senator challenged. "If they don't have the tax coins, make it a project for the local Legion garrison."

"You are correct Senator, however, the taxes are down in the Province. And normally, we would use the Legion. But the garrison has been mobilized to deal with the Boii," Lentulus explained. "The manpower needed to dig out the bridge are over a hundred miles north and the spring thaw is coming. We need funds to clean out the mud and debris. And possibly budget for building a stronger abutment on the upstream side of the bridge."

"Capital expenditures in a Province that can't support itself are a waste of coins," a young Senator proposed. "Cleaning is all I'll vote for."

"But aren't we just kicking the barrel down the road and leaving the problem for another year?" a legislator pointed out. "We should deal with the root of the problem before it blossoms into the loss of the bridge."

"Thanks to Scipio Africanus, our treasury is full of Carthaginian coins," another Senator pointed out. Several sections applauded Cornelius, recognizing his victory over Hannibal. Once the acknowledgements faded, the Senator continued. "What good is silver in the basement of a temple. Let's spend it on improvements to strengthen the Republic."

"If we allocate funds every time a Province comes up short," the youthful Senator advised, "soon there will be no silver under the temple, leaving none available for emergencies."

Sulpicius Galba stood at his chair and suggested, "I propose we vote on digging out the bridge and cleaning the approach for a half mile upriver."

Following the submission, the President of the Senate asked, "Consul Lentulus, do I call for a vote or do you have additional arguments?"

"Of course, I'd like to see the problem fixed during my term as Consul," Lentulus confessed. "But cleaning the muck is acceptable, if that's all we can agree on."

"Can I get a second?" the President inquired.

"I second the motion," the youthful Senator said, showing his acceptance of the plan.

"We have a proposition by Senator Galba and a second by Senator Marcus Lepidus to dig out the bridge and clean the Burano River for a half mile upstream," the President announced. "All in favor raise your hand. Clerks, please get a count."

While the Senate waited for the results, Publius Tuditanus leaned into the aisle and questioned, "You know the importance of the Via Flaminia, Marcus Lepidus. Why did you only commit to the lesser maintenance?"

"Because, Senator Tuditanus, if Consul Lentulus was serious about the building project he would have brought drawings and not imposed his dramatic hand gestures on us."

From the lectern, the President stated, "The motion passes. A committee will investigate the project, create a budget, and hire a contractor to clean out the river at Cagli. If there is no other business, I think we'll break until afternoon for meetings."

"Magister," Galba alerted the President, "before we adjourn, I'd like the floor."

"The Senate of Rome recognizes Senator Sulpicius Galba."

***

"Thank you. I want to talk about Macedonia," Galba stated.

Moans and outright jeers came from sectors of the chamber.

"It's understandable that you don't want the same, tired argument," Sulpicius told them. "I've just come from a meeting with three Ambassadors from Greece. One from Athens, another from the Isle of Rhodes, and the third from Pergamon. As you know, we have on display a statue inspired by victories of the Pergamon ruler. The Dying Gaul is a physical connection between our peoples. And when Rome was desperate, we sent ships to Pergamon to retrieve the Goddess Cybele to protect our city. In light of our close connection to Pergamon, I ask the Senate to give me leave to raise Legions and go against Macedonia to save Pergamon."

The President of the Senate glanced up and down the tiers, searching for any acceptance of Galba's impassioned plea. He saw none.

"Senator Galba, I see no enthusiasm for a campaign against Macedonia," he reported. "If you have nothing else, we'll break for a recess."

"One more item if you please," Galba begged.

Sharp breaths, signifying frustration, sounded throughout the chamber. No one, it appeared, wanted to hear more from Galba about Macedonia.

"You have the floor, Senator," the President allowed.

"During another meeting, the Ambassador from the Isle of Rhodes brought me up to date on the threat to shipping," Sulpicius Galba informed the chamber. "Every Roman citizen involved in commerce will pay a hefty price if Philip V of Macedonia continues his aggression. We can halt him in the Aegean before he reaches Egypt and interferes with the transportation of grain from the Nile River."

"Is the Aegean Sea part of our peace treaty with Macedonia?" Senator Claudius Nero questioned.

"Sadly, Senator, it is not," Galba admitted. "The Treaty of Phoenice prevents Philip from attacking Illyrian territory, and the west coast of Greece. And it bars him from the east coast of the Republic. But that shouldn't stop us from doing the right thing."

"The right thing is to not get us into another war so soon after Hannibal's War," Senator Publius Tuditanus advised. "It's costly in coins, resources, and human life. Our crops haven't recovered from having so many men gone for so long from our farms."

"I understand, Senator Tuditanus," Galba lied. Then to the President he asked. "Can we take a vote on declaring war on Philip V. I'll find a second."

The President of the Seante mentally counted the yawns and those jerking their heads, trying to fight off sleep. Seeing few with any signs of life or interest, he told Galba.

"Senator, after an impromptu pole of the Senate of Rome, I am denying your request. We are adjourning from the morning session. The Senate of Rome is secured from the morning session."

Clusters of Senators all discussed topics as they filed out of the chamber. Many remarked that their families and the citizens were exhausted by war and wanted peace.

Sulpicius Galba felt like the only sighted man in a world of the blind. He alone could see the threat, while the others stumbled through life, unaware of the danger of Macedonia. But he lacked the proper words to seize hearts and capture the imagination of the Senate. Feeling numb from the loss, he sent an assistant to collect the three Ambassadors.

"Perhaps a good midday repast will fix my attitude," he muttered while following Senator Cotta up the tiers.

***

The backroom of the restaurant was crowded with four Senators, five aides, and the three Greeks. Pairs of bodyguards waited at the two exits and at tables along the wall.

"It didn't go well," offered Ambassador Petridis.

"It's like combat," Sub-Commander Katsaros insisted. "You've got to keep attacking, Senator Galba."

"If I could, I would," Galba claimed. "But I've tried every approach to get the Senate to see the real King of Macedonia and nothing has moved the citizens or the Senators."

Cotta noticed the Stoic sitting in the corner of the room. Alone and silent, the Philosopher focused on the vegetables in his stew.

"We've heard from Pergamon and the Isle of Rhodes," the Senator stated, raising his voice to reach the corner, "but we've heard nothing from Athens."

"That's right," Galba injected. "You said if I didn't like what the others said, I should speak with you."

Tsolak rested his ladle beside the bowl and turned to face the big table.

"My words Senator were," the Stoic corrected, "if you don't find the answer in their testimony, I'll be available."

"I don't know what that means," Galba admitted.

"You're not alone," Katsaros tossed out.

But Petridis offered, "Senator Galba, ask the Stoic a question and listen to his response."

"I'm so far off the pace of this chariot race, I've nothing to lose," Galba confessed, using a sports analogy. Then he addressed the Stoic. "All right Tsolak of Fyli, why can't the Senate see what I see?"

"You've fielded Legions and commanded men in battle," Tsolak divulged. "Have you ever heard a coherent report from a frightened man?"

Galba smiled. He remembered how his Junior Tribunes stammered and lied to hide their inexperience during their first combat operations. After a moment of reflection, he agreed. "A frightened man is unreliable."

"Doesn't the process work in reverse?" Tsolak inquired.

The room fell silent until Galba replied, "You're saying the Senate of Rome is afraid. Afraid of what?"

"What do all men who live for glory fear?" Tsolak questioned.

"Shame, defeat, loss of honor," Galba listed. For several heartbeats, he sat moving his mouth as if forming words that wouldn't solidify. Finally, he ventured. "I need to make them unafraid of losing? I wouldn't know how to make such a shift in attitude."

"If a horse shies away from an obstacle, do you walk it back to the stable and feed it fresh hay?" Tsolak proposed.

"No, you make it more afraid of you than it is of the barrier," Galba described. He thought of his own solution before questioning. "But with my horse, I have a bridle and a whip. With the Senate, all I have are my words."

"Then you should have better words," Tsolak remarked.

Aurelius Cotta got angry and slammed a hand on the table.

"Better words is what he's trying to get from you, you slippery mud eel," Cotta exclaimed. "How about some plain language instead of the question for question exchange?"

"It is difficult for a stoic to lecture," Tsolak told him. "We live what we practice. We study what we live. I live in a sphere of control. My thoughts, judgments, desires, intentions, and actions fall under my control. I can't change what's outside of my being, only how I react to them. This leaves me unable to help others who aren't students of the school of stoicism."

Once finished with the speech, Tsolak returned to his bowl of stew and began eating.

Sulpicius Galba stared at Aurelius Cotta. After a moment of tension between the two Senators, Cotta stated, "I'll just finish my meal and keep quiet."

"Tsolak of Fyli, how do I put reins on the Senate of Rome?" Galba inquired.

Slowly, the Stoic turned and asked, "Which animal in a herd is most likely to be prey, a bull or a calf?"

"That's a ridiculous question," Galba commented. "Everyone knows predators go after the young."

"Exactly, Senator," Tsolak confirmed. "Now, which is more likely to be hunted, a young bull or a bull with a limp?"

"What do you mean, a bull with a limp?" Galba pushed back. "The answer is obvious."

"Suppose the bull had just come from a long battle," Tsolak responded. "Is the brute really weak, or simply perceived to be crippled by the wolves?"

Sulpicius Galba scrunched up his face in confusion, trying to dig meaning out of the pile of philosopher dung. But Aurelius Cotta, who had mostly tuned out the conversation, caught the implication.

"You're accusing Rome of being weakened by our war with Carthage," he stated.

"I'm alleging nothing," Tsolak protested.

Galba uttered in a halfhearted manner, "So what if our enemies think we're weak. Like the bull in your example, the Republic may limp but Rome is as strong as ever. Maybe more so."

"In that case, Senator," Tsolak advised, "Rome has nothing to dread."

"Dread makes it sound like we're discussing a child's nightmare," Galba argued. "This is serious business."

The Stoic got up and walked to the exit door. He stood in the doorway, as if debating whether to leave or stay. After a moment of the cool breeze fluffing his hair, he turned to Galba.

"Before he crossed the sea and violated and ravished your land, had anyone in the Republic ever heard of the Greek King, Pyrrhus? Do the voices of your Legionaries, put in the ground by Pyrrhus' army, not echo down through the years?"

"Our Legions build walls for marching camps each night because of King Pyrrhus' tactics," Galba admitted. "The mention of his name is used to scare children who misbehave."

The Stoic bowed his head either in recognition of the deceased, or to confirm the Senator's conclusion, or simply because he had a stiff neck. With philosophers, no one could tell. Lifting a finger and pointing at his empty bowl, Tsolak indicated that he wanted a second helping. A server poured from a pot, filling the Stoic's bowl.

"Before he crossed the Alps and violated and ravished your land, had anyone in the Republic ever heard of the Carthaginian General, Hannibal Barca?" Tsolak asked. He circled the table, heading for his second helping while inquiring, "Do the voices of your Legionaries, put in the ground by Hannibal's army, not echo down through the years?"

Sulpicius Galba sat limp as his mind raced. Eventually, he stretched his back and informed Cotta and the other Senators around the table. "Once elected Consul, I'll need your votes to have the Province of Macedonia assigned to me."

"Don't you need a declaration of war against Philip V before you can break the Treaty of Phoenice?" Cotta asked.

"The treaty, gentlemen, is as good as gone," Galba assured him.

Chapter 14 - The Boii Tribe

The afternoon session of the Senate, as with all afternoon sessions, was slow to form. From across the city, in groups of threes and fours, Senators meandered into the chamber. Galba and Cotta, being two of the early ones, were next to their seats.

"Sulpicius are you sure about this? You're putting your election to Consul at risk," Aurelius Cotta warned. "If you bring up Macedonia again, there are factions who will never vote for you for any office."

"I realize that possibility," Galba told his fellow Senator. "I tried financial and emotional pleas. They both failed. This time, it'll be different."

Galba spotted the President of the Senate coming down the tiers. He rushed to meet the man.

"I need the floor," he informed the presiding officer.

"Senator Galba, you're walking a dangerous line between passion and folly," the President advised.

"My presentation will be brief," Galba assured him, "and unoffensive."

"I'll call on you first," the President promised after a moment of reflection.

Seeing the Senate officer on the steps, individual Senators flocked around the President. Having completed his mission, Galba backed up and collided with a body. Turning, he came face to face with Gnaeus Lentulus.

"Excuse me, Consul," Galba apologized.

"No need, I wanted to speak with you about the bridge at Cagli."

"I thought we settled that," Galba stated.

"My family has farms on the eastern plains," Lentulus informed Galba. "The temporary fix of the bridge is just that, temporary. And remember, the Republic needs that bridge for the movement of the Legions."

"Had you told me it was that important to you, I'd have voted for the repairs," Galba proposed. "But I was going for a measure that would pass. Young Marcus Lepidus is your main opposition. Perhaps you should speak with him."

"I have. Lepidus is a student of finance and determined to cut costs no matter the value of the expenses," Lentulus grumbled.

"Perhaps we could send him on a journey," Galba suggested, an idea forming in his head. "Let's keep our ears and minds open for a Senate junket appropriate for Marcus Lepidus."

"With him out of the way, an amended proposal would certainly pass," Lentulus declared. "Thank you for your support. If you need my vote, just ask."

"It's fate that you should mention your vote," Galba remarked. Leaning in, he whispered in the Consul's ear.

***

Once the chamber had filled, the President called the afternoon session to order.

"Gentlemen, please settle," he declared. "The Senate of Rome recognizes Sulpicius Galba. Senator Galba, the floor is yours."

On more than one tier, a version of the same expression was heard. "What? More on Macedonia? Gods spare us."

"Thank you, Magister President," Galba acknowledged. He held up the flats of his hands as if to fend off the irritated statements. "I have a few quick comments about yes, Macedonia, but more so, remarks about the Roman Republic."

His latter assertion silenced his detractors, at least for the moment.

"Thanks to Cornelius Scipio Africanus, we won the war against Carthage," he asserted, then had to pause as cheers for Cornelius interrupted him. Before the enthusiasm ended, he crushed the excitement. "Our enemies, however, don't know we were victorious. As a matter of fact, the barbarians believe the Republic is crippled, weak, and ineffective."

Shouts challenging his remarks came at him from every tier, including his own sector. Senator Cotta dropped his head as if unable to look Galba in the eyes.

Waving down the aggression, Sulpicius Galba asked, "How could they believe such a fallacy? The answer, Senate of Rome, is simple. We have withdrawn from engaging with people who would attack us."

From an older Senator who stumbled over his words came, "you are, er, talking, er, about Macedon."

A spattering of "Macedonia again. Gods spare us" echoed around the chamber.

"No! You have it wrong," Galba grunted. "I am not speaking of Macedonia nor of their King, Philip V. My remarks referenced the Boii Tribe. A Po Valley nation where right now, we have Legions marching on the Gauls. But why would the Boii Tribe feel they have the freedom to break treaties and disrupt the good order of the Province of Gallia Cisalpina?"

Pointing to the old Senators, Galba waited for the old one to answer.

"Because, er, they think, er, Rome is, er, weak."

Sulpicius Galba slapped his hands together. The clap reverberated around the chamber. "Because they think we're broken after a long war with Carthage."

"But we aren't," Senator Claudius Nero objected. "As witnessed by our forceful response to the Boii."

"Senator Nero, you of anyone, with your victorious record of command during Hannibal's War and in Iberia should fear," Galba stated as if he'd made a valid point.

"Fear what?" Nero demanded.

"The fear of emboldening another Pyrrhus," Galba answered. "Tell me, before he crossed the sea and violated our sovereignty had anyone in the Republic ever heard of the Greek King, Pyrrhus? I can hear the voices of our brave Legionaries, put in the ground by Pyrrhus' army. They echo down through the years and haunt this very chamber."

"The appearance of weakness is undesirable," Nero agreed. "But King Pyrrhus' invasion was ages ago."

"You are correct, General Nero," Galba acknowledged. "But Hannibal wasn't ages ago."

Mutterings of discontent buzzed around the Senate. This time they weren't directed at Galba but at the memory of the hated Carthaginian.

"We have all lost brothers, fathers, uncles, and dear friends. So tell me, before he crossed the Alps and ravished our land had anyone in the Republic ever heard of the Carthaginian General, Hannibal Barca?" Galba asked. He waited a few heartbeats before adding. "The voices of our Legionaries, put in the ground by Hannibal's army, echo loudly in my heart. How about yours?"

Calls of emotional pain and prayers to dead relatives resonated around the Senate.

"Now, allow me to quote the venerable Legion commander Claudius Nero," Galba told the chamber. He saluted Nero and explained. "The appearance of weakness is undesirable. His is an undeniable truth. But now we have the Boii uprising, and in the past Pyrrhus' invasion and Hannibal's attack. All because Rome appeared weak."

The Senate hushed, as some guessed at the next remark, while other legislators hung on the edges of their seats.

"What of the future?" Galba exclaimed. Then, looking from section to section, he answered. "What creature will come calling next with bloody spears and solid shields. With fast cavalry, slingers, and siege engines? What creature indeed, we already know. Because he resides just east of our Republic. His name is Philip V Antigonid, the King of Macedonia, and inheritor of Alexander the Great's undefeated phalanx. And why would he attack us? Because Rome appears weak."

"I move to void the Treaty of Phoenice and declare Macedonia a rogue state," Cotta put forth.

"And I second the motion," Claudius Nero added.

The president of the Senate called for a vote and not long afterward, he announced. "The motion to void the

Treaty of Phoenice and declare Macedonia a rogue state has passed the Senate of Rome. But this leaves us short of a declaration of war. Do we call the priests and have them preform the ritual?"

Voiding a treaty that the Senate accepted had far-reaching ramifications. For one, it left the east coats of the Republic open to attacks and the Legions in Greece unprotected by an agreement. Of course, none of that mattered if there was war. But the people and Senate of Rome were leery of another major conflict, coming so soon after Hannibal's War.

"Magister, if I might," Gnaeus Lentulus requested.

"The Senate recognizes Consul Lentulus," the President acknowledged.

"Rather than a full declaration of war, we could send Ambassadors to Greece, Egypt, Pergamon, and Rhodes to ascertain the situation," he proposed. "And if need be, once they have firsthand knowledge, they can call for the Legions and the Republic's Eastern Navy."

"I move to accept the proposal," Galba announced.

"And I second it and volunteer to be an Ambassador," Claudius Nero told the President of the Senate.

"Perhaps, we should vote on the Ambassadors," Lentulus advised. "Let's say, Praetor Publius Tuditanus to accompany the senior statesman, Pro-consul Claudius Nero. And let's see, someone with the vigor of youth. Someone of quality, maybe a Tribune, like Marcus Lepidus."

At the naming of three Ambassadors, the Senate erupted in cheering. Especially for Marcus Lepidus, a well-spoken man many considered one of the most handsome men in Rome.

After taking a vote, the resolution passed and the three Ambassadors to the east were confirmed. Pleased beyond belief, Sulpicius Galba had what he wanted. Even if he'd need to wait until he was elected Consul to act against Philip V of Macedonia.

Gnaeus Lentulus strutted to the center of the chamber and raised his hands. The Senate calmed and listened to the Consul.

"Just a reminder that my Co-consul Paetus is marching to the Po River Valley," he told the Senators. "Please keep Aelius and our Legionaries, in your prayers and sacrifices as they go to punish the Boii Tribe."

***

One hundred and fifty-five miles northeast of Rome, the Legions of Aelius Paetus enjoyed the lower elevations near Cagli. Behind them was the spine of the Apennine Mountain and the toughest part of the march.

"This bridge is a mess," Consul Paetus remarked as his horse crossed over the Burano River. "Someone should dig out the mud before the spring thaw."

Riding beside the General, Colonel Gaius Ampius, commander of two auxiliary Legions, inquired, "Do you want me to assign a few Centuries to clean it out, General?"

"No. We need to reach the Boii, administer a little justice, and get back before winter sets in," Consul Paetus remarked. "I'm sure someone in Rome is already working on the problem."

"Yes, sir," the Colonel stated. "It's only fifty miles to Rimini. After that, the roads get worse."

The Via Flaminia stretched through the hills around Cagli to where it terminated at Rimini on the coast. The Legionaries and their animal handlers were grateful for the smooth, hard surface of the Flaminia as it cut along the heights and through the valleys.

"Colonel Ampius when we reach Rimini, I want your Legions to head west and drive the Boii into my shields," Consul Paetus described. "We'll smash them between our two forces."

"And where will you be sir?"

"My Legions will march northwest along the road from Remini," the Consul said. "Someday the engineers will make the Via Aemilia a proper roadway."

***

Two hundred forty miles northwest of Rimini, men of the Insubri prepared to fend off the Legions and protect their tribal lands. The one big flaw in their strategy, the Boii territory sat south of the Insubri. And on no map did the Legion's Planner and Strategies Department have the Insubri schedule for an engagement.

Yet around Lake Maggiore, the Gnātos Clan responded to the call of the Insubri King. Well, at least a third of their warriors prepared to battle the heavy infantry of the Legion. The other two-thirds, because of a lie and an oath, refused to answer the call. It caused splits in the Clan, pitting brother against brother and father against son.

Chapter 15 - Three Gifts

On the flatland bordering Lake Maggiore, a line of Gnātos tribesmen linked shields and stepped forward. As they moved in unison, their spears stabbed ahead as if prongs on the same thrashing board.

"Rearward, execute," their Captain shouted.

The line of Clan warriors punched with their shields, took two rapid steps back, pivoted, and sprinted away from the assault line. Rather than a mad dash, the warriors ran ten paces, and without an order, stopped. Turning around, they set a new defensive line. During the controlled retreat, two warriors tripped and stumbled, making them late for the new defensive barrier.

The clusters of spearmen watching from the side laughed out of sympathy. They had all practiced the unusual retreat maneuver until their legs were weak and they had nightmares about the exercise. All the warriors knew the penalty for not maintaining the line while running.

"Rearward, execute," the Captain ordered again.

The unit thrusted with their shields, took two steps back, spun around, and sprinted ten paces before coming to a halt and establishing a new assault line.

"That's it, right, Captain?" one of the tribesman inquired.

"You had two men delayed," the Clan officer explained. "The penalty for that is four additional rotations."

As the line of warriors moaned at more drilling, one of the spectators pointed to the lake.

"Boats coming from Arona," he announced.

"Dismissed," the Captain ordered his spearmen. "Get some water and dry off."

***

Shortly after the sighting, twenty boats nudged onto the muddy shoreline. Gnātos spearmen disembarked. Along with the Clan warriors came their Chief and his three War Chiefs.

"Oh look, everyone has come for a visit," a warrior sneered. "Maybe we can all hold hands and run backwards together."

"Last year when the Romans came, War Chief Jace Kasia planned the defeat of the Legion," Scanlan Kasia snapped, defending his adopted father. "If he thinks running to the rear is a good strategy, then he has a reason for it."

"Running to the rear isn't how you win battles, pup," the spearman growled. "As a matter of fact, it goes against a warrior's pride."

"What are you getting at?" Scanlan questioned.

"What you're doing kid is trying to justify a bad practice," the warrior scoffed. He glanced around at his file mates for confirmation. Seeing them making signs of agreeing with him, the spearman declared. "Once brain addled, always brain addled."

At the reference to Jace's befuddled condition when he arrived at Arona, Scanlan took offense. His training forgotten, the slight youth threw himself at the spearman. As easily as a bull throwing a squirrel off his back, the warrior tossed Scanlan over his shoulder. The lad landed hard, and the spearman planted a foot in the center of the youth's chest.

"You think running around the mountains day and night, putting holes in straw targets, and reading scrolls makes you a warrior?" the spearman sneered. "Only size and fighting with a shield and a spear will make you a warrior. Grow a bit then find people your own size to fight. Stop trying to be one of us."

The other spearmen cheered the warrior's comments. Surrounded by his file, the man strolled away, leaving Scanlan lying in the dirt. The cheeks of the youth flushed from humiliation. Before he pushed off the ground and suffered the embarrassment of brushing dirt off his tunic, the Clan Chief drew everyone's attention.

"Warriors of the Gnātos Clan," Samo Kentus called to the assembled spearmen. Using the shoulders of his sons, Abbo and Attalus Kentus, the Clan Chief hoisted himself to the bed of a wagon. Once stable on his good leg, he announced. "I've received word from King B'Yag. The butcher of Carthage is on the march. Our King has called for a gathering of the Insubri to defend our homeland."

"Then we march as Insubri," a spearman called out.

Rumblings from the Clan's warriors confirmed the spearmen's enthusiasm for a fight.

"If only I could order you to hasten to the defense of our people," Samo exclaimed. Then, softening his words, he admitted. "But I can't. My sons Abbo Kentus and Jace Kasia swore an oath not to take up arms against the butcher."

Grumblings of discontent ran through the warriors.

"When captured and taken to Rome, one term of their release was an oath of no aggression against General Scipio," Samo told the disappointed warriors.

"The Gnātos Clan hides from our responsibilities as Insubri for a Roman," a spearman challenged.

"My son, Attalus Kentus, is prepared to lead a band of Gnātos men to fight alongside the King," Samo informed the men. "While some will go and fight, more will remain here. We need extra spears on our borders during this period of unrest."

"We beat the Legions last year," Scanlan shouted in a moment of exuberance. Realizing the disrespect, he glanced around to find heads nodding in affirmation. With his confidence bolstered by the men surrounding him, the youth added. "And if enough of us go, we'll beat them again."

Samo pointed at Jace Kasia.

"Come explain the reality to the Clan," Samo urged.

In response, Jace Kasia, former Cretan Archer and Legion officer, leaped up to the wagon bed and scanned the defiant spearmen.

"The butcher of Carthage, as you call him, crushed Hannibal Barca and the Insubri in Africa. Before that, he defeated Punic armies and local tribes in Iberia," Jace explained. "General Scipio wins battles through the careful study of his enemies, the layout of the land, daring assaults, and bloody retribution. No matter what happens to the rest of the Insubri, our Chief Kentus will need warriors on the Gnātos borders."

"But if King B'Yag triumphs," countered a spearman, "the Gnātos Clan will be shamed for not fighting with the other Clans."

"B'Yag won't win but he will endure," Jace promised. "The other side of Roman General Scipio is his habit of keeping Kings in place if they sign a treaty with Rome. If Attalus and I go and fight Scipio Africanus, after his victory, the Roman will come for revenge against the Clan of oath breakers. And then King B'Yag, as a friend of Rome, will send Insubri warriors against us. We are in a no win situation."

"We need to go and fight for our homeland," a spearman shouted.

"Yes, we fight," Scanlan echoed the sentiment.

Samo Kentus waved down the outbursts.

"In the morning, my son, War Chief Attalus Kentus leaves to fight for the King," the Clan Chief informed the warriors. "Those who want can go with Attalus. Those who remain will begin guarding the trails and passes into the land of the Gnātos Clan."

***

Anger and pride split families. Nephews, brash and proud, went to stand with Attalus. Their uncles moved to Abbo and Jace, declaring their intention to remain with the Clan. Fathers and sons, as well, became divided.

Jace Kasia searched the shifting masses, looking for Scanlan. When he spotted his adopted son near Attalus, Jace motioned for the youth to switch sides. Scanlan placed his fists on his hips and stood defiantly.

"Scanlan Saltare Romiliia Kasia. You are in the wrong group," Jace suggested.

"You mean here with the heroes," Scanlan proclaimed. "Not there with the traitors and cowards."

A hush fell over the warriors of the Gnātos Clan. The youth had voiced the inner-thoughts of the spearman. Before Jace could argue, warriors flanked Scanlan, standing shoulder to shoulder with the fifteen-year-old lad.

"You could go and pull him out," Samo Kentus suggested. "I'll support your action."

"A hot headed young man can't be dissuaded from seeking glory," Jace responded to the Clan Chief.

"What will you do?" Samo asked.

"Give him gifts for his journey," Jace answered with a hint of sadness in his voice.

***

Late in the afternoon, one of the boats bringing supplies for the warriors going off to support the King arrived. Jace Kasia jumped to shore, adjusted the bags that hung from his shoulders, and marched into the camp. Spearmen, he had trained and fought with, greeted him. After searching several campsites, he found his adopted son with Attalus Kentus, the boy's uncle.

Anticipating Jace's argument, Scanlan braced and declared, "Don't try talking me out of this."

Jace shrugged the bags off his shoulders and faced his son. Remembering the last few years fondly, the Cretan Archer recalled the slender thief who approached him at his workshop.

***

"Teach me to fight," Scanlan had requested.

Recalling his own brutal training, Jace sought to dissuade the lad by giving him an impossible task.

"Bring me two eagle eggs," Jace told him, naming a high price for admittance into the warrior class.

After vanishing into the mountains, the young teen returned with two eagle eggs under his tunic and coat. The cost for training from then on was paid in diligence and caring for the pair of eaglets. Even when the eagles flew off to claim their place in the mountains, the instructions in archery, stalking, reading and writing Greek, Latin, Iberian, Insubri, and a little Egyptian continued. Along with the soft skills, Scanlan was attentive in practicing the bruising sports of boxing, wrestling, shield and spear work, and proudly carried scars from knife and sword fights. Unfortunately, while the talent was present, the lad hadn't hit a growth spurt. And while being undersized enhanced his natural talent for moving unobserved in the dark, the lack of muscle weight restricted his efficiency in unarmed combat and shield and spear training.

It was more the lad's size than his preparation for war that worried Jack Kasia.

***

Jace examined the defiant teen for a moment, before picking up a long case.

"I have three gifts for you, son," Jace explained. He handed Scanlan the case and described. "I present you with a new war bow. May it keep you safe, employed, and fed."

Scanlan accepted the gift but had to choke back a lump in his throat. He attempted to hide it when he wiped moisture from his eyes. Along with the bow, he was handed a quiver of arrows.

"Next, I present you with an identity," Jace informed him. He pulled a small scroll out of a waterproof case. "Here is a signed document making you my legal heir. You are the successor to the House of Romiliia, a noble Roman family, which makes you a citizen of the Roman Republic."

"I'm going to kill Roman's," Scanlan snapped. "Why would I want to claim such a heritage?"

"Because the official who signed the document is Cornelius Scipio Africanus," Jace whispered. "Do what you will with the scroll. But understand, it is the key to survival in the Roman Republic."

Reluctantly, Scanlan took the scroll and the waterproof case. When Jace stood for long moments with his head lowered, the youth reminded him, "You said three gifts."

Jace lifted his head, and with twilight reflected in his eyes, presented the third gift.

"Until you learn the only source to quench your thirst for adventure and war are the waters of Lake Maggiore, you are denied this valley," Jace instructed. "Until your heart yearns for a safe place to lay quietly and heal, your shadow may not darken my doorway or those of any member of the Gnātos Clan. Scanlan Saltare Romiliia Kasia, I grant you unencumbered independence."

With those words, Jace Kasia marched to a waiting boat, climbed in, took a seat on a rowing bench, and gripped an oar. Having said all he could, the Cretan Archer rowed for home, never looking back at his adopted son.

Chapter 16 - Where He Emerged

A week later, after the march from Lake Maggiore, seven hundred warriors of the Gnātos Clan arrived at the Po River. On the north bank, they set up camp during a rainstorm, while watching for Legionaries to appear across the river. Despite rushing to the aid of their King, they'd seen no sign of a Roman Legion, nor heard of any. They'd been assigned an advanced position, a place of honor, the King's son assured them.

Wet and miserable, the Clan warriors complained to War Chief Attalus Kentus about the poor conditions and the boredom.

"Scanlan Kasia," Attalus called to the youth. "Jace always teaches that a good leader should ask the youngest and the oldest in his command for their opinion. My elder spearman wants to go home. What do you think?"

"Do you need an answer right now?" Scanlan inquired.

"I did ask," Attalus told him as he adjusted an oiled cloth to keep the rain off his campfire. "If you don't want to offer an opinion, I understand."

Scanlan glanced at the gray sky, trying to judge the position of the sun. In the rain and muted light, it was near impossible.

"I'll have an answer in the morning," the youth informed Attalus.

"Always a good idea to sleep on an idea before venturing an opinion," the War Chief remarked.

"There is that," Scanlan muttered as he scooted away from the warm fire and vanished into the forest.

***

Raindrops beat a rhythm on the piles of leaves and branches. Where the rain ran off the roof of the King's pavilion, the leaves were soaked and dank. Just a half-step away, a warm glow bathed the dry interior of the big tent. Although open on three sides, the light stopped at the sheets of water coming off the top. The man and furniture inside appeared to be in a bubble of illumination as the light failed to penetrate farther than the downpour.

At the front of the tent, three guards stopped a new arrival. A moment later, they passed him through their security line. Once out of the weather, the man shrugged off a greased animal skin.

"We should be home enjoying a roaring fire," he complained while placing the wrap over a chair.

"Brocc, this was your idea," King B'Yag reminded his son.

The War Chief of the Insubri ran his fingers through his wet hair then dried them over a brazier. Ignoring his father's remark, Brocc reported, "The courier to the Lepontic Tribe left before dark."

"But Samo Kentus only sent seven hundred warriors to me," the King complained. "When I sent word that Scipio, the butcher of Carthage, would attack, I assumed Samo would send all three War Chiefs and more spearmen."

"It'll be fine. The Lepontics will lose more warriors when they attack," Brocc explained. "That'll make it easier for us when we arrive to reclaim the Maggiore Valley for the Insubri."

"And make you Chief of the Gnātos Clan," B'Yag commented.

"And expand your control over the unruly Clan," Brocc added. "But what if the Romans do attack?"

"Governor Gaius Helvius is a Praetor," King B'Yag assured his son. "He can call up the garrisons from towns, but he hasn't the authority to raise Legions. And my spies tell me the Senate of Rome is weary of war and has no plans to assign a Pro-consul General to the Po River Valley."

"Wine?" Brocc asked.

King B'Yag held out his goblet. "Top me off and we'll drink a toast to a good plan."

Where rain fell off the roof of the King's pavilion, the drops beat a rhythm on the piles of damp leaves. Shoved into mounds when the servants cleared a spot for the King's tent, the heaps of wet forest refuse drooped. Yet under one section, the mound shifted slightly. Between the rain and the sound of the drops on the leaves, the guards had no inkling of the disturbance.

Scanlan Kasia slithered back, being careful not to break the upper layer of leaves. Only when he reached the trees did he begin to crawl. And even far from the King's tent, Scanlan remained stooped as he slipped southward towards the camp of Clan Gnātos.

***

Sometime in the night, the rain stopped. At last, Attalus Kentus found a comfortable position in a relatively dry spot and drifted off to sleep. Moments later, a shadow snuck into his small tent. The exhausted leader was unaware of the intrusion.

"War Chief Kentus," Scanlan whispered. The youth placed a hand on Attalus' knife arm to prevent the man from stabbing him in the dark. "You should take the spearmen home."

Outside of the tent, water dripped off leaves. Attalus could only hear the drip, drip, drip as the overcast sky blotted out light from the stars.

"Can't we talk about this in the morning over breakfast?" the War Chief of the Clan whined. "I thought you were going to sleep on it before giving me your opinion."

"Never said that," Scanlan argued. "I went and listened to King B'Yag."

"How did you get an audience with the King of the Insubri?"

"You might say I tunneled my way into his pavilion," Scanlan replied. He removed the hand that held Attalus and poked the War Chief to be sure he was awake. "Brocc sent a runner to notify the Lepontic Tribe that the Gnātos Clan had sent their warriors away."

Attalus jerked upright. "He what? Why?"

"After the northern tribe thins our number of warriors, they plan to remove Chief Samo and replace him with Brocc B'Yag," Scanlan revealed.

"Let me think about this for a moment," Attalus pleaded.

"Lepontic warriors could already be on the descending slopes to the valley," Scanlan warned. "Once you break camp, B'Yag's scouts will warn Brocc. You'll need to be across the Ticino before the main body of the Insubri catch you."

"What about the Roman, Scipio? Isn't he marching on us?"

"Turns out the plan was too clever," Scanlan declared. Then he whispered. "*Mēden agan.*"

"What's that?" Attalus questioned.

"A quote from the Oracle of Delphi. It means, *Nothing In Excess*," Scanlan replied. "By invoking the butcher of Carthage, King B'Yag named an extreme enemy. He hoped the threat would draw all the warriors of the Gnātos Clan away from the valley."

"But Jace and Abbo didn't come on the expedition because General Scipio holds their oath," Attalus whispered. Then to the youth, he pointed out. "But we'll never escape. Brocc will have scouts on us before we can cross the Ticino River."

"Maybe not," Scanlan told him. "Wake the spearmen and leave everything except your spears and shields."

"We can't fight and swim," Attalus scoffed.

"You can if the scouts are delayed," Scanlan suggested.

"Before I can stop and cripple the King's scouts, I'd have to know where the main body of the army is located," Attalus stated. "It'd be a mistake to try a delaying tactic on a shield wall."

"I can help with that," Scanlan Kasia offered.

***

Sneaking seven hundred warriors out of the camp along the Po River did not go unobserved. Just as

Attalus Kentus feared, before he and his spearmen reached open farmland, Brocc B'Yag called the light infantry together.

"The Gnātos Clan are cowards," he accused the fleeing spearmen. "They've deserted their King and their Insubri brothers when war is imminent."

The tribe's War Chief sent the nine hundred infantrymen after the escaping Clan. Moving quickly, Brocc's scouts caught up with the spearmen, a roman mile from the Ticino River. Dawn was just breaking.

"We can beat them," a Gnātos spearman boasted to his War Chief. "This place is as good as any."

Attalus glanced across the open field. The fastest infantrymen appeared between the trees.

"Yes, we could," he confirmed. "But the light infantry doesn't need to win the fight. They just need to hold us here until King B'Yag's infantry arrives."

"In that case, we are as surely cooked as a holiday goose," the spearman said.

"Form an assault line," Attalus ordered. When he caught the confused looks on the spearman's faces, he added. "We're better than a goose. We get to choose where we're cooked."

The seven hundred Gnātos warriors linked shields, creating a shield wall. With their targets in sight, the King's light infantry bellowed a challenge and ran at the double rank of shields.

"We are surely cooked now," the spearman told Attalus.

Shortly after the statement, the infantrymen and spearmen clashed. Chiefs and Captains, on both sides, shouted to keep up the courage of their fighters. The grinding of shields against shields overcame the grunting of men pushing and the cries of shock when a spear slipped between the shields and found flesh. Wounded warriors fell back from the assault lines. Quickly, others took their place. Locked in a dance of death, both sides pressed forward.

"We need to get some of us to the river," several spearmen shouted to Attalus.

Disregarding the suggestion, the War Chief bellowed, "Hold your line."

Then, as if a shooting star flashing across the morning sky, an arrow trailing a linen tail arched over the small battle. At the signal, Attalus Kentus roared, "Rearward, execute."

The forward line of Gnātos warriors punched with their shields, smashing their fellow Insubri in the face. The spearmen took two rapid steps back, pivoted, and sprinted away from the assault line. Confused by the action, but assuming they had broken the Clan, the King's light infantry forgot their discipline and sprinted after the spearman.

Rather than an uncontrolled dash, the spearmen raced away for ten paces. Next, without an order, they stopped, spun around, and set a new assault line.

Caught by surprise, the fastest infantrymen ran into the spears of the Gnātos Clan. The light infantrymen rushed to reform their own shield wall. But the wounded got in the way and chaos sowed confusion.

A moment later, another arrow towing a linen flag streaked across the sky. Attalus Kentus roared, "Rearward, execute."

The line of Gnātos warriors punched with their shields, but there were few infantrymen to catch the abuse. The spearmen took two rapid steps back, pivoted, and sprinted away from the assault line.

Afraid of another turn and a new attack line, the light infantrymen didn't pursue the spearman. Besides, couriers arrived, informing them that the rest of the Insubri were close behind. The light infantry helped their wounded while waiting for the tribal War Chief and the army.

With no one challenging his spearmen, Attalus instructed, "To the river."

As the light infantry watched, seven hundred Gnātos warriors raced for the Ticino. Unencumbered by an enemy, the warriors made their escape across the river. In two days of hiking, Attalus and his spearmen would reach Lake Maggiore and alert their Clan to the King's treachery.

***

At the top of a massive oak, Scanlan Kasia unstrung the war bow and slipped it into the case. Then he watched the spearmen vanish into the trees, heading for the river. In the middle of the field, the light infantrymen meandered around. Farther to the east, the Insubri army moved through the trees, their passage marked by flights of disturbed birds.

Scanlan put his feet up on a thick branch, braced his back against the tree trunk, and relaxed. He couldn't go anywhere until nightfall.

Moments later, King B'Yag, the potential murderer of the Gnātos Clan, arrived with his son. Deeper in the field, they paused a distance from the light infantrymen.

"Attalus and his spearmen escaped," Brocc told his father. "Do we march on Maggiore Valley?"

"Not unless Clan Chief Samo Kentus sends for help," B'Yag told him. "If anyone mentions it, we will deny any knowledge of the attack by the northern tribe."

"What about all this?" Brocc inquired. He waved his arms at the army.

"Send the Clans home," B'Yag instructed. "This war is over."

From his perch in the tree, Scanlan couldn't hear the words. He noted Brocc's body slump. The posture of the Tribe's War Chief wasn't that of a victorious commander.

**

Darkness fell and Scanlan descended from the high branches. To the east of the tree, he encountered several camps. Where many Clans had marched home after being dismissed, those from farther away set up for the night. They would head for their clan territory in the morning.

The youth could have passed by the cook fires unobserved. But he was hungry. The aroma of roasting lamb, drifting on the night air, stopped him at a large encampment. Scanlan moved east of the position and stowed his gear and bow in the fork of a tree. Next, he dropped to his hands and knees, and like a forest predator, listened and waited. Long moments later, a commotion at one campsite lured Scanlan towards the disturbance.

**

Bannus, Clan Chief of Lugus Leno, planted a foot in the backside of a servant. With a shove, he propelled the man out of the circle of light.

"I asked for a slice of lamb," Bannus complained. "Not a sliver or a taste, but a slice. Now get back here and cut me a man-sized slice."

All the spearmen's eyes were looking at the humiliated cook. Unnoticed, Scanlan eased into the camp from the other side. A flash of his knife cut off a portion of cooked lamb. It dropped it into his left hand. Then he lifted the big knife, lowered his head, and loudly smacked his lips.

"What?" Bannus growled. Seeing a figure near the roasting meat, he ordered. "Get away from that lamb. No one eats until I have my share."

Nodding his lowered head, Scanlan backed out of the camp. The spearmen watched the would be thief leave. As the youth moved to the edge of the light, the cook stepped into the circle of light.

"How big a slice?" the embarrassed servant asked his Clan Chief.

At the question, the spearmen in camp refocused on the cook. They missed Scanlan, holding a big chunk of meat, as he backed out of the firelight and vanished into the darkness.

Not long after the theft, Scanlan Saltare Romiliia Kasia strutted down a moonlit trail. While chewing on the lamb, he thought about the seaside port of Rimini. Full of meat and confident, Scanlan had no doubt that the skills he developed on Lake Maggiore would transfer to a position on a merchant ship as an oarsman.

***

Dawn found him on the bank of the Po. With his bow and bags on a small log raft, Scanlan kicked across the wide river. On the far side, he collected his gear and headed southeast. According to the maps his adopted father showed him, the home port of Rome's Eastern Fleet sat one hundred and forty miles from where he emerged from the Po. Moving farther south, he skirted the Latian settlement of Piacenza. After a night spend under a pine tree, the needles made for a soft bed, Scanlan awoke, and while stretching noticed movement on the foothills.

He should have continued on his journey eastward. But tribal warriors of the Boii, enough to hint at forces preparing for a major battle, appeared on the far slopes.

"May be King B'Yag had been mistaken," Scanlan thought. "General Scipio Africanus might be coming to punish the Insubri. But why cut through another tribe's area?"

Curious about the movement of spearmen, Scanlan changed directions. At a jog, the youth headed south across the plain and into the foothills of Boii territory.

Chapter 17 - Faded Horsehair Plume

Gaius Ampius trotted at the head of his two auxiliary Legions. Scouts ranged ahead of his light infantry while his heavy infantrymen struggled through the hills and the broken terrain. Being auxiliary, the Colonel commanded lesser trained and badly equipped infantrymen. Out of necessity, Gaius Ampius filled out his staff with transient staff officers.

"First Centurion," Ampius ordered, "send out the camp scouts and find us a place for the night."

"Yes, sir," the senior combat officer said before noting. "It might take a while, sir. The ground isn't level anywhere that I can see."

"I'll go with them," Senior Tribune Moresina offered.

"Since when does a Fleet Planning and Strategies officer volunteer for marching camp duty?" Ampius inquired.

Clario Moresina had latched onto the auxiliary Legions for a specific reason. The Senior Tribune ran spy networks throughout the Adriatic region. Under his control were agents along the east coast of the Republic, down the coast of Illyria, and southward to the town of Vlore, where the Ionian Sea mixed with the Adriatic Sea. Because the Consul Legions were made up of farmers with connections to property, they were unlikely candidates as spies. Moresina looked for recruits in the auxiliary Legions where the infantrymen were under-funded and less professional.

"Consul Aelius Paetus ordered you to take your Legions through the rough country," Clario Moresina reminded the Colonel. "While we're climbing hills and unable to see the wings of our Legions, the Consul is parading his Latin Legions down a roadway."

"He said we'll come at the Boii like a clamp," Ampius described. He held up two fists and put them together at the knuckles. "The Consul said we'll catch them between us and crush them like a grapes in a press."

"I have little confidence that the four Legions will ever meet up," Moresina proposed. "The route of the auxiliary takes us into highlands controlled by the Boii. On the road, the Consul Legions march along the edge of the territory. Unless the Insubri decided to interfere by moving southeast, General Paetus would never find an opposing force of tribesmen."

"That's a cynical view of our strategy," Gaius Ampius pointed out. "So why, Senior Tribune, do you want to help find the location for our next marching camp?"

"Colonel Ampius, I want to sleep behind walls tonight," Clario Moresina told him, "and not roll downhill if I stumble getting out of bed."

A sour expression passed over Colonel Ampius' face. Not because he thought the joke about getting up and falling downhill was bad. Rather, he feared it might be closer to the truth than he cared to admit.

***

Typically, a Legion on the move would send out staff officers, engineers, and a cavalry detachment. The officers would find a flat spot of ground near a water source and the engineers would stake out the marching camp. While the team worked, the cavalry would patrol for enemy activity. In the mountains, horsemen couldn't ride security. They got replaced by a Century of heavy infantry and four squads of light.

When the Legions stopped for a rest, Clario Moresina dismounted. After handing the reins to a Junior Tribune, the spy master hiked to the Centurion in charge of the detail.

"Welcome to the infantry, sir," the combat officer greeted him with mistrust.

"I may not look it, Centurion, but in my younger years, I was an Optio," Moresina assured him. "This old Sergeant won't slow you down."

"That's good to know, sir," the Centurion said without a lot of conviction. Then to his light infantry, he instructed. "Optio of Velites, take us forward."

The one hundred and twenty infantrymen, staff officers, and engineers started forward and immediately headed uphill, through a narrow valley.

***

Scanlan Kasia watched the spearmen vanish behind the next rise. All morning, he followed the warriors as they moved deeper into the high country of the Boii Tribe. Other large groups joined the one he tracked until they became long lines of spearmen on the trails. Although he didn't know where they were going, he was positive, just as streams flowed together to form creeks, the army of the Boii was gathering with a destination in mind. Climbing to high ground, the Insubri youth watched the march from above the warriors.

Late in the day, the horde stepped off the trail, set up camps, and built fires. Scanlan untied a blanket from his bundle, wrapped it around his shoulders, and shivered. From below, wisps of smoke, aromas of spices, and boiling grain reached him. With a tree trunk behind his back and his legs dangling off an overhang, he watched the Boii settle in for the night.

***

Many evenings, Scanlan sat in the forest without a fire to warm his body or flames to cook a meal. If he had any food. He recalled one night when they weren't on sentry duty at an access trail into the valley, but on a hunt.

"Envy is a waste of your evening," Jace Kasia had taught. "If an enemy has comforts and you don't, figure out why. And as always, resentment is not knowledge."

"Why are we sitting here in the dark?" Scanlan asked. "What harm would it do to make a fire?"

Down in the valley, warm glows from the windows of houses cast light into yards and gardens. The spots of illumination appeared as bright squares around the village.

"Knowledge goes both ways," Jace lectured. "You gain it to your advantage or you give it away for the benefit of your enemy."

"But bears sleep in their dens at night," Scanlan protested. "What knowledge are we withholding by being cold?"

"If we light a fire, the bear will smell wood smoke on our clothing in the morning," Jace replied. "Who gains the advantage with that knowledge?"

"When we stalk the beast as it goes to scavenge in the village," Scanlan commented, "the bear will smell us. And maybe attack before our arrows are notched."

"Still want a fire?" Jace inquired.

"No father," Scanlan answered, "I'd rather keep the knowledge of our presence a secret."

***

The youth pulled out a dried carrot and sat chewing the vegetable. He should head for the coast. But apparently the Boii had a plan and Scanlan wanted to know what it was.

"Envy is a waste of my evening," he whispered while chewing.

As the sun went down, the night turned chilly, and Scanlan Saltare Romiliia Kasia shivered.

***

The sun topped the mountain before the light penetrated the walls of the Legion stockade. Not until the ramp dropped and patrols of auxiliary infantrymen marched out to begin patrolling did the light reach the commander's pavilion. Several lanes away from the Colonel's compound, Senior Tribune Moresina and a single bodyguard walked through the infantry area.

Clario Moresina noted the ragged, patched, and aging tents. Even the servants, lounging in the Century areas, wore threadbare tunics handed down from secondhand users. He paused to examine a stack of broken spear shafts and rusty spearheads.

"I hope their training is better than their gear," Moresina remarked.

"Did you say something, Senior Tribune?" Gaius Ampius questioned.

The Colonel appeared from between tents. His face showed he hadn't slept well, which explained his early morning stroll.

"Just an observation about the age of the gear, sir," Moresina told him.

"It's why I took this command," Ampius disclosed. "If I capture enough gear and valuables, I can equip and pay the Legionaries. Once they accept me beyond the Consul's authority, I'll build them into a formidable force."

They walked to where the lane ended at the main road of the marching camp.

"Carthage is defeated and the Po Valley tribes are not united. Why build a formidable force in this area?" Moresina asked. "To what end is one needed, Colonel?"

"I wouldn't expect a naval officer to understand, but the east is full of turbulence," the Colonel told him. Moresina, the spymaster for the fleet, made a face as if surprised at the unrest in the east. Ampius missed the irony and added. "The Republic doesn't have a large presence there this year. But in a few, we'll have to go and defend the grain fields of Egypt. And that's where a popular commander with loyal Legions can earn glory and make a name from himself."

"It's good to have motivation, Colonel," Moresina granted. "My ambition is to get back to my office, my view of the ocean, and the eastern fleet."

"Senior Tribune, that's not a very grandiose plan," Ampius teased.

"Sir, look around," Moresina recommended. "We're deep in Boii territory on landscape where you can't see what's happening beyond your nearest flank. From my point of view, simply getting back to Classis sounds rather ambitious."

Down the main roadway, two riders came through the gate. One slightly ahead of the other. Both drove their horses hard.

"That can't be good," Moresina suggested.

The scouts galloped to the two officers and reined in their mounts.

"Colonel, we've located grain houses and an armory," one reported.

"And a stockade with structures filled with dried meat and bags of silver," the other conveyed.

"Where? How far?" Gaius Ampius asked.

"Three miles to the north," the first replied.

"Five miles to the south," the other revealed.

"If we're going to collect on the bounty," Colonel Ampius proposed. "I'll need to split my Legions in two."

"Three," Moresina commented. "One for each prize and a group here to defend the stockade."

"Three sounds right," Ampius agreed. "I expect, Senior Tribune, you'll be staying in the camp."

"No way, Colonel," Clario Moresina disagreed. He pointed to the lane they had come from and the stack of broken spears. "I want to see those sacks of grain and the war gear."

***

By mid-morning, the four wagons the Legions had pushed and shoved up and then brought down the hills, left the marching camp, heading for the Boii grain reserve and armory. Under eight hundred ill-equipped Legionaries guarded the wagons. The undersized Maniple of heavy infantrymen had four hundred light infantrymen flanking their formation. Colonial Ampius didn't have problems with math. His Legions simply lacked a full complement of Centuries for both Legionnaires and Velites. Dividing the Legions by three left each unit woefully shorthanded.

The brush on the side of the narrow cart trail squeezed the wagons, making the progress slow. By mile two, the lead element of the heavy infantry had moved far ahead. Taking their cue from the forward Legionaries, the light infantry maintained the forward formation. Unfortunately for Senior Tribune Clario Moresina, security at the wagons became thinner and thinner.

***

After trailing the Boii warriors and observing them gathering at positions on the hills behind a village, Scanlan focused on the reaction of the spearmen. None attacked the Legionaries, lounging in the village square. The spearmen greatly outnumbered the Romans. Yet the tribal leaders failed to order an attack.

It struck Scanlan as odd. No matter how much he thought about it, the youth couldn't figure out why the Boii ignored a perfectly good target.

Near midday, Boii scouts hurried through the forest. Moving from the south, they circled the village, climbed the slope, and met with the War Chiefs. Moments after the scouts arrived, a good distance to the south, splashes of color appeared between trees.

"An ambush," Scanlan answered the question that plagued him. Unable to affect the developing battle either way, the Insubri youth watched from his perch on the hilltop. With a panoramic view of the hills behind the village and across the face of the forest to the clearing, he settled in to learn from the engagement.

"*Every fight, whether between rutting bucks, massive armies, or combatants from neighboring villages, teaches a lesson,*" Jace Kasia instructed.

***

Far behind the red cloaks of the forward Legionaries, a transport and mule team entered a clearing. Their presence identified a narrow track through the woods. To the rear of the wagon, a mounted staff officer with a faded horsehair plume on his helmet rode near the tailgate.

Back on the hills, as if a beaver dam had been breached, the Boii raced downhill, flowed around the village, and vanished into the woods. Where the warriors had ignored the hamlet, they now made up for the neglect.

A war-band stormed down the slope and ran through the hamlet. Too late to defend against the advancing spearmen, the Romans stood in an uneven line, two missing their shields. They might have held, if they squeezed tightly together, something Jace Kasia would applaud.

But a pair of the Boii warriors leaped over the Legion spears and their flying weight drove the infantrymen back. As the Legionaries fell away, the rest of the spearmen entered the line and turned the fight into a melee.

Scanlan's mind drifted to the voice of his father shouting during drills, "Hold your line. Shields tight. Hold your line."

In those moments, the concept had been an imagined ideal. Scanlan swallowed a lump in his throat as a warrior speared a Legionary in the neck. In the spurts of blood, the ordered line of shields broke. The spearmen washed over the Legionaries, leaving broken and dead infantrymen in their wake.

Tearing his eyes away from the village, Scanlan searched the forest. But the trees blocked his view of the fighting in the woodland. Drifting farther south, his eyes located the clearing. He searched for the officer with the faded plume on his helmet.

Beyond a line of Legionaries and over their shields, Scanlan noticed Boii tribesmen bunched up at the edge of the clearing. A solid wall of interlocking shields prevented the spearmen from advancing. Two combat officers stalked behind the infantrymen, directing their spear thrusts and warning when a file of Boii warriors surged forward.

The staff officer in the faded helmet moved at the rear of the Centurions, almost as if he was attempting to stay out of their way. The concept of a Tribune not interacting with his Centurions went against Jace Kasia's teachings about Legion officers. Scanlan was fascinated by the dynamics of command while in combat, and especially, the lack of control by the old Tribune.

He could see the back half of the wagon but not the mules. Then, the wagon elevated on its rear wheels. Obviously, Boii spearmen had reached the harnesses and were driving the mule team backward. As if a giant hand had slapped shields aside, the rolling wagon knocked Legionaries down. Boii warriors leaped through the gap, destroying the shield wall. In an instant, individual fights broke out in the clearing. Remembering the old officer, Scanlan searched for the helmet with the faded horsehair plume.

Caught by surprise, the top edge of the tailgate collided with the Tribune. Between the impact of the wagon which doubled him over and the weight which knocked him off the trail, the old staff officer rolled into the woods and tumbled down the hill. His helmet with the faded plume landed beside the wagon.

With the shield wall decimated, the Boii rushed forward and slaughtered the Legionaries. After years of being taught and lectured by his father about the discipline of the Legion, Scanlan found himself disappointed by the performance of the Legionaries.

The fighting shifted to a slope before vanishing over a ridgeline. Scanlan peered at the area below the clearing and the wagon.

"The fall probably killed him," he thought. "If not, then by tomorrow the Boii will round him up. I wonder how much ransom they'll get for an old Tribune?"

While thinking about the monetary reward, Scanlan caught a glimpse of red material and a flash of a steel band from armor. Moving downhill, the old staff officer stumbled and tripped as he staggered away from the fighting.

"The Boii will catch him before I can get down there," Scanlan concluded.

But even as the negative thought crossed his mind, the youth shouldered his pack, tied the quiver around his waist for ease of access, and opened the case of his war bow.

Chapter 18 - Comedy or Tragedy

Clario Moresina tripped over a root and fell to his knees. The fall jarred his ribs, which sent another wave of throbbing up and down his chest. Involuntarily, he cried out. From the slope above, a pair of Boii warriors mimicked the Senior Tribune's cry of pain. Then, as they adjusted their route to intercept him, they chuckled.

Since he woke on the hill below the clearing and the wagon, the Senior Tribune had taken the path of least resistance. It was easier to stagger forward than to lift his feet and ascend the slope. But his moans and occasional cries of pain alerted the pair. They began stalking him like a wounded boar. Except he wasn't as dangerous as a wild hog, and after a short period, they realized it.

A branch emerged from leaves and caught Moresina's leg. He started to tip over. But hands latched onto his arm and swung him sideways. He found himself pushed into a depression. Agony from the rough treatment brought another cry of pain. Before it cleared his throat, a thick piece of leather was shoved between his teeth.

"Bite on this, keep quiet, and be still," a voice instructed.

Clario Moresina might have fought the hands and ignored the directions. But the speaker's inflection came from central Rome, or possibly one of the wealthy suburbs.

Trusting the upscale Latin, he ducked his head as leaves and branches were shoved over his legs, back, and head.

"Don't move until I get back," the Latin speaker urged.

"As you wish, Dominus," Moresina whispered.

His savior gave a little chuckle at being called Mister. The Senior Tribune fought the urge to moan as the man's footfalls faded.

***

Moments earlier, Scanlan Kasia heard the Tribune crashing around as he bounced from one tree trunk to another and stumbled over bush after bush. It was the worst example of hunting skills he'd ever seen or heard. Originally, Scanlan thought to let the officer come to him. But two eager Boii warriors had picked up on the sounds of the wounded man and took up the chase.

Now, with the old guy safely buried in leaves and branches, Scanlan needed to guide the spearmen away. Once clear of the old officer's hiding place, the Insubri youth would convince the Boii warriors to give up the hunt. To keep the chase going, he issued little yelps of pain, much like a hunter spreading bait for prey along a chosen route.

The branch was low enough that a short hop allowed Scanlan to reach it with both hands. A single swing of his legs whipped him up and around. He ended the loop on top of the branch. A stretch allowed him to pull up to a higher limb.

He plucked the war bow off two pegs he'd pounded into the trunk earlier. After notching an arrow, Scanlan held a second shaft between his fingers. His father, a Master Archer, always held four arrows in his forward hand. But

Scanlan found one was his limit. Once set in his tree stand, he waited for the two Boii spearmen to arrive.

"The description of this play," Scanlan proposed in the direction of the pair, "will depend on you. Will it be a tragedy where the heroes die in each other's arms? A comedy, where one helps the other limp away, both escaping danger and living to laugh about it in years to come? Or a satire where one runs for help while his companion dies alone? And for the rest of the coward's life, he lives with the guilt? Come players, the performance is about to begin."

Scanlan drew back on the bowstring as the pair of spearmen came through the brush.

Zip-Thwack!

The shaft flashed from the tree, caught the spearman on the side of his chest, and drove the arrowhead under the man's ribs. As if on a slide, the sharp point rode the inside of a rib, warping the shaft before the arrow stopped.

The Boii spearman dropped to his knees, screaming while grabbing his side. The tension of the bent arrow pried on the rib, trying to separate the bone from underlying tissue.

"It's an ambush," the other blurted out. "Run."

He raced away.

"A satire," Scanlan whispered as he drew the bowstring and sighted in on the injured man.

But the coward found his nerve and returned.

Scanlan held the tension while mouthing, "Tragedy or comedy?"

Even though visibly shaking, the returning warrior scooped up his wounded companion and the two Boii limped away, fast.

"Bravo," Scanlan stated while releasing the tension on his bow. "A well-acted comedy, even if the dialogue lacked a proper soliloquy and originality."

He un-strung his bow, wound the string, and placed the war bow in its case. Next, Scanlan climbed down and went to fetch the old Tribune.

***

As if his heel had been struck by a club, a bolt of fear raced through Clario Moresina's body. But it wasn't a strike but the movement of a branch being lifted off his legs and tossed aside. Then, panic set in as the leaves were brushed away, leaving him exposed to whoever was uncovering his body.

"They're gone sir," a voice remarked.

Moresina turned his face to the side and studied the Latin speaker. The articulate individual was a young tribesman. Above average height but thin with mid length brown hair and light skin. Even though his Latin held an educated tone, he displayed no features of Latin heritage.

"Where's your war-band?" Moresina asked, believing he'd been captured by a competing group of Boii.

"In the Maggiore Valley," the youth answered. "If they made it home."

"You're not with the Boii Tribe," Moresina offered.

"Not yet, Tribune. But soon, if we don't get moving, we'll be guests of the Boii. Not a good idea for a Latin or for an Insubri."

The Legion officer pushed to his knees and groaned.

"I hurt but I can walk," Moresina stated, his voice quivering with emotion.

"Drop your armor and we'll cover it," the Insubri recommended.

"You're pretty loose with my belongings," Moresina said, showing a little temper.

Based on what he'd experienced and the narrow escape, it stood to reason the staff officer was agitated.

"It is nice armor," the well-spoken youth told him. "Are you perhaps addicted to wearing it? Do you suffer from irregular sleep, obsessional thinking about armor, paranoia, and lack hygiene from hoarding armor."

"What are you talking about?" Moresina demanded.

"It's from *The Wasp*, a play by Aristophanes," the youth answered. A smile showed he was enjoying the exchange. "Although in the play, the author was referring to the addiction of Philocleon to the courts of law. And not a Senior Tribune addicted to armor."

"The play is familiar. However, I am not obsessed with my armor," Moresina declared. He reached for a strap and moaned. "I don't have the dexterity to remove it."

"Good, you've settled and are calmer," Scanlan noted. "Here let me help."

Aided by the tribal teen, Clario Moresina removed his armor. After covering it with leaves, he leaned on the Insubri. The two headed north.

"I'm Senior Tribune Clario Moresina," the Legion officer introduced himself. He left out the nature of his occupation as the commander of the Eastern Fleet's Planning and Strategies Department.

"Scanlan Kasia," the youth stated. "Adventurer, scribe, and oarsman of renown."

"And a patron of the theater, it seems," Moresina added.

"I'll have to remember to use that," Scanlan mentioned. Next, he repeated the phrase. "And a patron of the theater. Yes, sir, I like the sound of that."

It was as if the youth had been educated in isolation and dropped into the world without experiences. Moresina offered a silent prayer to Mercury, the God of Messengers, Commerce, and Trickery. For a youth who had already shown bravery and resourcefulness, the God's blessings added to Scanlan's attributes as a potential spy.

***

After a hard climb out of a valley, Scanlan allowed the Tribune to rest. He lowered the injured man to a place under a tree and dropped his pack.

"We need meat," Scanlon stated while opening the bow case.

"Meat has to be cooked," Moresina warned. "Isn't a fire risky?"

The youth indicated the far ridges across the valley and the tree-covered slopes.

"If the Boii were close, we'd see cook fires," he explained. "After the hike they made, and the uncomfortable nights on the hillside, they'll camp early."

"How can you know that?" Moresina challenged.

"Because I tracked them for two days," Scanlan responded. "They'll settle in early after a day of hard fighting. And we'll keep the fire low and hot."

"For one so young, you are wise beyond your years."

"It's not me," Scanlan deflected as he tied his quiver to his hip. "My father was a Legion officer. He taught me to know my enemy."

"A Centurion?" Moresina questioned, thinking a combat officer would teach his son about war.

"No, sir," Scanlan corrected. "My adopted father is Colonel Jace Romiliia Kasia. He was a Legion commander under the Butcher of Carthage. Oh, sorry, under Pro-consul Scipio Africanus in the Republic, Iberia, and at Carthage."

When the Senior Tribune fell silent, Scanlan slinked away on a hunt for small game. Moresina had heard about a Colonel vanishing before the assault at Zama. It appeared the Legion commander hadn't died. Somehow, Colonel Kasia ended up among the Insubri as a father to a special lad.

If his ribs didn't hurt so much, Clario Moresina would have built an altar to the God Mercury in gratitude. As good as the intention was at the moment, later that evening, he would learn about Scanlan Kasia's talents.

**

The hole was deep but narrow, with three tunnels in the hillside that fed air to the glowing wood. The air flow allowed the fire to burn hot and clean. Two rabbits, skinned and dressed, rotated on a spit over the flames. And what little smoke there was drifted up and disappeared among the branches of the tree.

"Surely, a Legion officer didn't teach you about hot fires holes and hunting rabbits so efficiently," Moresina remarked. To him, the youth returned with the game almost as soon as he left.

"Before the Colonel was a Legion officer," Scanlan bragged. "He was a Cretan Archer. Beyond archery, they're trained to live off the land."

"Are you a Master Archer, then?" Moresina asked, becoming a little leery of the fantastic story.

"No, sir. Jace insisted that reading and writing were better skills for survival than mastering a range weapon," Scanlan confided to the staff officer. "But I'm a competent archer."

Moresina peered over at the garbage hole where Scanlan had tossed the fur, feet, guts, and heads of the rabbits. Arrowheads had split both craniums, attesting to Scanlan's competency with a bow and his desire to not mangle the flesh of the rabbits.

"You mentioned scholastic work. What languages do you read and write?" the Senior Tribune inquired. "Obviously, Greek because of your knowledge of plays, and Latin because of your speech."

"I write and speak Insubri, Latin, and Greek," Scanlan listed. "A little Iberian and less Egyptian. We didn't have any samples of writing to study for those two."

"Run short of coins, did you?" Moresina teased.

"No sir. Jace and I crafted Cretan hunting bows and sold them. It was just no traveling merchants ever brought scrolls from Iberia or Egypt."

"How did a Legion officer become a Cretan Archer?"

"He was orphaned on Crete and didn't learn about his Romiliia family until he went to Rome," Scanlan described. "I have the name on my adoption scroll. It was signed by Cornelius Scipio Africanus."

"That makes you," Moresina whispered as if keeping the information a secret, "a citizen of the Republic."

"Yes, sir, I am," Scanlan confirmed without thinking about his earlier stance on fighting the Legions.

***

Left on his own, Scanlan could have reached the Latin settlement of Piacenza in two days. Between hunting for two people and assisting the injured officer up and over the hills, the pair took four days to reach the gates of the city.

"Senior Tribune Clario Moresina of Ampius Legions," Moresina reported to the guards at the gate.

Although his dirty red tunic carried no rank, his gladius, bearing, and stern gaze convinced the guards to grant him access to their command office.

"Senior Tribune, you have my deepest sympathies," the Centurion of the Guard offered.

"Contact with the Boii was bad, certainly. But sympathies?" Moresina questioned.

"Sir, Colonel Gaius Ampius was killed by the Boii," the officer explained. "Only part of his Legions made it out of the mountains. We took in several Centuries before Consul Paetus called them to join the Consul Legions."

"Where are they staging for the next assault?" Moresina inquired.

"They aren't, Senior Tribune," the Centurion informed him. "The Consul has disbanded the auxiliary Legions and sent them back to their tribes. He marched for Rome with his Legions yesterday. We can equip you and you're servant with horses if you want to catch up."

"I'm in need of medical attention," Moresina told the officer. He touched his ribs tenderly before assuring the Centurion. "I'll send a letter to Consul Paetus and tell him about my situation."

"Very good, sir."

"Thank you for your assistance," Moresina gushed. "You and your men are a credit to Rome. I'll mention you in my report."

Clario Moresina and Scanlan Kasia left the guard's office.

"The guard officer straightened up and his eyes showed your compliment meant a lot to him," Scanlan observed.

"People respond to kind words," Moresina said.

As they neared the doctor's office, the Senior Tribune asked, "How many guardsmen were in the building?"

"Five in armor and two in the back lounging," Scanlan answered. "Plus the Centurion."

"How many cups were on the table?"

Scanlan thought for a moment before stating, "Nine mugs."

"Who did the ninth mug belong to?"

After several steps, Scanlan ventured, "There must have been a guard out of my sight. Why do you ask?"

"No reason," Moresina commented.

They reached the door to the doctor's office and entered.

***

By midafternoon, Scanlan and Moresina had bathed in a private bath and had their skin oiled and scraped by household slaves. The same wealthy merchant donated clean linen tunics. He explained, without Rome's Eastern Fleet, his merchandise couldn't reach markets. The gifts to the Senior Tribune were a small price to pay for his shipping enterprise.

Sitting at an outdoor cafe, Scanlan and Moresina enjoyed the peace and the sun after escaping through the mountains.

"Considering the bruising over your ribs, I'm surprised none are broken," Scanlan offered.

"The doctor was confident, but to me, my side hurts as if several ribs were broken," Moresina grumbled. Then his mood brightened, and he remarked. "You like plays. Ever think of a career on the stage?"

Chapter 19 - For This Mission

Bowls of stew and rounds of bread were served, along with a pitcher of wine and a container of water. Moresina hesitated while Scanlan served himself.

When the youth added a lot of water, the Senior Tribune nodded and remarked, "It's very civilized of you to add water to your vino."

"Cretan Archers are against anything that dulls their reflexes," Scanlan informed the officer.

"A good habit," Moresina offered as he watered his own wine. After a sip, he asked. "What are your plans, Scanlan Kasia?"

"Rimini is a big port and merchant ships dock there," Scanlan responded. "I had figured to get a job on one as an oarsman."

"Had figured?" Moresina questioned.

"Now, I'm thinking about going to Athens and becoming an actor," Scanlan told him.

"Scanlan, you know I'm a Senior Tribune," Moresina revealed.

"Yes, sir, you command a half Maniple," Scanlan volunteered. "Fourteen hundred and forty Legionaries, eighteen Centurions, and three Tribunes report to you."

After a sip to hide his grin, Moresina got control of his expression. He placed the mug on the table.

"That is the job of a Senior Tribune in a Legion. My position is different," he divulged. "In the Eastern Fleet, I'm in command of the Planning and Strategies Department."

"I don't know what that means, sir," Scanlan admitted.

"My department plans fleet attacks and makes maps of where an enemy might attack our warships," Moresina explained. "Doesn't sound too exciting, does it?"

"No sir, it does not," Scanlan stated.

"I understand," the Senior Tribune pointed out. "It's certainly not right for an adventurer, a rower, and an actor. I would say."

"Sir, why would I consider joining the fleet?" Scanlan inquired.

"You shouldn't. Except." Moresina paused to allow the word to hang in the air between them. Next, he repeated. "Except. Have you thought of where I get the information for the maps and the plans?"

"Senior Tribune, up until a moment ago, I'd never heard of a Planning and Strategies Department. How would I?" Scanlan stopped in mid-sentence. He continued on a different track. "A fleet covers thousands of miles of shoreline and seaports. I've seen maps. How do you collect information for your maps."

"Legions use forward scouts, moving a day or more away from the main body of the force," Clario Moresina told him. "They are there to warn if an enemy approaches. It seems, Colonel Gaius Ampius failed to send his scouts out far enough. For a garrison Legion, they place men in villages or hire craftsmen around their area. These men send information in to help the patrols plan routes and stay safe."

"Those are defined areas," Scanlan proposed. "Whether the Legion is on the march, or fixed in a garrison, cavalry can ride either zone. What do those scouts have to do with the fleet?"

"The Republic sails over a vast region," Moresina answered. "Rather than gathering information for immediate use, my forward scouts send me political trends, the movement of armies, reports on the building of warships, and sea wall construction."

"How do they do that?" Scanlan asked.

"Think of a play where the actors die if they fail to stay true to their characters," Moresina described.

"You're talking about spies," Scanlan blurted out. He thought for a few heartbeats, which worried Moresina. But the youth wasn't deterred by the word spy. Scanlan broke the silence and recalled. "In the Iliad, Hector sends Dolon to spy on the Greek Camp. He's captured and questioned. After Dolon tells the Greeks about the Trojan forces and the location of the Thracian camp. Diomedes and Odysseus murder Dolon. Because he was a spy who got caught."

"How do you feel about Dolon?" Moresina asked.

"He got caught," Scanlan stated.

"Concerning Homer's character Dolon," Moresina inquired, "what are your thoughts?"

"He got caught," Scanlan repeated. "I won't."

***

They spend the afternoon walking through Piacenza, stopping at buildings made of different materials. At a brick structure, Senior Tribune Moresina gripped a brick in the wall.

"Imagine if this brick was loose," he described. "You pull it out, place a note in the hole, and after reinserting the brick, you walk away."

"What happens to the note?" Scanlan asked.

"Someone you don't know, and who doesn't know you, comes by and picks up the note," Moresina replied. "It's called a dead drop."

"What if the area doesn't have any brick walls?" Scanlan questioned.

Senior Tribune Moresina guided the youth to a rail fence. After an inspection, he eased open a narrow split.

"Insert a note here and this becomes your dead drop," he instructed.

"There's one flaw in the plan," Scanlan noted. "The other spy needs to know the location of the drop. And when there is a note to be picked up."

"Now you're getting into identifying compatriots, passwords, and identifying items," Moresina cautioned.

"What about them?" Scanlan demanded. "Don't I need to know how to find the other spies?"

"No, you do not. Because like Dolon, everyone who is captured and questioned could tell the authorities about you. Besides, to protect your true identity the passwords, signs, and countersigns change."

"Passwords, signs, and countersigns?" Scanlan asked.

"Like the call and response of the choir in a Greek play, when spies need to meet, they need a system," Moresina advised. "Say you spot a special pouch on a stranger. How do you know if they're safe to talk with? You state a prearranged word. If they reply with the countersign, you've made a connection."

"What if they don't know the countersign?" Scanlan proposed.

"You cough into your hand and walk away," Moresina replied, "as if you hadn't said anything."

For days, the commander of the Eastern Fleet's Planning and Strategies Department and the young Insubri lad walked the streets of Piacenza. From dawn to dusk, they discussed the art of acting in the deadliest of dramas.

"Tomorrow, I leave for Classis, the port of the Eastern Fleet," Moresina announced. "What will you do, Scanlan Kasia?"

"I thought I was going with you?" the youth questioned.

"It would be bad spy craft for a secret scout to be seen with the Commander of the Planning and Strategies Department," Moresina suggested. "Perhaps, you should take a horse from the garrison stables tonight, ride to Classis and sign onto a warship as a rower."

"But how will I contact you?" Scanlan asked.

"You don't contact me," Moresina told him. The Senior Tribune handed Scanlan a piece of birch paper and explained. "When I have need of you, I'll contact you. The person will mention Nightjar and say, they have soft feathers."

"And how do I reply?"

"Very good, you remembered that the call requires a response," Moresina confirmed. "You reply, their feathers make poor fletches."

Moresina strolled away while Scanlan looked at the message written on the birch.

Rider,

You are dispatched to take a horse and a saddle from the stables at Piacenza and deliver them to the stables at Classis.

The directions were signed by the Garrison Commander of Piacenza. It gave no indication of a connection between the Senior Tribune of Planning and Strategies and Scanlan Romiliia Kasia.

Early the next morning, Scanlan rode out of Piacenza on the southeast road, heading for the port city of Classis.

***

The barracks and administration offices occupied buildings inside the stone walls. From the top of the walls, officers overlooked the city of Classis, the shipyards, the docks, and the wide, flat shoreline where Rome's warships rested. But they weren't casual observers.

The garrison of Classis provided order and infantry protection for the port city. Unlike other shipping ports, Classis existed solely to supply the Eastern Roman Fleet. As a result, the streets and businesses were crowded with rowers, sailors, ship's officers, and infantrymen to maintain order. Control was necessary as rowers, vast in numbers, came from three distinct groups.

Muscular men made up the Engines of the warships. They sat midship and provided the oar-power to drive the ship steadily through the water. In front of the easily identified physiques of the Engine, the Stroke provided the best and most experienced oarsmen. As expert rowers, they set the pace for the other oarsmen on the warships. Being selected for their skills and assigned to specific warships, they strutted through the streets of Classis, taking offense at any slight to their ship. On any given day, depending on how many Roman warships put in at Classis, the press of bodies could make the streets impassable.

For example, when beached, each three-banker trireme deposited one hundred and twenty Engine and Stroke oarsmen on the streets of Classis. And for every five-banker quinquereme on the beach, the number of Strokes and Engines increased by two hundred. But the skilled oarsmen weren't the most plentiful bunch of rowers.

The Bow section constituted the entry level for a position on a warship. Hoping for a seat on a rowing bench, youths and desperate men flocked to Classis, seeking a job. Thus, while Bow rowers added a third more bodies to the streets from each beached warship, candidate rowers added even more to the multitude.

***

Three days after leaving Piacenza, Scanlan Kasia arrived at the Fort of Classis. He located the stables and turned over the horse and saddle. For his delivery, the stableman counted out three bronze coins.

"I'm new in town," Scanlan told the groom who took the mount. "How do I get a rowing position on a warship?"

The groom moaned.

"When you find out, let me know," he replied.

"The Naval schedulers only want rowers with experience," the stableman told Scanlan.

"How is anyone supposed to get experience," the groom complained, "if the scheduler won't hire us for a crew?"

"But if you're going to try, go for a trireme," the stableman offered. "The three-bankers stay near shore so you'll sleep on dry land at night."

"Plus, they patrol the coastline for pirates," the groom said with a glint in his eyes and excitement in his voice. "You might earn some salvage coins."

"Where do I find a scheduler?" Scanlan asked.

***

A Naval officer sat at a table with a long scroll, a pen, a bottle of ink, and a stern expression on his face. Just off the boardwalk, a line of Roman warships rested on the beach. Scanlan approached the Centurion.

"Scanlan Romiliia Kasia. I'm seeking a position on a warship," Scanlan announced. He placed the small scroll, identifying him as a citizen of the Roman Republic, on the table.

"Are you a sailor?" the officer inquired.

"No, sir. I'm an oarsman," Scanlan answered. "And I want to row for the *Hawk of Peace*."

"We already have an experienced crew," the Naval scheduler informed him. He pushed the identity parchment back across the table. "Go try a civilian shipper. King Phillip of Macedonia won't have to fear you for a few years. Come see me when you have more experience and more muscle."

Scanlan fumbled his identification scroll and it unrolled across the table. While retrieving it, he scrutinized the scheduler's scroll, the list of rowers' names, and the Stroke,

Engine, and Bow placements in a diagram of the warship. In addition to the substance of the scheduler's list, the youth studied the handwriting style of the Centurion.

"We are done here. Move along," the Naval officer directed.

Scanlan stepped away from the recruitment table, but he didn't leave the area. Instead, he walked along the pier, looking down on the beached warships. If any had been named *Eagle*, he would have targeted that warship for a rowing position. But *Accipiter de Pax*, the *Hawk of Peace*, had sailors hammering in caulking, sanding the deck, and rolling ropes. It appeared ready to launch.

After watching the preparations for a while, Scanlan faced out to sea. Spy or not, the Adriatic was his future. To the west was his home and mixed feelings for the Insubri Tribe. After lingering for a period, Scanlan walked back into the crowds of Classis.

***

On the street of sail makers and rope makers, and other shops supplying equipment to the warships, Scanlan headed for a three story structure.

"Excuse me," he questioned the guard at the entrance. He licked his lips and held his eyes downcast as if he was extremely nervous. "I've come to see someone called the scheduler. I'm told he's on the second floor. In the northeast corner."

"You've been given wrong information," the guard chastised him. "First off, the scheduler is down on the boardwalk. Second, his office is on the third floor, and it's in the southeast corner so he can see the harbor. You aren't too bright are you?"

"What?" Scanlan asked while letting his mouth hang slack.

"Nothing. Move along," the guard ordered the slow-witted youth.

As if afraid he'd bump into someone, Scanlan slouched away from the doorway. At the corner of the building and blocked from the guard's view by the crowd, he squeezed into a narrow alleyway. Extending his arms, he measured the distance between the three story Naval administration building and its two-story neighbor. After making a judgement, Scanlan returned to the dock. He snacked on a honey cake while keeping the scheduler under surveillance until the Centurion finished his day.

***

Lamps and candles in windows of shops where workers toiled pushed back the coming night. In restaurants, diners lingered over platters of food, and in pubs, sailors and rowers hovered over pints of beer and wine. Despite the artificial radiance, as the sun dipped below the horizon, the streets of Classis grew dark.

Along with the setting sun, the scheduler appeared in the doorway of the Naval administration building. His day finished, he nodded to the guard and hurried down the street.

Scanlan Kasia waited until light from windows created easily avoidable pools of illumination. Then he eased out of the recess where he'd spent the early evening. At the corner of the admin building, the youth squeezed into the narrow alleyway.

The first step was always the hardest. He extended one foot and planted it against the wall behind him. Next, the youth leaned forward until his arms took his weight. Then he lifted the other leg and pressed the ball of his foot against the bricks. In an awkward crawl, Scanlan Saltare lifted a foot higher, followed by a hand up. Next came the other foot and once it was braced, he moved the other hand. Through the process of keeping three points of contact on the hard surfaces, he scaled the walls.

Once near the top of the neighboring building, Scanlan planted a hand on the tile roof. Walking his feet higher, he inverted until he looked down on the tiles. With a kick, his feet left the admin building, and he balanced in a handstand less than a hand's width from the gap over the alleyway.

Twisting his arms, he reversed the way he faced, dropped to a crouch, and scanned his surroundings. Once sure he was alone on the tile roof, he leaped across the gap and grabbed onto the windowsill. Hanging by his fingertips, Scanlan dangled off the third floor of the admin building, hoping the bricks were laid by a master craftsman.

***

Reaching up, he tapped on the shutters and they swung open. Scanlan shimmied up and through the window. Not by chance, he emerged in the naval admin building on the southeast corner, third floor.

Conveniently, a scroll marked *Accipiter de Pax* lay on the Scheduler's desk.

After unrolling the roster for the *Hawk of Peace*, Scanlan struck a flint and by weak candlelight, he uncapped the ink container. After dipping the pen, he wrote his name on the ship's list in a perfect copy of the scheduler's writing. Waving the scroll to dry the ink, he prevented smudging before rolling it and placing the document on the desk. Exactly as he found it.

***

Shortly after dawn, the rowing officer of the *Hawk of Peace* unrolled the scroll and began reading off names. As he read, the Stroke and Engine rowers boarded. Part way down the list of Bow rowers, he announced, "Scanlan Romiliia Kasia."

"Here, Second Principale," Scanlan responded.

"Bow section. Sort out your seating with the lead rower," the ship's second officer instructed.

"Yes, sir," Scanlan confirmed.

He lifted his bags and walked up the ramp of the trireme. In his mind, he thought about chasing down pirates, boarding their single-decker ship, sword fighting with their best, and being rewarded for capturing stolen cargo. In all the dreams of adventure, Scanlan had no idea how far off his vision was from reality.

***

Looking down from the third floor of the administration building, two men observed the youth as he strolled up the ramp. From the east window, the scheduler glanced at the older man standing next to him.

"How did you know he'd find a way onto that three-banker, Senior Tribune?" inquired the officer in charge of staffing warships.

"There's only one Romiliia family," Clario Moresina replied. "Any son of Jace Romiliia Kasia must be a special lad. I needed to know how special."

"And your evaluation?"

"Could you separate his writing from yours?" Moresina asked.

"No sir, he matched my handwriting to the letter," the scheduler admitted.

"He's apparently that special," replied the head of Naval Planning and Strategies. "Scanlan is a good addition to the trireme for this mission."

"How do you figure that, sir?" the Centurion asked.

"Because Colonel Jace Kasia was extraordinarily resourceful. And apparently, so is his son. And he'll need it for where he's going."

Chapter 20 - During Every Cruise

At the forward seat on the lowest tier, where the frame and boards curved around to form the bow of the warship, the crowded rower's position butted against the hull. During hard strokes, the oarsman's feet, if he wasn't careful, would slip off the rib of the ship and splash into the bilge water. Plus, due to the cramped position, if he retracted his arms too far, his elbow would beat against the hull.

"That's your home for this cruise," the lead oarsman said, introducing Scanlan to the least popular rowing bench. "If you want out, leave the ship now, or show me you deserve better."

On the starboard side, a hesitant rower stared at the equally miserable position across from Scanlan's. The lead oarsman of the Bow section climbed over a thick cable of hemp, horsehair, and fiber to reach the other side of the ship.

"What is that?" Scanlan questioned. He patted the cable and felt tension.

A face dropped from above, as a middle tier rower leaned down.

"It's our hypozomata," the oarsman explained. "If it snaps, the hull will flatten and we'll all drown. But don't worry about the water because you'll be dead from the snapping of the cable."

Scanlan studied the knots that secured the cable to the raised section of the forward keel. They appeared secure. Following the length of the cable, he lost sight of it long before the cable attached to the stern section, one hundred and thirty feet back. While the bottom tier of rowers could see the hypozomata, it rested below the rower's walk, meaning the top and middle oarsmen couldn't see the cable.

From the other side of the hypozomata, the lead Bow rower repeated to the new oarsman, "That's your home for this cruise. If you want out, leave the ship now, or show me you deserve better."

Both oarsmen at the undesirable positions were thin, young, and from appearances, weak. One lacked experience as an oarsman. Although Scanlan had skills, he wasn't sure if rowing on a lake with a small boat crew would translate to rowing a massive warship.

***

There was one benefit to being lower tier and at the front. Scanlan and the other youth went down to their out of the way positions first. While they settled in, along the length of the rower's deck, one hundred and eighty oarsmen shuffled down to the rowing decks and jostled to get onto their benches. If it was only finding a seat on one of the three tiers, it wouldn't be chaos. But they had to step over and around oars, hang water and wineskins overhead, as well as string up their food and possessions. What little headroom the warship allowed quickly vanished. Looking down the length of the ship, the hanging gear gave the appearance of clothing and salami loafs displayed in a bazaar.

"I'm glad I'm not in that mess," Scanlan declared. Oarsmen above and in front of him, the ones close enough to hear, laughed. Puzzled, Scanlan asked. "What? Did I say something funny?"

A moment later, the Second Principale shouted down from above, "Bow section. Get to the beach and get us wet."

Immediately, the fifty-nine oarsmen around Scanlan scrambled upward. Scanlan had forgotten that the warship needed to be pushed off the beach.

As if a nest of snakes, they weaved between water skins, hanging hams, and sacks of grain. Using deck braces and the sides of benches, they pulled, climbed, and shimmied to reach the rower's walk. Once on the planks, they hurried to the main deck.

Scanlan, unaccustomed to the maze, fell behind. He reached the deck just as the last Bow rower jumped over the side.

"Did we wake you from your beauty rest, sweetie?" the warship's second officer sneered. "Perhaps a dip in the sea will freshen you up. Over the side oarsman. Now."

Scanlan rushed to the edge, and just before jumping to the beach, the Second Principale decided, "There's a loser on every cruise. I guess, I've found him."

***

On the beach, the sixty inexperienced rowers put their shoulders to the hull.

"Steady," the Third Principale alerted them. From above, the first officer called down, get us wet. In response, the third officer ordered. "Push. Free the *Hawk of Peace* from the sand and let her float. Push."

At first the trireme resisted. But as the rowers dug their feet into the sand and pebbles, the keel began to slide. And once momentum took hold, the warship slid into the water.

"Unless you truly enjoyed your stay in Classis," the Third Principale warned as he climbed up the hull. "Get on board."

Sixty men grabbed the lower rails, pulled up, found footing, and swarmed to the deck.

"I've got a count of sixty, sir," the Second Principale informed the Ship's Centurion.

"Very good. Now get me out of the shallows," the ship's officer instructed.

The Bow rowers dropped down the forward ladder, heading for their positions.

"Stroke, stroke," the officer called the rowing cadence. "Keep it light and don't break you oars on the bottom. Stroke, stroke."

By the time the Bow section had found their benches, run out their oars, and joined the Engine and Stroke sections, the *Hawk of Peace* had powered into deep water.

***

"Stroke. Stroke," the Second Principale chanted. He stomped his feet in rhythm as he strutted back and forth on the rower's walk. "Bow section, get it together, stroke, stroke."

Despite his encouragement, the inexperienced individual oarsmen failed to move together. Some pulled too hard, others too soft, and for the most part, they were equally short or long strokers. If not for the Engine and Stroke in the stern, the warship would have floundered.

Stroke and Engine leads took the upper and middle of the Bow section to coach. The lead Bow dropped to the lower tier and moved first to one side of the cable and then to the other. At each bench, he placed his hands on the rower's arms and guided him to the proper rhythm and stroke length. Once the man rowed along with the commands of the Second Principale, the lead moved across to the next oarsmen.

Just as he reached the worst of his rowers, the Bow lead had reached the end of his patience. The last ones in the rear got his short-tempered instructions.

"I told you if you didn't like the position to get off my ship," he shouted at the Starboard rowers near the rear. Not in a gentle fashion, he slapped, jerked, and growled until they almost matched the experienced oarsmen.

Scanlan found the balance of the oar and moved it in time with the call, "Stroke. Stroke."

The lead of the Bow climbed over the cable, glared at the last three rowers on the Port side, and started to unload his pent up frustration.

"I told you if you didn't like the position to get off..." the lead fell silent when he noticed the last oarsman.

"The balance of the oar is a little off," Scanlan Kasia told the lead. "But the length isn't much different than an oar on a lake boat."

Of all the inexperienced rowers, Scanlan matched the oars of the Engine and Stroke sections and kept pace with the rhythm.

"Keep it up and I'll move you up a tier and back," the lead told the Insubri youth.

A quick glance over his shoulder at the broad expanse of the inner hull brought a smile to Scanlan's face. Although the position was cramped for the rower, the hull provided space for his bow, quiver, bundle, beverage, and food sacks.

"I'm fine right here," Scanlan assured him.

***

The oarsmen of the *Hawk of Peace* rowed most of the morning. Sweat dripped from rowers above, which irritated the lower tiers, but droplets also flew from the ends of oars. Everyone got a nasty taste of their neighbor. Breathing hard but rowing together, the oarsmen were too weary to complain and too exhausted to cheer when the First Principale ordered the sails raised and the oars withdrawn.

"Kasia, get topside for two turns of the sand dial," his lead instructed. Then he addressed the rest of the Bow section. "The best rowers from the Stroke and the Engine are going up. Scanlan will meet them and they'll get a look at him. Row better and you might win the first position for the next break."

Scanlan crawled around rowers and up braces until he reached the rower's walk. Coming from farther back, a large man with great hairy arms and a tall, rawboned rower met him.

"Rufus Alfena, Engine lead," the center section rower introduced himself. "I hear you understand the power of varying hard and soft strokes."

"It's a long ways up Lake Maggiore," Scanlan told him. "A rower has to know when to battle the wind coming down the mountain and when not to exhaust yourself in a fruitless fight."

"Wise words," the Engine lead agreed.

He headed up the ladder while Scanlan waited for the Stroke lead.

"Folia Minicia," the man said his name before challenging. "You aren't ready to join the best rowers in the fleet."

"I never said I was," Scanlan pushed back. "As a matter of fact, I have a cozy corner with wall space for my gear. Plus, no one expects much from me."

"Unpretentious, now that is refreshing," Folia ventured. "Come on tell me where you learned to row."

Scanlan followed the first rower of the warship up the ladder.

***

On the top deck, the ship's second officer warned, "Stay on this side of the sail. The Marines are practicing archery. I can't afford to lose any rowers to a wayward arrow."

"Second Principale Tapsennia," Alfena remarked. "This is Scanlan. If he had more meat on his bones, I'd pull him into the Engine."

The ship's second officer studied Scanlan for a moment.

"Weren't you last up at launch?" Tapsennia inquired.

"Yes, sir. It was the first time I ever crawled out of a giant spider web," Scanlan offered.

"I remember my first time climbing up from the bottom," Minicia reminisced. "I wasn't last but I was close."

From the other side of the sail, a voice snapped.

"If you slip like that when we engage raiders, I'm going to offer you in trade for a crippled pirate," the man suggested. "It'll be an unfair trade. The pirate throwing rocks will do more damage than you are doing with that bow."

Scanlan looked from Folia Minicia to Rufus Alfena and decided he had nothing more to say to them.

"Second Principale, do you mind if I watch the Marines?" Scanlan inquired.

"Be my guest," Tapsennia invited. "But stay out of Optio Vibia's way or he's liable to make you hold the targets while his Marine's practice."

"Yes, sir," Scanlan conceded.

He hadn't realized being a new oarsman on a warship would tighten his gut so much. Simply ducking under the big sail and getting away from the rowers eased the tension. And then he saw the Sergeant and a feeling of calm washed over him. Combat leaders came in every size, but they all had one thing in common. They wanted the best from their underlings with the least amount of flying bull excrement.

***

If the sight of numerous scars and old war wounds gave Scanlan comfort, it was all due to the scars on his stepfather's body. Optio Vibia carried trophies from years of shield wall battles.

The Optio stood looking at the throat of a Marine. Obviously, he refused to look up at the taller man.

"That's a bow. That's an arrow. That's a bowstring," Vibia listed. "Over there is a target. Why can't you put the shaft through the target, Pacius?"

"Optio, I'm trying," the Marine pleaded.

"Well, try better," the NCO instructed.

The Marine named Pacius notched an arrow, and pulling with his long arms, he drew the bowstring back to his cheek. But the motion bent the weapon beyond the normal curve. Even then, the man pulled until the notch and bowstring rested by his ear. The form matched a master archer's ideal. But when he released the arrow, the bow wobbled before returning to the curve of a strung bow. During the momentary shake, the shaft adopted the wobble. The flight of the arrow resembled a moth around a flame. It oscillated.

"I didn't think anyone could get worse with practice," Vibia swore, his frustration apparent.

Behind the Marine and the Optio, five more Legion Marines stood with their heads down. They seemed nervous. Perhaps they feared for the fate of the tall man. He must be popular with the other infantrymen.

"Optio Vibia. My father, Colonel Jace Kasia of Scipio Legion," Scanlan advised, "says if your instructions aren't working, let another fool try."

Vibia's head pivoted so fast, it looked as if someone had slapped his face around.

"What did you say?" the Optio thundered.

"Let another fool try," Scanlan answered.

"And you are?"

"The son of Jace Kasia," Scanlan answered. "A Legion officer and a Cretan Archer. So you know I've been over-trained."

"Over-trained in what?" Vibia asked.

Scanlan pointed to the bow and said, "Over-trained for a lot of things, Optio. But for the purpose of this discussion, in archery."

Vibia waved Scanlan forward. As the youth moved, the Optio warned, "If Pacius doesn't hit the target, after your lesson, I'm throwing you over the side."

"I'm a good swimmer," Scanlan promised. "But a better archer."

The youth took the bow from the Marine, notched an arrow, pulled, and released.

Zip-Thwack!

The arrow hit in the center of the target.

"Nothing wrong with the bow," Scanlan announced.

"The problem is with the archer," the Marine whined.

Scanlan walked to a cool brazier and ran the tip of his right finger around the rim. Black soot clung to the fingertip. After notching another arrow, he drew and held. With a flick of his finger, he marked the arrow shaft near the handle of the bow.

"Here, draw the arrow to the mark," Scanlan advised while handing the bow and arrow to the big Marine. "I know the Legion taught you to pull to your ear. Don't do that, your arms are too long. The side of your nose is far enough back."

The long arms of the Legion Marine pulled the arrow until the mark reached his forward hand. Resting his jaw on the top of his hand, he released the almost half-drawn bowstring.

Zip-Thwack!

The shaft appeared in the target next to Scanlan's arrow.

"You were overextending the bow and causing the arrow to wobble," he described. "If you mark a few shafts for the shorter draw, you'll soon learn what works for you."

"Rower Kasia," Tapsennia called from the other side of the sail, "your sand is running out."

"Nothing wrong with the bow or the archer," Scanlan assured Pacius. Then he jogged under the sail and raced back to the ladder.

"I see you didn't get thrown overboard," Second Principale Tapsennia noted.

"Does he really toss people over the side?" Scanlan asked.

"At least once during every cruise," the rowing officer replied. "Get below, your time on deck is over."

The ship's second officer turned the sand dial as another trio of rowers came up the ladder. Scanlan dropped below the deck on his way back to his corner position.

Chapter 21 - Marcus Lepidus

Over the following days, the warship drilled and challenged its oarsmen. The *Hawk of Peace* rowed straight, then made sharp turns to Port and to Starboard. They rowed against the wind and stroked with it, catching the breeze from both sides. After fifteen days of rowing in circles, but mostly down the coast, their training paid off. To the satisfaction of Ship's Centurion Bavius, the rowers solidified into a crew of oarsmen.

"First Principale, play days are over," Centurion Bavius directed. "Take us to Brundisi. And remember, we'll be under scrutiny as soon as we come over the horizon."

"Second Principale Tapsennia, we need the best from your oarsmen," the first officer alerted the rowing officer.

"You'll have it, First Principale."

Seamlessly, as soon as the sailors rolled the sails, the oars flashed in the morning sun. Wet and glistening, the blades splashed, leaving parallel wakes behind the warship. At the beach, the vessel spun as if balanced on the center of its keel. Next, as if they were on fire, sixty Bow oarsmen raced to the deck, ran to both sides, and jumped to the beach.

"Nicely done," Bavius congratulated the first officer. "My compliments to the crew."

"Thank you, Centurion," the first granted. Then to the sailors, he directed. "A ramp for the Ship's Centurion."

The sailors ran long planks to the edge of the deck. They tilted over until the ends dropped to the beach. Centurion Bavius left the warship and marched into the city of Brundisi. Tailing him were two Legion Marines in polished and oiled gear.

***

Refilling their freshwater containers, washing their bodies and shaving were priorities for the oarsmen. Feeling refreshed, six of them dropped their gear and bedrolls, designating an area as a campsite. Scanlan and another rower dug a firepit on the beach and lined it with rocks.

"The Centurion was in a rush," one suggested as he lit the fire.

Another oarsman poked a skewer through a hunk of lamb and held the meat over the flame.

"I heard it from a Stroke rower," he whispered as if wanting to protect his source. "We're going across to Illyria and patrolling north. The Centurion went to get instructions on how to be a good ambassador."

"Does that mean we won't be chasing raiders?" Scanlan asked.

"You are either touched or have a death wish," two rowers ventured. One finished the thought. "No one wants to die fighting raiders, except maybe you."

"But you've got to fight if you want prize ships, bounty, and to get rich," Scanlan responded. "My father said Cretan Archers are sworn to earn a profit every day."

Around the campsite, the five rowers each held out a hand with the palm up. Resting in the cupped hands were pairs of denarii. The new bronze coins reflected the midday sun.

"We get paid every day for being Roman Republic oarsmen," the one holding the meat over the fire stated. "Most of us keep our signing bonus as a reminder that were are employed. Sure, we won't get back pay until the end of the cruise, but in theory, we earn a profit every day."

"Where are your denarii?" inquired a rower on the far side of the firepit.

No one was in the Senior Centurion's office that night when Scanlan forged his name on the ship's roster. He didn't have two new bronze coins to show the rowers.

"Don't tell me the Insubri gave his bonus to a barmaid," teased a rower.

Grabbing onto the lifeline, Scanlan held his breath and squeezed his chest until he felt his cheeks flush.

Several rowers pointed and observed, "He's blushing. Ah, it was a girl."

"But, but," he stammered, "she was very pretty."

"Lad, they all look pretty after too much wine," sympathized an older oarsman. "It's a costly lesson but one worth remembering. Water your wine and keep the ties on your coin purse knotted."

"That is sage advice," Scanlan admitted.

They each poured a portion of grain and a few vegetables into a large pot of water. Several added herbs to season the soup. The oarsman with the lamb cut the fist-sized piece in two and tossed one half into the pot. While waiting for the food to cook, he went back to roasting the other half. Most rowers stretched out and let the afternoon idle away while waiting for the soup to boil.

***

"Yo, Bow section," the rowing officer greeted them as he approached the campsite. "We're going to be on the beach for two days."

"Did the fleet get lost, Second Principale?" an oarsman teased.

"No, we're waiting for a couple of five-bankers," he told them.

"If we're traveling north from Illyria," Scanlan questioned, "why are we waiting for the quinqueremes?"

"North," Second Principale Tapsennia repeated. "We're not going north. The *Hawk of Peace* is being designated a Senate Tribune vessel. We're sailing with Ambassador Marcus Lepidus to Athens. And from there to anywhere he wants to go."

"Does that mean we won't be hunting raiders?" Scanlan suggested.

"I see it's hot violence and a challenge you seek," Tapsennia exclaimed. "Well, Bow rower, I have just the mission for you. Over the next two days, the first officer wants the ship waterproofed. Hot birch tar, wades of hemp fiber, a big hammer, a broad chisel, and the entire hull of our three-banker as your battlefield. That should satisfy the adventurer in you, Kasia."

Scanlan slumped down and scolded himself for opening his mouth.

"What about the rest of us, Second Principale?" an oarsman inquired.

"The first officer wants the deck, the ladders, and the rower's walk sanded and oiled," Tapsennia told him. "Other than Kasia and his squad of tar warriors, the rest of you will be making the *Hawk of Peace* look like a new ship."

The oarsmen around the campsite began talking when the rowing officer turned to leave. But Tapsennia stopped and spun around.

"And Kasia, I want the blades on the bronze ram scraped, buffed, and polished," the Second Principale added. "If the rest of our ship is going to be beautiful, then our primary weapon should be as well."

"Yes, sir," Scanlan acknowledged with little enthusiasm. After the second officer left, he moaned. "I should have kept my mouth shut."

***

When Ship's Centurion Bavius returned, he brought with him a handsome staff officer. Attractive and muscular, Tribune Marcus Lepidus wouldn't look out of place on a stallion, leading a Legion into combat, or posing for a sculpture as an epic hero. Along with Ambassador Lepidus came a combat officer, five infantrymen, two men in robes with ink stains on their fingers, and a Greek who seemed amused by the others. Behind the entourage, porters hauled bundles and chest of belongings.

"No offense, Ambassador, but why a three-banker," Bavius commented when they arrived at the beach. The Ship's Centurion nodded towards the two five-bankers that had arrived while the crew cleaned the three-banker. While the deck of the *Hawk of Peace* stood thirteen feet off the beach, the decks of the two quinqueremes towered twenty feet overhead. "My ship is sturdy and my crew tough and efficient. But, a trireme hunts raiders in coves, rows messages between ports, and acts like a ferry service for officials."

"Am I not an official?" Lepidus questioned.

"Yes, sir. An Ambassador is certainly an official," Ship's Centurion Bavius confirmed. "But why my ship? Why a three-banker?"

They crossed the beach, approaching the trireme.

"Pro-consul Claudius Nero and Praetor Publius Tuditanus need big, impressive warships to show the might of Rome when they enter a harbor," Marcus Lepidus informed Bavius. "While they attend feasts, listen to political speeches, and fend off pleas for help, they have limited power."

"Limited power, Tribune?" the Ship's Centurion asked.

"They're diplomats in the truest sense of the word. Pro-consul Nero and Praetor Tuditanus can offer advice, spread coins among our allies, and sign letters of trade. But I alone hold the proxy of the Senate of Rome. If there is to be war with Philip V of Macedonia, the declaration of war will come through me."

Bavius thought for a moment before offering, "In a trireme, you can move in and out of a harbor and not be noticed. And you can blend in with a squadron of warships and look around before the ships of the diplomats arrive."

"Now you understand," Lepidus confirmed. "Your *Hawk of Peace* is a beautiful ship and well cared for. Especially the bronze ram. Let's get aboard. The sooner we get launched the sooner we can get to Vlore."

At the ram, Scanlan Kasia buffed one of the cutting blades. From pitted and coated in a green film, the Insubri youth had scrubbed until the bronze showed dull metal, which served to highlight the pits on the ram even more.

"Where's Vlore?" he asked a sailor as he buffed a spot.

The crewman checked the beam that supported the ram before replying.

"It's an overnight sail directly east," the sailor told him. "The city has been Greek, Illyrian, Macedonia, and now owes allegiance to Rome."

"Think we'll stay there?" Scanlan inquired.

"The fleet is wintering at Vlore," the sailor answered. "So we could winter there as well."

"Scanlan Kasia stay on the beach," the ship's third officer called out. He climbed down the hull while informing the youth. "We're getting our feet wet."

Thirty rowers vaulted from the deck and landed around Scanlan. Moments later, the hull slid off the shore, the warship splashed into the water, and the rowers scrambled aboard. Afraid of being last, Scanlan reached the deck at the head of the pack and sprinted for the ladder. Before reaching the opening in the deck, a voice stopped him.

"Kasia. Come over here," the first officer shouted.

Scanlan stopped short, forcing the rushing oarsmen to flow around him.

"What did you do wrong?" Tapsennia demanded.

"I have no idea, Second Principale," Scanlan admitted. Running oarsmen bumped into him and cursed because he stood between them and the ladder. When the last one went by, he suggested to the rowing officer. "Maybe the Ambassador wants to congratulate me on the superb job of polishing the ram."

"Not likely, Kasia," Tapsennia said, denying the concept. "Go, don't keep the First Principale waiting."

Scanlan marched to the steering deck and halted in front of the raised platform.

"Sir, Oarsman Kasia," he said with his arm posed in front of his chest. There shouldn't be an expectation of a salute. He wasn't Legion. But Scanlan had taken up the habit when greeting Jace Kasia. Deciding it couldn't hurt, he displayed an open hand to show he held no weapon and slapped his chest with the hand, "reporting as ordered, First Principale."

The ship's first officer returned the salute, then informed the youth, "Tribune Lepidus wants a word with you."

"Yes, sir," Scanlan stammered. He couldn't figure why the Ambassador from Rome had singled him out.

***

People of exceedingly pleasing features, just as with paintings and sculptures of handsome men and beautiful women, drew other's eyes to their expression. Marcus Lepidus raised an eyebrow in an amused manner and allowed a lopsided smile to bend his full lips. The effect relaxed Scanlan, as if he knew the Tribune from his past. He didn't, but people of exceedingly pleasing features befriended others quickly.

"Scanlan Kasia. Was it you who cleaned and polished the ram?" the Ambassador inquired.

At the sound of a cough from Tapsennia, Scanlan almost turned and winked at the Second Principale. But the shock of hearing the very words that he joked about froze him in place.

"Yes, sir," Scanlan confessed. "But the green tarnish wasn't that thick on the bronze."

Agile as a cat, Marcus Lepidus walked off the four-foot-high platform. He landed with no more bounce than if he paced forward one step on level ground.

"Tell me, Oarsman Kasia, how you managed to get such a shine on the ram." Lepidus pulled two new denarii from his purse, placed them in Scanlan's hand then draped the arm around the youth's shoulder. Bending over, he remarked. "Is that so?"

Scanlan hadn't said anything to elicit a response. He was too flustered to speak. The strong arm on his shoulders turned him and he strolled away from the steering platform with the Tribune.

"Oh, I can see the usefulness of that," Lepidus responded to the one sided conversation. Again, Scanlan hadn't said anything. Next, the Tribune leaned in close and whispered. "Scanlan, did you know that Nightjars have soft feathers."

"Yes, sir," Scanlan replied to the code, "but they make poor fletches."

"Oh, that's a relief," Marcus Lepidus breathed out, the tension leaving his arm. "I wasn't sure you were Nightjar. All I had was a description and it matched twenty rowers on this ship."

The first officer called for oars. Quickly following the command, the sounds of trimmed and dried fir trees being shoved through oar holes reached the deck.

"How did you know it was me, sir?" Scanlan inquired.

"I didn't. But I know Senior Tribune Moresina. He has a weakness for men who attack even small jobs with zeal."

"So it was the polish on the ram," Scanlan asserted. He bounced the new bronze coins on his palm. "What now, sir?"

"Nothing yet," the Ambassador admitted. "But now I know you and you know me. I'll let you know when I need you."

"Yes, sir. Am I free to go?"

Marcus Lepidus pushed Scanlan away while nodding his understanding. "San, salt, and vinegar, you say. And lots of sweat, I'd venture. Return to your station, Oarsman Kasia."

Scanlan raced for the ladder. It was hard enough to climb down to his position on the lowest level and in the front. And now, with everyone rowing, the maze took on a new dimension of difficulty. He reached the rower's walk as the cadence began.

"Stroke, stroke, get it together people," Tapsennia threatened. "We've got a long cruise tonight. If you need the practice, we can row the whole way."

"Excuse me, Second Principale," Scanlan requested as he came up behind the officer.

Tapsennia turned slowly and ran his eyes up and down the youth.

"The Tribune really did want to ask you about polishing the ram?" he inquired.

"Yes, sir. But he already knew the answer."

"Get to your station," Tapsennia instructed. He stepped aside to allow Scanlan to pass on the narrow walkway. Before Scanlan had gone far, the second officer called out. "I didn't think you did such a great job on the ram."

"Yes, sir," Scanlan acknowledged as he squeezed the bronze coins.

Chapter 22 - A Code Mark

The *Hawk of Peace* had ventured far from shore during training maneuvers. Yet, every afternoon, they returned to the coast of the Republic for the night. But on the crossing to Vlore, the sun touched the unbroken line of the western horizon. No land was visible from the deck of the warship in any direction. Before the sea doused the daylight and plunged the ship into darkness, Ship's Centurion Bavius prepared to offer sacrifices and prayers.

Second Principale Tapsennia perched high on the ladder above the rowers' walk and waited. From his vantage point, he would describe the ritual for the rowers.

Although speeches delivered on the steering platform would reach the foredeck, they became muffled to the rowers below.

"The Centurion is holding dried mint and spearmint leaves, salt, and a container of olive oil above his head."

"Luna, Goddess of the moon, may you light the night and shine on our ship," Tapsennia repeated Bavius' prayers. "Salacia, Goddess of Seawater and the calm aspects of the sea, allow our passage to be uneventful."

Silence fell over the warship as Bavius approached a lit brazier.

"The Centurion is sprinkling the mint and spearmint leaves into the fire," Tapsennia reported. "Luna and Salacia, may you find the fragrance of these herbs pleasing. The ground leaves are rising into the air as tiny sparks. A glorious sight as the sun begins to set."

Below, religious or fearful rowers whispered Goddess Luna and Goddess Salacia accept these gifts.

"Now the Centurion is sprinkling ground salt over the flame. As if water, the flame falters in the presence of the mineral," Tapsennia described. "Goddess Salacia, we offer the return of salt to your dominion. The same salt we extracted from your seawater."

Two sailors tilted the brazier and shifted the charcoal and wood from the iron basin to a deep ceramic bowl.

"The Centurion is pouring olive oil into a bowl, being careful to float the fire and burning wood chips on top of the oil," Tapsennia explained. "Goddess Luna, please accept this olive oil, which was picked and pressed at night under your radiance. We ask for clear skies during our crossing."

The sailors placed the bowl in a rope sling and lowered it over the side.

"The ceramic bowl, holding our sacrifices, is being lowered to the sea," Tapsennia alerted the rowers. "Goddess Luna. Goddess Salacia. Will you accept our sacrifices, grant passage to our vessel, and guide us across the sea?"

Below deck, the rowers held their breath, as did the sailors, officers, infantrymen, scribes, and navigators. The only one seemingly unconcerned if the sacrifices would sink or be accepted by the Goddesses, sat waiting for the stars to fully emerge. For those points of light alone, he held out hope. He left the safe passage of the ship in the hands of the fates.

Despite Tsolak of Fyli's disinterest in the sacrifices, the stoic leaned over the edge and watched the ceramic bowl settle in the water. Not until the bowl with the low flame on the layer of olive oil floated free of the rope sling did the Philosopher lean back and begin his examination of the heavenly bodies.

"The bowl floats, allowing our sacrifice, like our ship, to hover between the sea and the night sky," Tapsennia declared. "The Goddesses have accepted our sacrifices and our prayers."

Comforted by the good omen, the *Hawk of Peace* settled in for a long night of sailing on open water. The sun dropped into the sea, the stars came out, and the navigators sighted on specific points of light for direction.

***

The Goddesses had surely blessed the crossing. In the morning, the sun appeared above distant mountains. Although still half a day's sailing from land, the warship enjoyed fair weather and calm seas.

Marcus Lepidus rolled back his blanket, stood, and stretched.

"Ship's Centurion," the Tribune addressed Bavius, "when we arrive at Vlore, I need to gather some information. If I walk around with veteran Legionaries, it'll be obvious that I'm more than a staff officer. Yet, if I go about my business with no bodyguard, I'll be seen as a victim."

"You could take one of your scribes," Bavius suggested before looking at the pair of frail scribes. "No, that won't work. How about an oarsman? They are strong and can fight."

"I can fight," Lepidus argued. "I need someone who speaks and writes Latin and Greek. A second set of ears as my witness and someone to watch my back."

"Let me check." Bavius pardoned himself and went to his first officer. "I'm not sure what you can do. But see if we have an oarsman who can write and speak Latin and Greek. And it has to be kept quiet. He'll be accompanying the Tribune into Vlore."

"Typically rowers aren't scholars," warned the First Principale. "But I'll see what Tapsennia has in his stables."

***

Second Principale Tapsennia sat on the deck with his feet on the steps of the ladder. He chewed a piece of dried meat, savoring the rich flavor and a few moments of solitude before the day started.

"Tapsennia. The Ship's Centurion needs an educated rower, but this is a secret," the first officer described. "We need one who speaks and writes Greek and Latin to accompany the Tribune."

"From this bunch? Oarsmen are known for their broad backs, not broad minds," the rowing officer advised as he climbed to his feet. "I don't know of any philosophers in my crew, but I'll check."

"It cannot become common knowledge," the First Principale reminded him.

At the mention of philosophers, Tsolak rolled out of his blanket and crawled on his hands and knees over to the ship's officers.

"Are you in need of a test to find a man of talent?" Tsolak questioned.

Tapsennia squinted in the early morning light as if the voice came from the ether. Only after looking down did he notice the man sitting at his feet. Although the material of his tunic appeared new, it hadn't been washed for several weeks.

"You're with the Tribune's party," Tapsennia ventured.

"How astute of you," the Stoic offered. "Now, do you need a test to find one man in one hundred and eighty, or not?

"Yes, we do," the ship's first officer granted. "But you can't just ask for him."

Tsolak rolled over, put his face down into the ladder well, and shouted, "I need someone who can transcribe Aristotle's three principles of rhetoric into Latin. I only have one scroll in Greek. It pays poorly in coin but the rewards for your intellect are vast."

"Who are you?" a sleepy voice inquired.

"I am Tsolak of Fyli," the Philosopher answered. "A student of the School of Stoicism."

"You mean a poor beggar," another rower commented. "Go away and let us sleep."

Tsolak rolled away from the opening and resumed his sitting position.

"That went well," Tapsennia volunteered.

From the rower's walk, a youthful voice remarked, "Sarcasm doesn't suit you, Second Principale."

A moment later, Scanlan Kasia came up the ladder.

"What are the three principles of rhetoric?" Tsolak quizzed.

"The credibility of the speaker, the speaker's ability to connect to the emotions of his listeners," Scanlan responded. "And the use of logic and reasoning for his arguments. I'd like to read the original in Greek."

"Other than Latin and Greek," Tsolak questioned, "what other languages?"

"Sir, I speak, read, and write Greek, Latin, Iberian, Insubri, and a little Egyptian. But I'm weak on the letters from the Nile region."

"There is the result of your test," Tsolak announced before crawling back to his blanket. "Now can you keep the noise down so I can sleep?"

The two ship's officers exchanged amused glances before the First Principale indicated the steering platform.

"Go see the Ship's Centurion," he directed.

Scanlan marched to the platform and saluted. To his surprise, it was Tribune Lepidus who returned the salute this time.

"You'll need a new tunic, a pair of combat sandals, and a box of writing materials," Marcus Lepidus observed. "Can you handle a dagger?"

"I'm proficient with a skinning knife, dagger, sica, gladius, spear, and javelin," Scanlan reported. "I'm well trained with blades, sir. But I'm better with a bow."

"This shouldn't require bow weapons," Marcus Lepidus told Scanlan. "If it goes wrong, it'll be close up and personal. Are you okay with getting your hands bloody?"

"I've battled in fighting circles, Tribune," Scanlan replied.

"I'm not sure what that means," Lepidus admitted. "But it sounds ominous enough."

***

The warship reached a short strip of wooded land. After passing the shoreline, three Republic triremes rowed out to challenge them.

"We found the Eastern Fleet," Bavius announced. "Flag them, First Principale, so they can go back to sleep."

"They seemed to be quick to come at you," Marcus Lepidus suggested.

"Tribune, that trio of three-bankers should have been on the western side, not hiding on the eastern bay. Being safe allows them to sleep all day."

"Why would they," Lepidus began, but changed his mind. "On the western side they have to be on the watch for pirates, raiders, and maybe, Macedonian ships-of-war. Do I put them in my report or would that cause too many problems."

"The problem, Tribune, are treaties that only partially end wars," Bavius explained. "Maybe in Pella and Rome, the leaders think there is peace. But on the bleeding edge of diplomacy are nervous warship Centurions and anxious Legionaries."

"Point taken," Tribune Lepidus conceded. "I'll hold off for now. When do we reach Vlore?"

Bavius looked at the sky and declared, "When the sun is directly overhead. Where will you go?"

"Ship's Centurion that is something you don't want or need to know," Tribune Lepidus told him.

***

Sixty Republic warships almost filled the broad sandy shoreline. The *Hawk of Peace* carved a half circle in the water and backstroked to the shallows. Rowers and sailors from those ships shouted at the *Hawk*.

"What took you so long?"

"Got lost on the crossing?"

Thirty-nine rowers joined the Third Principale in the water. They pushed the hull up onto the beach of Vlore. Before the ramp dropped, Marcus Lepidus and Scanlan Kasia leaped over the side, rushed across the beach, and vanished into the port city. Their casual clothing and sturdy footwear allowed them to blend into the crowds.

"Where are we going, sir?" Scanlan inquired once they slowed.

"Do you know what a dead drop is?" Lepidus asked.

"Yes, sir. It's a loose brick, or a loose rail of a fence," Scanlan replied. "But you need to know where to look."

"We're going to a cafe and have lunch," Lepidus stated, as if ignoring the statement. "I was told a scout dispatched by Senior Tribune Moresina left a location for a drop. He claimed it's in plain sight. The problem is I don't know what I'm looking for."

"I read Greek and Latin," Scanlan advised, "but, Tribune, I'm not a mind reader."

"Neither am I," Lepidus confessed.

"Tribune, why don't we ask the scout?"

They traveled by old brick buildings along narrow streets for a few more blocks. Finally, Marcus Lepidus broke his silence.

"Clario Moresina received a scroll from the scout," Lepidus explained. "The Senior Tribune sent a reply. Weeks later, he got word that his scout was dead, a victim of street violence."

"Do you believe that, sir?" Scanlan inquired.

"Not in the least. Just the fact that he sent a scroll to Classis, tells us he didn't trust anyone in Vlore," Lepidus proposed. "Not the Republic Navy, officers in the Legion garrison, or anyone on the staff of the Praetor of Illyria."

"That explains why you're traveling without the trappings of an Ambassador," Scanlan theorized. "What did the scroll say about the dead drop, Tribune?"

"Nothing specifically, only that from inside a restaurant, an educated man would know the location where the message is hidden," Lepidus told Scanlan.

***

Only a few blocks from the east gate of Vlore, the Tribune turned down a side street.

"Tapsennia told me it was around here somewhere," Lepidus confessed. "But I'm not sure, we could be heading towards the wrong gate."

Scanlan looked ahead to where two roads joined with the street. If not for a plaza, they would converge to form a Y-shape. Then the youth reached out and stopped the staff officer.

"Tribune Lepidus, what's the name of the restaurant?"

"The scout named it as *The Theban*," Lepidus answered. "Why do you ask?"

"*Seven Against Thebes* is the third book of the Oedipus trilogy by the Greek writer, Aeschylus," Scanlan told him. "Look ahead, we have *The Theban* cafe. There are three roads. If we find anything gate related, we'll have clues to the dead drop."

"Aren't you reaching a little to make those connections?" Lepidus questioned. "Afterall, three books is far from three roads, *The Theban Cafe* is not the city of Thebes, and there are no gates that I can see."

"It's not just those items, Tribune," Scanlan cautioned. "Take notice of the residential district we're in. Now explain away the armed and muscular men lounging around the plaza. Do they fit the feel of the neighborhood?"

As they approached the entrance to the restaurant, Lepidus declared, "I'm hungry. Come scribe, we'll take our midday repast here."

"Yes, sir," Scanlan agreed.

Inside, they saw another armed man sitting at a bench near the entrance.

"Too much coincidence," Lepidus said while guiding Scanlan to a bench in the rear. "What are the chances a military unit would be watching this plaza?"

They sat, and a server walked over.

"Good fortune shines on you, sirs," the server announced. "Today, we have baked chicken stuffed with garlic and leeks. And a vegetable soup with asparagus, artichoke thistle, and celery. Plus fresh rounds of bread."

"Good fortune indeed," Scanlan suggested. "I count seven blessings."

"Seven blessings?"

Marcus Lepidus cleared his throat before ordering from the confused server, "We'll split a chicken plus we'll each have a bowl of soup. I'll take wine. Scanlan?"

"Fruit juice," the youth ordered. "I've got a busy evening ahead of me."

"Pomegranate juice?" the server inquired.

"That's fine," Scanlan said, his mind not on the beverage.

From the bench, he looked through the restaurant, beyond the soldier at the entrance, out through the façade, across the plaza, and down the angled road. Rows of doors for shops were visible from the restaurant. There were ten entrances visible along the road. Scanlan stopped counting at door seven.

"Explain your seven blessings comment," Lepidus challenged.

"In *Seven Against Thebes*, the King of Argos sent seven heroes against the seven gates of Thebes," Scanlan recited. "Each hero died at his chosen gate. One of the heroes was the rebellious brother to the King of Thebes. Both brothers died fighting each other at a gate. Brother against brother was the point of Aeschylus' tragedy. But years later, Sophocles in his play *Antigone*, picked up the tale. Antigone, the sister of the dead brothers wanted to bury both in the city. But she's told one brother was a traitor to Thebes and she could not properly bury him."

"What does that have to do with our current situation?" Lepidus demanded.

"Door seven, down the street, is the entrance to the shop of a funeral mask craftsman," Scanlan described. "Do you think the soldiers keeping watch over the plaza have puzzled it out?"

"If they had, they wouldn't be hanging around looking for a Roman scout," the Tribune granted. The chicken arrived, along with two large bowls of soup and two rounds of bread. Before eating, Lepidus questioned. "But how am I supposed to collect the message?"

"Tribune Lepidus, you don't retrieve the message," Scanlan told him. "Tonight after sunset, I'll bring it to you."

"So that's it? I leave everything to you. There must be something more I can do?"

"Yes sir. After this fine meal," Scanlan suggested, "we'll stroll by entrance number seven. Without being obvious about it, we'll look for the code mark on the stonewall."

Chapter 23 - Ruination of Attica

Long after sunset and half a block from the angled streets and the cafe, Scanlan Kasia pulled a warm iron pan from a bag. After scooping out a handful of the fresh fig pie, he dumped the rest in the alleyway.

"If I have a chance tomorrow," he promised as he chewed, "I'll go to the baker and buy a pie and pay double for it."

He tested the direction of the night breeze. Once sure he was upwind, the Insubri youth placed chunks of beeswax and a linen rag in the pan. Next he soaked the items with nasty olive oil he dredged up from the bottom of the cask.

"For cooking, you want clear olive oil," Jace Kasia coached, *"for this application, the darker and dirtier the oil the better."*

With a small bar of iron and a piece of flint, Scanlan stuck sparks until the pan smoldered around a low flame. When the smoke began stinging his eyes, he carried the iron pan to the end of the alley and slid it behind a tree. Then he backed away.

***

The plaza in front of *The Theban Cafe* caught a little starlight through tree branches. To a lesser extent, illumination from lanterns and candles in windows cast pools of light. While the light showed the stones of the streets, the rays served to deepen the darkness in the shadows. None of the light sources revealed the smoke drifting in the air.

Scanlan Kasia eased up to the corner of the cafe and squatted. Carefully, he studied the black patches around the plaza, easily picking out the soldiers hidden around the intersection.

"The description of this play will depend on you," Scanlan whispered to the hidden men. "Will it be a tragedy where heroes die by a ghost brandishing a blade? A comedy, where soldiers watch and watch but nothing happens, ever. Perhaps a satire, where the soldiers race off in different directions, chasing shadows. Come players, the performance is about to begin."

***

When blinking, the eyelids caused vision to flash rapidly between seeing and blackness, leaving the mind slightly befuddled. As the smoke from the pan settled around the plaza, the soldiers blinked more and missed more. Taking advantage of their interrupted sight, Scanlan Kasia crossed the plaza slowly, moving from one deep shadow to the next. To the soldiers watching for someone to come and reveal the location of the dead drop, the youth moved unseen during the blinks of their irritated eyes.

***

Earlier that afternoon, Scanlan and the Tribune had strolled by the seventh door and noted the code marks. A single scuff below knee level seemed unnatural. But when added to the vee, two stones up and to the left, it became an arrow, identifying the direction of the dead drop.

Now, using the night, the youth remained in the shadows and moved to the marks. Which stone was the loose one concealing the message?

"Were you a consistence fellow?" Scanlan questioned the dead scout. From the scuff mark, he counted diagonally to seven, the bases for the play, the *Seven Against Thebes*. Wrapping his fingers around the edges of the seventh stone, he shook it. The stone failed to wobble in the least. "Perhaps not so consistent, my fellow spy. Oh, but wait."

Counting again to the seventh stone, but this time from the vee mark, the building stone jiggled. Next, it slid out smoothly, leaving the mortar in place. After fishing a piece of parchment out of the void, Scanlan inserted the stone, slipped the message into a pouch, and started to walk away.

But he couldn't allow the deed and his stealth to go totally unacknowledged. Or for the soldiers, the actors in his play, to go without an ovation.

"Fire. Fire. Do you smell the smoke?" Scanlan shouted as he raced away from the door of the funeral mask maker. Behind him, soldiers came out of the shadows and began searching for a fire. After rushing around a little, one of them found the smoldering pan and wondered why it was there. Scanlan smiled and proclaimed the type of play. "I hope you enjoyed the satire. Take a bow, players."

Bending at the waist, he bowed to an imaginary crowd. Then the youth sprinted into a lane and left the surveillance in the plaza far behind and unaware that the dead drop had been looted.

***

The villa hovered over the fleet on a hill above the beach. Although a poet could easily write verses about the magnificent view of the sea to Optio Vibia, it soured his stomach. Marching from the rear of the house, he crossed the courtyard to the gate.

"Optio, why are we guarding a compound and not our ship?" the tall sentry asked. "Aren't we Legion Marines?"

"Pacius, if the Ship's Centurion and the Tribune wanted you to know, they would have told you," Optio Vibia scolded the young Marine. "Report."

"It's been quiet all evening," Pacius assured him.

"Stay awake, the courier should be here before daybreak," Vibia told him.

Walking away, the Optio went to find the two Marines he had assigned to a roving patrol. Even though Pacius had voiced the concern, Vibia couldn't admit to his own worries about being away from the *Hawk of Peace*. The Legion Marines under his command were sworn to protect the warship, and they couldn't very well do that from a villa high above the beach.

***

Deep in the night, Pacius rested a shoulder and his head against the bars of the gate. Typically, he'd have a navigator or a sailor to keep him company. Here at the entrance to the villa and alone, he drifted off.

Something tugged the side of his armor. Fearing an attack or discovery by his Optio, the lanky Marine stepped away from the gate, spun around, and lowered his spear.

"Who or what is there?" he demanded.

From beside him, Scanlan suggested, "Perhaps a spirit or a bear."

Pacius squinted to bring the starlit figure into focus.

"Oarsman Kasia, what are you doing here?" he gasped.

"Marine, what are you doing here?" Scanlan asked in response.

"There's a courier coming before daybreak," Pacius told him.

Scanlan looked at the moon and then the dark eastern sky.

"It appears the courier is right on schedule," Scanlan declared. "Oh, I'm the courier."

"But the gate is barred," Pacius remarked.

"I didn't want to disturb your nap," Scanlan explained as he headed for the villa, "so I came over the wall."

Pacius cast his eyes upward to the top of the wall that was twice his height.

"No way," he decided. "There must be a side gate."

***

The patio on the villa allowed for the best view of the water. Tribune Marcus Lepidus spent part of the night sitting and watching where the stars vanished into the black sea. After a breeze came up, rather than putting on a robe, he went into the great room, wrapped a blanket around his shoulders, and laid down on a couch.

After a short nap, the Centurion of his bodyguard alerted, "Tribune Lepidus, the courier is here."

Sitting up, Lepidus shrugged off the blanket, rubbed his eyes, and ordered, "Bring in the courier. And light some candles, I'll need light. I hope."

Scanlan walked in with a veteran Legionary on his right side. Even though he wasn't Legion, the youth saluted.

"Tribune, I have a message for you," Scanlan said, as if he was simply carrying a scroll from one villa to another.

"How is my old friend?" Lepidus asked, maintaining the act of hiding the true source of the message.

"There was some confusion among his household guards," Scanlan responded while handing the message to the Tribune. "But his situation remains the same as before."

"I see," Lepidus accepted the news, figuring Scanlan went undetected and the dead drop remained operative. He took the small piece of parchment, gently unrolled it, and studied the Greek words. After several readings, the Tribune offered it to Scanlan and instructed. "Tell me what you think it says."

Scanlan Kasia translated the Greek words.

"Arsenal and siege engines for the attack on Athens at Chalcis storehouses," the youth reported. Then dramatically, he added. "*Leviter custodiri.*"

Tribune Lepidus repeated the Latin, "Lightly guarded."

"Where is Chalcis, Tribune?" Scanlan inquired.

"Good question. I'll check with the ship's Principale."

"What now, sir?" Scanlan asked.

"I'm going to meet with Ambassador Nero when he arrives," Lepidus answered. "A preemptive strike to protect an ally would fall under the powers of a Pro-consul. Return to the *Hawk of Peace* and resume your duties as an oarsmen."

"Yes, sir," Scanlan acknowledged.

He started for the door when Marcus Lepidus called after him, "The Republic owes you much, Oarsman Kasia. Thank you."

"Yes, sir," Scanlan repeated as he left the great room.

***

Not long after leaving the villa, Scanlan came from the center of Vlore, carrying another stolen iron pan. At the beach, he paused for some much needed soul searching.

"You can lie to an enemy, a competitor, or to a known liar," Jace Kasia had coached. *"But never lie to a family member, a trusted acquaintance, someone you are doing business with, and most important of all, do not lie to yourself."*

"Too late," Scanlan whispered to the night. He inhaled the fragrance of the fig pie and chastised himself. "I said I would pay double for the next pie. But I didn't. I didn't even pay for this pie. That was bad of me."

Once done reprimanding himself for stealing another pie, Scanlan went to the *Hawk of Peace* and took the ramp to the deck.

"No fire, no loud talking," the sailor on watched instructed.

"No dancing or singing, I imagine," Scanlan added.

"Those as well," the sailor said, not seeing the humor in the rower's statement.

"No worries," Scanlan told him. "The Republic's gratitude only goes so far."

"What?" the sailor asked.

Scanlan ignored the question and strolled around sleeping bodies until he reached the foredeck. Once on the raised platform, the youth dropped to a sitting position and hung his legs over the side. With a million stars overhead, he dipped two fingers into the pie and lifted out a handful.

"If I'm not mistaken," a voice queried, "that's a fig pie."

"Who is asking?" Scanlan inquired.

The Stoic Tsolak crawled onto the foredeck, spun around and allowed his legs to hang over the side of the warship.

"I'm Tsolak of Fyli, a student of stoicism," he introduced himself.

"The man with the works of Socrates on ethos, pathos, and logos," Scanlan recalled.

"You're referring to the ancient master's three rhetorical appeals," Tsolak suggested.

"No, I'm referring to a man who promised a valuable intellectual lesson and failed to deliver," Scanlan told the Stoic as he licked his fingers.

"For that selfish act, I apologize. It was beneath my goal in life."

"What is your goal in life?" Scanlan asked.

"At this very moment," Tsolak confessed, "it's to get a bite of that fig pie."

Scanlan held out the pan, and the stoic gouged out a piece.

"Now, young man, you tell me, what is your goal?" Tsolak questioned as he chewed.

"My adopted father is a mighty warrior. When two women were carried away by raiders, Jace Kasia went after them, alone. He emerged from the mountains with both women unharmed. I went to him and begged to be trained in warfare," Scanlan answered. "He told me the mind is the most decisive weapon on a field of battle."

"No philosophers or wise men in history would argue against that," Tsolak assured him before venturing. "Thus you became a scholar and not a warrior."

"The balance of learning weapons and the way of war," Scanlan described, "hinged on learning languages, and how to read and write them as well."

"Few men, even advanced students, know Socrates' three rhetorical appeals," Tsolak said, then paused as his hand reached for more fig pie. "If your training balanced martial skills along with scholarly endeavors, you must be a formidable warrior."

"My father agrees save for one issue," Scanlan admitted. "I haven't hit a growth spurt. At fifteen years, I don't have the mass for battle. I hope to grow more, much more. Unless the fates have condemned me to being a thin man without the breath of shoulders to dominate in a shield wall."

"You certainly talk like a warrior and think like a scholar," Tsolak complimented the youth. "I'd say you are prepared for manhood. Yet you stand on the edge of a personal gulf. Will you becomes a fighter or a thinker?"

"Why not both?" Scanlan insisted.

"You are so very young," Tsolak offered before asking. "You never told me. What is your goal?"

"I've read scrolls from temples, from traveling scholars over long winters, classic and epic poems, and my favorite, plays. The enactment of a tragedy, comedy, or satire has captured my imagination since I first read a play," Scanlan told the Stoic.

"But what is your goal?" Tsolak questioned.

"I'd like to see a live performance," Scanlan revealed. "Actors, a chorus, a stage, and me in the audience caught up in the emotions of the playwrights words."

"Lad, a stage performance is much more than words," Tsolak proclaimed. "The actors wear masks, they mimic fights, dying, and things you've only read about. Plus, the elocution of the actors are living examples of Socrates' rhetorical appeals of ethos, pathos, and logos. Live theater is much more than words on a scroll. But hold on, you are in luck. Soon the fleet will sail to Athens. And in March, the city puts on the Festival of Dionysus. The events include playwriting competitions. You'll be able to feast your mind on three days of plays performed at the Theater of Dionysus."

"That sound wonderful," Scanlan announced.

From the dark, a voice ordered, "Keep your voices down. People are trying to sleep."

***

One hundred and seventy miles eastward from Vlore and over the rugged mountains, the sun had yet to rise over Pella. In the darkness, General Philokles and his staff rode south from the Macedonian Capital. Ten miles from the Pella Lagoon, they arrived at a camp. Tents for two thousand infantrymen and two hundred cavalrymen were visible in the low light of dying campfires. Dismounting at his compound, the General marched into the pavilion. As soon as he entered, a cluster of his Captains surrounded him.

"Will it be Athens?" one file commander inquired.

"Not with only two thousand infantry," Philokles told him. "Even with quality siege engines, we'll need more than a couple of thousand to take the Long Walls."

"Will King Philip be joining us, General?" another inquired.

"The King has business to the east," Philokles explained. "Our job is to destroy towns in Attica. Gentlemen, we will deny Athens reinforcements, grain, and other supplies from her rural allies."

"When will we take Athens from those arrogant promoters of democracy?" a third Captain demanded.

"I can always tell our noblemen by their animosity towards the government of Athens. It's too bad you aren't a fan of the theater," Philokles suggested. "Then, at least, you'd look forward to our visit to Athens."

At the idea of calling their conquest of the ancient city a visit, the Captains chuckled.

"Get the infantry up and on the march," Philokles ordered.

Shortly after the meeting, the fifteen hundred members of the Phalanx, the five hundred shield bearers designated to protect the flanks of the dense formation, and a majority of the calvary packed up and marched south. By then, riders were far down the road, looking for the first city the detachment would ravage. With the ruination of Attica underway, the first stage of the siege of Athens had begun.

Chapter 24 - Enchanting Priestess

Three days later, twenty Roman warships rowed out of Vlore and sailed south. Under the command of Claudius Nero, each evening the fleet beached early and the next morning launched late. According to the Pro-consul, he wanted the crews rested and the ships in top shape for whatever he encountered in Athens. After fifteen days of traveling, the Roman fleet rowed into the Harbor of Piraeus and the crews got their first glimpse of the long walls of Athens. And Nero received proof that sparing his crews was the correct strategy.

Upon landing, Pro-consul Nero got accosted by a committee of Athenians. Quickly, Tribune Marcus Lepidus was sucked into the mob of frightened men. The cluster of loud voices moved from the beach to a port building commandeered by one of the Athenian magistrates.

Not far into the discussions, a messenger departed the office and hurried to the beach.

"Ship's Centurion Bavius and Second Principale Tapsennia," the courier announced when he reached the *Hawk of Peace*, "by order of Pro-consul Nero, you and Scribe Kasia, are ordered to report without delay to the People's Committee to Save Athens."

"The People's Committee to Save Athens," Bavius commented. "What an odd name for a joint command staff."

"It's the Athenian way," Tapsennia explained. "Every action must be presented and voted on by a majority. They call it Democracy. I can't imagine the system is sitting well with Pro-consul Nero."

"Nor with Tribune Lepidus," Scanlan added. He shifted the strap of the writing kit to a more comfortable position over his shoulder.

The three followed the messenger up the beach and across the docks to a set of low buildings. Typically used by traders to discuss buying and shipping goods, the building now had Roman guards at the entrance. The Legion red of their capes stood out from the pedestrians working at the port and the few Athenian hoplites in the area.

***

In the conference room, Pro-consul Nero and Tribune Lepidus occupied one side of a table. Almost as if an invisible barrier ran down the center of the tabletop, the Athenian representatives sat crowded together across from the Romans.

"Ship's Centurion Bavius and second officer Tapsennia, reporting as ordered," Bavius announced when they entered the room.

Before Nero could say why the ship's officers were there, Tribune Lepidus indicated a chair at a side table.

"Take notes, Kasia," he directed.

"Gentlemen, we have a problem," Nero told Bavius and Tapsennia. "The Macedonians have a large force rampaging through the countryside. From our Athenian allies, we know the purpose of the campaign. Philip V is softening up the rural villages and towns to prevent them from helping Athens when Philip comes to lay siege to the city."

"How does that concern the *Hawk of Peace*, sir," Ship's Centurion Bavius questioned.

While the senior officers talked, Scanlan approached the small table. Briefly, he wondered where to layout his writing utensils. Strips of papyrus and parchment had been glued together with beeswax to form a large map. Then he noticed distances and directions sprawled on the patchwork material. Quickly, he memorized the distances and directions to the city of Chalcis. Someone had lettered pirates next to the symbol for the town.

"You lad, it's labeled in Greek," an Athenian with a booming voice remarked. "Don't try to decipher it. Just bring it over here."

Careful to keep from separating the sections or cracking the wax, Scanlan carried the map to the big table.

"Here," Nero pointed to the town before the map had settled on the tabletop, "is Chalcis. We need to know what is going on in there. Ship's Centurion, any idea how to get a man inside and back out with information?"

As Scanlan stepped away, Tribune Lepidus nodded at him. It was obvious who was going into Chalcis. The question for Scanlan: How was he getting there?

"I know those waters well," Tapsennia volunteered. "Two years ago, when I served on the *Wings of Luna*, we chased pirates up the Euboean Gulf. On the northeast corner of the upper lobe is Arethousa Park. It's a mile from the defensive walls of Chalcis."

The city representative, who over projected his voice, cleared his throat as if preparing to give a long speech.

"I've heard you Romans were rambunctious and careless," the Athenian ventured dramatically. "But rowing a warship up to the side entrance of a fortress is, well heroic. Maybe you could skip the whole subterfuge thing and row to the main beach and march in through the front gate."

His sarcasm at the expense of the Romans caused him to beam proudly across the table.

Pro-consul Nero, a General of the Legions, who had commanded at Nola, laid siege to Capua, survived dozens of campaigns during Hannibal's terror reign, and finished the Carthaginian army in the north at the battle of the Metaurus slapped the tabletop. The sound reverberated around the room as if an actual assault.

"It's theater Ambassador Nero," another magistrate said, excusing the insult. "Not to be confused with accusations."

"Mockery taken to new heights, most excellent," a fourth representative offered, addressing the guy with the big voice. "I see you are sharpening your pen for the playwright competition."

"Thank you, dear friend," the man offered. "You, of course, are correct. The Festival of Dionysus is only a couple of months away."

Scanlan took a small piece of papyrus and wrote five words on it. Then he handed it to Lepidus. The Tribune read the note before dropping it into a pouch.

"Scribe Kasia, the latrine is outback," the Tribune directed, as if referring to the note. Next, as Scanlan slipped out the back door, Marcus Lepidus cleared his throat in the manner of an orator. "I have a thought on what we'll need to reach Arethousa Park undetected and gather information about Chalcis."

"Do tell," Nero invited.

"A fishing boat with extra nets and a set of extra-long oars."

"I'm familiar with oars of that size," the Greek writer remarked. "They're designed for fishing far out to sea. There isn't that much offshore wind on the Euboean Gulf."

Tribune Lepidus hesitated. Truly, he had no idea why Scanlan needed the long oars. But if his scout wanted a piece of equipment, the staff officer wanted him to have it.

Scanlan Kasia strolled in, but the Tribune couldn't very well ask his spy why he wanted a set of long oars.

"Are you saying sir, there's never any wind in the gulf?" Lepidus asked. "And there is no, absolutely, no chance the operation will be delayed by the wind?"

"Never say, never," the playwright commented. Then his face brightened, and he declared. "That's a good line. I need to use it in my play."

Scanlan handed him a note with the words "Never say never" written on it. The would-be playwright realized at that moment, the youth he scolded could read and write Greek.

***

The *Hawk of Peace* rowed from the Port of Piraeus the next morning. Two days later, the warship rounded the tip of the Peloponnese peninsula and beached at the Temple of

Poseidon. The vessel and crew lingered there for a day and a half before a four-man fishing boat arrived.

As the boat eased alongside, Bavius called down. "What took you so long?"

"The vote went against the idea for two rounds," a Greek fisherman told him. "But on the third ballot, it passed."

"Tie your boat to the stern," Bavius directed. When the fishermen came on board, he noted. "I only count three. Where is your fourth man?"

"He'll be along when we need him," Tribune Lepidus assured the Ship's Centurion. "Right now, we need to get to mouth of the southern gulf of Euboean and cut the fishing boat loose. And then get back while it's still dark."

"Second Principale to the steering deck," Bavius instructed Tapsennia. "I'm counting on you to keep us off the rocks and out of the shallows."

"Yes, sir, I'll do my best," Tapsennia said with hesitation.

"Now, I wish I had a vote on this mission," Bavius declared.

"How would you have voted?" Tribune Lepidus questioned.

"Truthfully, sir, I don't know," the Ship's Centurion admitted, now realizing the complex nature of the politics involved.

***

At twilight, the warship passed a rock of an island. Not a rocky island, but a block of granite jutting from the surface. The opposite shoreline consisted of a rock slope that entered the gulf at an angle. This made the shallows hazardous.

"We've little enough light," Bavius warned. "It'll be full night when we return."

"I'm noting the location, sir," Tapsennia assured him. "If this is going to work, the fishing boat needs to be as close as possible to Chalcis."

The warship moved beyond the rock and progressed until the shoreline vanished in the dark. Not much farther north, they pulled the fishing boat up beside the trireme. Four men climbed down and pushed the boat away from the warship's hull.

"Who is the fourth man?" Bavius inquired.

"Oarsman Kasia," the Tribune told him.

"We shouldn't miss him, he's just a Bow rower," the Ship's Centurion suggested. Then he stated. "Second Principale Tapsennia. Turn us about and find me some open water."

"Yes, sir," Tapsennia acknowledged.

***

The fishing boat glided away from the trireme. With four men rowing, the vessel glided north at a constant rate.

"From the way you're rowing, I assume you're Athenian Navy," Scanlan suggested to the three rowers, before adding. "I'm Scanlan."

"Bouras, Hatzi, and Gabris," Gabris replied. "You wanted oarsmen. Here we are."

"Is there a problem?" Hatzi inquired.

"I had hoped for fisherman," he admitted.

"Why?" Bouras asked.

"I need a load of fish for Chalcis," Scanlan informed the three Greek sailors.

"Two rowing and two on the net," Gabris directed. "We'll troll for fish as we travel."

After shuffling seats, the fishing boat rowed north while dragging the net behind the vessel. As they traveled, Scanlan and Bouras hauled in fish, tossed back the small ones, and kept the large. Long before dawn, the pair of fishermen wrapped the fish in a double layer of net, grabbed oars, and added their blades to the rowing.

***

Rays of a new day brushed the blue sky with streaks of pink. The fishing boat glided under overhanging branches before the bow rode up on the bank. While Scanlan gathered the ends of the net, Bouras, Hatzi, and Gabris pulled the boat out of the water and hid it in the bushes.

"How long do we wait?" Hatzi asked.

"Two days," Scanlan replied. He hooked the ends of the doubled nets on the two long oars. Then he placed the ends of the shafts on his shoulders with the fish suspended between the poles. "If I'm not back at dawn in two days, row away, fast."

"No worries about that," Bouras assured him. "Nobody wants to get caught spying."

"Thanks for that," Scanlan complained. He pulled on the ends of the oars, moving the load of big fish and leaving two furrows in the grass behind him. Gabris followed for several paces, erasing the marks of Scanlan's passing with a tree branch.

A half mile from the water, the defensive wall of Chalcis appeared above the trees. Not long afterwards, Scanlan stepped out of the forest, located a wagon trail, and followed it to a side gate of the city.

As he approached the portal, a sentry came out of a shed.

"Where did you come from?" the guard demanded.

"Lake Maggiore Valley," Scanlan answered quickly.

"What?" the guard asked.

"Po River Vally," Scanlan practically spit out the words.

"Hold on," the sentry spoke slowly. He pointed behind the youth and said. "The trail and forest behind you. What direction did you come from?"

Scanlan's eyes opened wide with understanding. Walking a half circle to show the load of big fish, he hooked a thumb over his shoulder.

"From the water," he declared with a stupid grin on his face.

"The marketplace is to the right of the main gate," the guard directed. "If you get lost, just ask for the forum."

"Marketplace," Scanlan shouted as if he just discovered the word.

"Move along," the sentry ordered. Scanlan did a full circle with his load of fish before dragging it through the gateway. As the youth passed him, the guard muttered. "It's going to be a long day."

***

Shops and businesses filled the streets just inside the gate. Angling to his left, Scanlan came up behind a large compound. Based on the number of men in robes attended by servants, he figured it had to be a government complex. While pulling the pair of oars and the load of fish, he looked around but couldn't find a likely warehouse that might hold Philip's arsenal. But his view was limited to a few blocks. At the government complex, he turned right and noticed three buildings around a plaza. They wouldn't have stood out from any other city building, except for the pairs of soldiers at each structure.

The sentry at the city gate held an old shield, and his spear had a warped shaft. In comparison, the soldiers at the plaza were dressed in torso armor, toted new shields, and carried spears with deadly straight shafts.

"What is so valuable in a city that it requires protection from the populace?" he thought. "And demands better outfitted guards than the city could provide?"

Beyond the guarded buildings sprawled the city's forum. On the far side of the square, stalls and open spots created a marketplace. He headed towards the area.

***

A bare spot of ground between booths cost two bronze coins. Scanlan made that back when he sold three fish. Adding the limb of a tree to his long oars, he created a tripod. With the fish in the net, hanging in the center, he had a display of his wears.

"Those are nice sized fish," a farmer in the next space noted.

"I had to haul them to Chalcis from the water," Scanlan explained. "It didn't make sense to tote small fish."

"An excellent use of your labor," the man complimented Scanlan. "You'd make a good farmer."

"I like rowing, fishing, and being on the water," Scanlan countered. From deeper inside the city, a line of unkept, limping, and half-starved men stumbled towards the forum. Soldiers flanks them, using the butts of their spears to keep the line moving. Scanlan indicated the pitiful prisoners and asked the farmer. "Who are they?"

"Rhodians, from the Island of Rhodes," the farmer replied. "Taken after their shipwrecked on Chios Island."

"The guards aren't treating them very well," Scanlan observed.

"The guards are Macedonian soldiers," the farmer warned. "They don't treat anyone very well. Stay away from them."

"I'm not staying in the city long," Scanlan informed the farmer. "Just so I don't wander into them, where are their barracks and the holding area for the prisoners?"

"They're billeted by the southeast gate. The prisoner compound is next door at the corner of the defensive walls."

"I'll avoid that area," Scanlan lied.

A group of women, talking and laughing, came to the fish stand.

"You're a cute one," one said with a wink. Her perfume drifted to the youth, and he almost missed her question. "Staying in the city, are you?"

Scanlan meant to say he had to get back to the gulf to fish. It wasn't what came out of his mouth.

"Those fish don't catch themselves," he offered.

Rather than confused, the woman advised, "No they don't. But neither do mates or husbands."

"Husbands do what?" Scanlan asked.

"Catch themselves," the lady responded, while her friends giggled. "It takes a woman to catch a husband."

"I don't understand," Scanlan admitted.

The women moved to the next booth, leaving the youth confused and still smelling the heady perfume.

"You handled her correctly," the farmer suggested.

"I don't understand," Scanlan revealed. When he noticed a blank look on the face of the vegetable seller, he insisted. "Really, I don't know what they wanted."

"The God of Wine, Theater, and Revelry has female Priestesses. And they have young male servants," the farmer informed him. "Those were Priestesses of Dionysus. If you had flirted with her, she would have lured you to their Temple and enslaved you."

"She was pretty and smelled good," Scanlan commented.

"All traps set by the female of the species to capture a man," the farmer cautioned. "The Temple of Dionysus is near the northeast gate. That's another location to avoid."

"Sage advice," Scanlan conceded.

All afternoon, he sold his catch. But his mind wasn't on the price of fish. The youth's thoughts meandered around plays, the God of the Theater, and the enchanting Priestess who spoke to him.

Chapter 25 - The Tall Tale

The fish were sold, his purse reflected a good day of selling, and the blanket he bought rested comfortably over Scanlan's shoulders.

"Are you going to use your spot tomorrow?" the farmer asked. "I mean, you are out of fish."

"You can spread out your goods but I need something in return."

"I can't afford more than a bronze coin," the farmer stated.

"It's not about coins or fees," Scanlan told him. "I need your word."

"My word is my business," the farmer assured him. "Ask anybody who knows me, they'll tell you I can be trusted."

Scanlan reached out an arm and opened his hand. A pile of coins from the day's earnings covered his palm.

"The booth and these coins for a favor," Scanlan emphasized, upping the reward.

"For what?" the farmer asked, suspicion creeping into his voice.

"To say you watched me sleep here all night long," Scanlan answered. "Or at least as far as you know, because you were asleep as well."

"The space and the coins just to say I saw you sleeping?" the farmer summed up. "Where would you go in the middle of the night?"

"Perhaps to the Temple of Dionysus," Scanlan suggested.

"You young people never listen," the farmer scolded as he took the coins. "Just don't wake me when you get back."

"How could I?" Scanlan inquired. "I never left the booth or the marketplace."

***

At dusk, the Rhodian prisoners returned. They appeared more miserable than when they left on the work detail. Scanlan purchased two baked turnips and a couple of boiled onions. He settled down under the blanket, ate, then took a nap.

When he woke, darkness veiled most of the streets of Chalcis. But at the main gateway, torches burned and guards walked along the top of the wall. They patrolled while keeping eyes towards the beach outside the walls and the North Euboean Gulf beyond the shoreline. Attacking the main entrance to the city would be costly in the lives of Legion Marines and Athenian hoplites.

Glancing away from the gate, Scanlan studied where the torchlight ended on the forum. The illumination didn't reach the heavily guarded buildings at the plaza. Moving backward, he tied the blanket around his waist before slipping away from the marketplace.

"When you're on a reconnaissance mission or trying to blend in with a population," Jace taught him. "Always have a prop. A *basket, a clay jug, a cap, or just a blanket. Having an item, and not using it, is preferable to needing an item and not having one."*

Several streets later, the Insubri youth arrived at a sealed building. There was no mystery as to the function of the structure. A sleepy guard sat out front. Although relaxed, his presence meant the contents were valuable, but not worth enough to rate a Macedonian sentry.

"Granary," Scanlan decided.

Moving around the grain storage facility, he located the corner of the defensive wall and followed it to the east. A few homes later, he approached a line of massive bushes. On the other side of the hedgerow, candlelight marked levels of a terraced building. Based on the farmer's description, the structure had to be a temple.

"Maybe I should leave an offering to Dionysus. I could ask him to bless the play I'll see in Athens," Scanlan pondered the action. Then he became cautious. "But sneaking into the temple would be careless. Even if the Priestess had kind of invited me."

He smiled, patted his coin purse, and dropped to his knees. Crawling between the bushes, he came out the other side. Across a lawn, he saw a beautiful woman standing in a ring of candles. She held a whip.

"You are celebrants of Dionysus," she instructed four young men. They weaved, held each other up, and giggled. "The God of Wine provides but it doesn't mean you have permission to overindulge."

She slapped their backs almost playfully with the whip.

Scanlan tried to imagine himself standing in the line of drunken youths. Shaking his head no, the Insubri crawled along the bushes to a path. Veering away from the hedgerow, he followed a stone walkway to a low wall. On the other side, a patio stretched to the lower level of the temple.

After placing coins on top of the wall, he started to turn away. But, his performance had been so good this evening. A few coins wouldn't do. To honor the God of the Theater required a small feat of art.

Using a stone chip from the pathway, he inscribed Greek letters on top of the stone wall, "FISH DON'T." He moved the coins to the message and crawled off into the night.

***

The guard at the northeast gate leaned against the side of his shelter. Scanlan waited long enough to appreciate the man's talent for sleeping while standing. In three looping strides, the youth crossed the street and vanished into the shadows on the other side of the gate road.

Even in the dark, and long before he reached the compound, Scanlan smelled the stink of unwashed and unhealthy bodies. Animal aromas from nearby pens of goats, horses, mules, and pigs blended in to soften the reek. But tormented human flesh heightened nerves and provoked avoidance in most men. After observing the beautiful Priestess, the youth had no desire to see the prisoners from Rhodes. But he needed to count the guards and to reach the barracks from the least likely approach. And that would be from the prisoners' area.

***

Looking at the prisoners through a hole in the stockade fence, Scanlan understood the huddled mass of sleeping men. Pack animals clustered together for protection against predators and violent weather. The mimicry of grazing animals by the Rhodians demonstrated the abuse they suffered under the care of their Macedonian jailers. Weary of the sickening sight, the Insubri youth continued on his mission.

One edge of the prisoner camp ran near the southeast corner of the city's defensive wall. Scanlan slipped between the wooden timbers of the stockade and the stones of the defensive wall. A glance upward showed no sentries patrolling where the walkways came together at the corner.

"They use guards at the main gate and watch the gulf," Scanlan muttered. "But place none on the rest of the walls. Are they confident or incompetent?"

Putting the unknown away, Scanlan eased around the stockade and got his first view of the Macedonian barracks. A long three story building of planks and lumber filled the area behind a commercial district. All the services needed to make Chalcis a self-supporting city were present. Stalls for ironwork and leatherwork to bakers' ovens and other shops, the area reflected the services available to the population and to the Macedonians sleeping in the barracks.

A guard stood at the entrance to the quarters. Spotting an outbuilding, Scanlan waited for the sentry to look away before rushing from the shadows and entering the structure. A moment later, he came out of the latrine with his blanket over his head and strolled to the entrance of the barracks.

"Don't let anyone go in there," he warned, indicating the entrance to the latrine building. Explaining further, Scanlan reported. "Too much garlic and onion on that lamb. And the oil might have been rancid."

"Thanks for the warning," the guard responded. "Hope you feel better."

Scanlan Kasia marched into the Macedonian barracks and began counting beds. Three levels with seventy beds on each floor gave him a count of two hundred ten soldiers. But nowhere in the barracks did Scanlan see private apartments for their officers. Either the Macedonians didn't separate their officers from the soldiers or the commanders were quartered in a different location.

Leaving a facility, compared to the difficulty of tricking a guard to get inside, didn't come close. While he used a joke to enter the barracks, walking out required only a grunt at the guard on the other end of the quarters. Seeing as he came from a Macedonian facility with burning braziers, the youth strolled across the access road at the southeast gate. In the light of a couple of more braziers, he noted the guard, a local guardsman, nod in greeting.

"Being a Macedonian in Chalcis is good duty," Scanlan reflected as he lifted a hand in greeting.

Once away from the gate guard, Scanlan stepped into the shadow of a villa. Ahead, a pair of Macedonian soldiers loitered by another set of braziers. Looking back, Scanlan identified a lighted path between the barracks and the villa. He'd found the officers' quarters.

From boldly marching down a street, the Insubri youth slipped into the bushes. Under a side window, he stopped to listen.

"Lieutenant Aetos, King Philip assigned us to Chalcis for three reasons," an older man explained. "To guard his siege engines, artillery, shields, and spear hoard. To protect the grain needed to feed his army and the war chest needed to pay his soldiers and sailors."

"Yes, Captain Sopater," File Leader Aetos acknowledged. "But we're near Athenians not Pella?"

"What position did you have in Pella?" Sopater asked. He paused before answering his own question. "Like me, you were regulated to a low level position in the guard. Now you are a File Leader and I'm Captain of a city. Would you trade the new you for the old?"

"No, Captain, I would not," Aetos assured his commander.

"Good. Now stop complaining about being officer-of-the-guard overnight and get back to the main gate," Sopater instructed.

Scanlan slinked away from the window, located a bush with branches that drooped to the lawn, and crawled under the living curtain. Once hidden from a chance discovery, he allowed his mind to ponder the ramifications of what he overheard.

The weapons and siege machines were dangerous and needed to be destroyed to protect Athens. Discovery of a larger grain stockpile, much more than a city would store, added to the reward of raiding Chalcis. But the presence of King Philip's war chest heightened the importance and the urgency of the attack. By any measure, Scanlan should have left and taken the information to Tribune Lepidus. But the three warehouses at the plaza had yet to be explored. And Scanlan was curious.

***

Reaching the side of the first single-story building proved easy. The guards had clustered in the front and were talking. It appeared that while Captain Sopater radiated confidence, Lieutenant Aetos, as officer-of-the-guard, leaned towards the incompetent.

"All the better for me," Scanlan decided as he ran at the building. Planting a foot high on the wall, he jumped and pushed with his toes. Although only his fingertips caught the edge of the tiles, he pulled hard and vaulted to the roof. "Now to have a look."

Sticking his head between the cover of the vent and the hole in the roof, Scanlan peered into the gloom. Even in low light, the heavy beams of the siege towers and artillery pieces were visible. At the next building, the shields and shafts revealed the armory.

After satisfying himself of the content for the first two buildings, he hesitated. What could be in the next structure?

A short run and a leap landed him softly on the roof of the third building. Peering down, he noted two guards sitting beside a chest. Iron bands clamped the leather surfaces together. Only one item required close up guards and iron bands. A door to a royal chamber, or a war chest full of gold. As most young men would do in a situation like this, Scanlan dreamed for a moment.

"With a five-banker of my own, I could sail the seas," he fantasized. "Or maybe build a mountain top fort and defend it. Or, buy an army and conquer Rome."

The last idea gave him pause. Did he hate Rome? He started out with the aim of fighting the Legions, but now he worked for Romans. And here he sat on the roof of the most guarded building in Chalcis, thinking of ways to spend a fortune in coins, but unsure where his loyalties landed.

"I'll worry about who my Master is after breakfast," he thought before scaling down the back of the building and running away into the night.

***

"You young people sleep too much," the farmer mentioned as he shifted produce into the empty spot next to his booth.

"What's good for breakfast?" Scanlan inquired as he rolled to a sitting position.

"Follow your nose," the farmer instructed. "At the end, you'll find honey cakes."

Scanlan, with the blanket over his shoulders, sniffed, stood, and as if in a trance, followed the fragrance of baked goods to a booth at the end of the marketplace.

Others, spellbound by the delicious aroma, had already formed a line. Some pushed forward, impatient for a honey cake.

"Take it easy," the baker instructed. "I made enough for everyone."

People walked away, their fingers bathed in a sticky, sweet coating as they ate their honey cakes. Scanlan stood four people from the front, his stomach grumbling and his mouth watering.

"Baker, hold the sale," a familiar voice directed. Scanlan peered around to catch a glimpse of Captain Sopater. A tall man with a gray beard, the garrison commander at Chalcis stood with five Macedonian soldiers. Next, he stated. "Here baker, take my coins, I'm buying all the honey cakes."

"But the crowd," pleaded the baker before complaining. "And this isn't near enough to pay for all the cakes."

"Lieutenant Aetos. Arrest the baker for overcharging for his products," Sopater ordered.

Aetos paced forward and the crowd waiting for the sweet treats grumbled and surged forward as well. Shorter than the Captain, the File Leader had slim shoulders and a lean, hungry face. When the File Leader drew his sword and signaled the four spearmen, Scanlan tossed the blanket over his head and backed out of the crowd.

"Maybe a nice piece of fruit," he muttered while heading for a fruit stand. Behind him, people shouted and spear shafts knocked citizens to the ground.

***

At midday, the stream of traffic through the main gate caused an impasse. Scanlan shouldered the fishing nets, rested the long oars on one shoulder and left the market. At the southwest gate, he joined a line of people looking to avoid the crowd at the main gate.

Scanlan smiled a too wide grin, and the guard waved him through without a conversation. Few people wanted to engage with an individual touched by the Gods.

A mile from the gateway, Scanlan disturbed the midday naps of Bouras, Hatzi, and Gabris.

"How did it go?" Bouras asked.

Hatzi and Gabris looked behind Scanlan to see if he was being followed.

"The fish sold and the city revealed it's treasures to me," Scanlan answered. "It went without a problem except for the Priestess."

"Priestess?" Gabris repeated. "What Priestess?"

"Of Dionysus," Scanlan boasted. "Everything went as planned until the Priestess made me a temple boy one evening. It was difficult to sober up enough to break the spell and escape. Here look, are there any scars on my back?"

Scanlan pulled up his tunic and exposed unblemished skin.

"No marks of any kind," Hatzi reported.

"It's a miracle," Scanlan exclaimed. "Between the wine, the kisses, the perfume, and the beatings with the whip, I was positive the Priestess had marked me for life."

The three Athenian sailors stood gawking at the Insubri youth.

"We should go," Scanlan encouraged. "I'm not worried about the city guards or the Macedonian soldiers. It's those beautiful and enchanting temple Priestesses that have me worried."

"Were you really a temple boy for a night?" Bouras questioned.

"Yes, I was," Scanlan lied. "I'll tell you more about the whipping part later. For now, we need to get going."

With four men pushing, the fishing boat moved easily to the bank. They soon had it launched, and the sail raised and bloated with wind.

"We've got two days of sailing," Hatzi declared. He used one of the long oars to steer the boat from the stern. "That's plenty of time to tell us about the Priestess of Dionysus."

"Well, first they ply you with deep red wine to lower your resistance to their advances," Scanlan told them. "Remind me to tell you about the ring of candles."

His eyes were as open with excitement as the eyes of the three sailors as he told them the tall tale.

Chapter 26 - Let Me Judge

If left to the Romans, the raid on Chalcis would have happened a week earlier. But the Athenians not only held votes on each part of the plan, they voted some down based on the language of the pact between them and Ambassador Nero. Eventually, the campaign received approval from the committee, the council, and the assembly.

On the morning of launch, ten Roman three-bankers with one hundred and fifty Legion Marines, Nero's quinquereme with his personal guards, and a handful of five-banker warships from Athens rowed out. The Greek ships carried two hundred shield bearers. Once clear of the shoreline, they set sail on a course to the Gulf of Euboean. On the lead warship, Ship's Centurion Bavius scowled at Oarsman Kasia.

"Are you sure there are only two hundred and ten Macedonian soldiers in Chalcis?" he commented, before worrying aloud. "We have no guarantee that we can get off the beach and escape a slaughter by the Macedonians, if things go bad."

"Sir, I counted their cots myself," Scanlan told him for the tenth time. "I can't attest to what's changed in the past week but when I was there the numbers were accurate."

"When did you go into the barracks?" Tapsennia asked, with a lot of suspicion. "Weren't you with the Priestess all night?"

Scanlan's gut twisted at having to admit the truth. Tribune Marcus Lepidus crossed the steering platform and saved him.

"We don't have enough infantry to garrison Chalcis once we take the city," the staff officer warned. "If we can't get the gates open, we'll abort the mission."

"The guards on the secondary gates are lax at night," Scanlan insisted. "We can get one open, sir."

"I hope for the sake of the Athenians, you're right," Lepidus stated.

***

At seventy-five miles from Athens, the assault force beached for the day. Tribune Marcus Lepidus went to the Ambassador's five-banker to consult with the experienced Legion commander.

"According to the Athenians, we're close enough to row in and attack today," Proconsul Nero argued. "In my day, I'd go for the throat and not play with a target."

"Sir, although we're close enough to start an attack, the walls of Chalcis would stop us," Tribune Lepidus countered. "We don't have the men or the equipment for a long siege. I recommend we start the attack at night and be done and gone shortly after sunrise."

"You're suggesting we row the narrow Gulf of Euboean in the dark," Nero remarked. He put a finger on a map and traced a line up the gulf to a drawing of the city. "One bad stroke and we could wreck our force on the rocks."

"Even taking into consideration the dangers of navigating at night," Lepidus contended, "darkness is our best chance of success."

"If my knees were stronger, I'd climb the assault ladder with your team," Nero boasted. "And if my heart was stronger, I might argue with you about a nighttime attack. But it's your campaign, Tribune. We'll stick to your schedule."

"Our schedule, General Nero," Lepidus corrected the decorated campaigner. "I couldn't do it without your counsel."

"Nice of you to say," Pro-consul Nero acknowledged. "Now tell me again where we'll start the attack."

"The barrack houses the Macedonian soldiers, and according to Oarsman Kasia, they are the largest force in Chalcis," the Tribune answered. He pointed to the square Scanlan had drawn to designate the quarters. "It's our biggest challenge once we're in the city."

"Are you sure about that?" Nero contested. "This information came from an unknown lad. Who, I might point out, only spent a day in Chalcis. Shouldn't we question reconnaissance gathered in such a casual manner?"

"Scanlan Kasia is the adopted son of Jace Kasia," Lepidus reminded the senior diplomat. "He's not untrustworthy, Pro-consul."

"I remember his father as a Centurion of Legion Marines on my brother's warship," Nero stated. "I found him impulsive and not a good officer. He was too independent."

"The independent streak must run in the family," Lepidus said, turning towards the ramp. Before leaving the warship, he offered. "Be careful tonight, General Nero."

"May the blessings of the Goddess Bellona go with you," Nero declared as he scattered herbs in the air. "Let her spill the blood of our enemies and not of our men or that of our allies."

"Know that we war in your name, Goddess Bellona," Marcus Lepidus intoned before saluting and marching down the ramp.

Both Legion commanders failed to notice one thing on the drawing, the villa housing the Macedonian officers. At sundown, the armada launched and rowed north up the Euboean.

***

Bathed in weak moonlight, the *Hawk of Peace* turned out of the main channel and glided slowly towards the bank of the gulf. Gray shadows moved about the deck, dodging around unarmored Legion Marines. When the bow nudged the shoreline, the shapes leaped to the grass. Still appearing as shadows, the sailors stretched lines from the ship to the closest trees. After anchoring the warship, they whistled softly.

The unarmored Marines jumped to shore, and ladders were handed down from the ship. Then, in a single file, they hiked away from the southern Euboean Gulf.

"Kasia, you better know where we're going?" Vibia warned.

"Optio Vibia, we'll cross a trail up ahead," Scanlan told him. "On the other side, we'll find the corner of the defensive wall."

"During a night operation, a simple yes is enough," Vibia told the youth. "Slow your pace. The ladder bearers are rushing to keep up."

Having learned that a reply wasn't necessary, Scanlan shifted the war bow case to settle it against the quiver and shortened his steps. Once over the wagon trail, he picked the widest route between tree branches to keep the noise level down. When the looming wall of Chalcis arose out of the darkness, he stepped to the side. Optio Vibia used grabs, shoves, and nudges to line up the bearers.

Once the ladders were against the wall, Vibia hauled Scanlan in close and whispered in the youth's ear.

"You're not qualified for this. You don't have to go up."

"Tell my spirit that," Scanlan declared. His excitement overriding his common sense.

Stepping on the first rung, Scanlan climbed steadily. At the last rung, he reached to the top of the capstone and hoisted himself up and over. The wooden walkway wobbled, letting him know why the city guard and the Macedonians didn't post sentries on these walls.

"I can see the gate," Vibia whispered, looking over the side of the walkway and farther north. "And the gate guard."

As his Marines reached their Optio, he directed them to the walkway's ladder and pointed to positions for an attack on the guard.

"He needs to be removed silently," the Optio remarked. "If he gets loud, we could have Macedonian company before we get the gate open."

"I've never killed a man," Scanlan admitted as he eased the case off his shoulder.

"Then don't start now. Taking a man's life is not something to be done lightly," Vibia advised. Despite the scars, numbers of battles survived, and his warrior attitude, the veteran Optio's recommendation came from his heart. "Most people go through life without the nightmares."

When the last of the Marines had slid down the ladder and staged for the attack, Scanlan walked beyond the ladder to get a better view of the gate road. Below him, the Legion Marines closed in on the sentry while Scanlan watched the empty intersection. Next, a block from the gate, moonlight reflected off a moving object.

***

The saving grace for the Marines, the helmet on the relief guard, showed him strolling up the road. It appeared the man wasn't in a rush to assume the sentry duty at the southwest gate.

Without forethought, Scanlan flexed and bent his war bow to warm up the wood. Automatically, he placed the bow behind his knee and hooked the bowstring over one end. Carefully, so as not to overstress the limbs and the handle, he bent the bow and connected the bowstring to the other end. Stepping out of the strung bow, Scanlan reached for an arrow, but stopped.

Vibia's caution about killing a man ran through his mind. *"Most people go through life without the nightmares."*

Each step the relief guard took carried him closer to the Marines. And with every pace came the likelihood of the man sounding the alarm about the attackers.

Could he kill? Scanlan had the training, and he'd hunted since he was a small lad. If a deer was venison to nourish the body, what was a human carcass good for? What could it foster? What benefit would it bestow on the killer?

Yet, the Marines were about to be discovered. Found out before they could remove the guard and open the gate for the rest of the Legion Marines and the Greek shield bearers.

The relief guard moved closer, threatening to end the raid before it started. And possibly ending Optio Vibia's life, the lives of Pacius the Tall and the other Marines from the *Hawk of Peace*.

Zip-Thwack!

In reaction, the relief guard threw himself to the side and away from the pieces of flying pottery. Dirt and gravel released when the arrow exploded the hanging plant, scattered outward, further peppering the man.

"Phantasos," he cried out to the God of Deceptive Shapes in dreams.

From a neighboring building, a sleepy voice scolded him, "Be silent, dreamer. Some of us are trying to sleep."

Shaken by the violent destruction of the clay pot, the relief guard stood staring at the empty rope that once held the potted plant. He never thought to look for the arrow embedded in the street behind him.

The shout of surprise did alert Vibia. He dispatched three Marines to deal with the relief guard while the Optio and the other three charged at the duty gate guard.

Scanlan rushed to the ladder and missed the assaults as he slid down the rails to the ground. Sprinting to the gate, he helped remove the locking beam and pushed with the others to open the gate for Tribune Lepidus and the raiders.

"What now, Optio?" Pacius asked as the armored Marines and shield bearers jogged into Chalcis. "We should get into the fight."

"We'll stay behind the shields of the others," Vibia told him. When his Marines complained about missing out on the fighting, their Optio reminded them. "No matter how well I trained you, we have no spears, shields, or gladii. We have dagger. And what good are daggers in a shield wall battle?"

"We could go look at the plaza," Scanlan suggested. "They have spears and shields stored there. If the guards leave, you'll have access to weapons."

"Fine. Two of you get those poor excuses for spears from the guards but leave the shields," Vibia instructed. "A weak shield gives a false sense of protection. Oarsman Kasia, show us the plaza."

***

The seven men of the gate assault team followed Scanlan towards the government building. As they moved cautiously down the street, the sounds of battle from the barracks reached them.

"Give me a spear and a shield," Pacius exclaimed, "and put me in that fight."

Feeling confident in his standing with the Marines, Scanlan reached back as if presenting the bow to the tall Marine. "How about a different weapon?"

"No thanks, I'll only touch a bow and arrow when it's an emergency or in the case of a pirate attack," the tall Marine said, declining the offer.

Scanlan led them to a spot around the corner from the plaza and the three warehouses containing the arsenal and war treasure.

"Macedonian soldiers guard King Philip's siege engines, artillery, shields, spears, and war chest," he told them while indicating the side of the building. "The shields and spears are in the second building. You can see all three buildings from the plaza. Farther away, across the forum is the main gate."

Vibia gently moved Scanlan to the side and stepped around the youth. Pacius and two others joined their Optio at the corner.

"What are they carrying?" Vibia asked.

Curious, Scanlan eased between the Marines and peered around the corner.

From the third warehouse, soldiers huddled around a suspended chest with iron bands. Captain Sopater directed the movement of the war chest while Lieutenant Aetos commanded a line of retreating shields, protecting the porters.

Stepping out from concealment, Scanlan searched the far side of the plaza and the forum. There were no armored Athenian shield bearers or Legion Marines in sight. Without a challenger, Captain Sopater and King Philip's war chest had a clear path to the gateway and to the ships on the beach.

With practiced hands, Scanlan unstrung his war bow and placed it in the case. After sealing it, he handed Pacius the bow and the quiver of arrows.

"What's this?" demanded the tall Marine.

"Marine Pacius, this is an emergency," Scanlan told him. "Save the bow and quiver for me."

"What are you doing, Oarsmen Kasia?" Vibia questioned.

"Tracking King Philip's war chest," Scanlan replied. Then he requested. "Optio, say these words to Tribune Lepidus, Nightjars have soft feathers."

"I don't understand," the Sergeant of Marines admitted.

"The Tribune will," Scanlan stated before sprinting to the government building.

Moments later, the Insubri youth vanished behind the compound. In the air, the first whiffs of smoke from the burning barracks reached them.

"Scanlan said the second building has the spears and shields," Vibia directed. "Let's collect weapons and get into this fight."

The seven Legion Marines came around the corner and ran for the warehouse door. Lieutenant Aetos noticed the movement and pointed out the threat to his Macedonians. But the Marines had no weapons and were just opening the door. The soldiers, on the other hand, had almost reached the gateway. What Aetos didn't see was a slim figure dash from around the government building and slip through the open gates.

***

While outwardly, Tribune Lepidus remained detached, playing the unemotional commander. Inside, he seethed with anger.

"The Rhodian prisoners will need help getting to the ships," the Centurion of his bodyguards volunteered. "We ought to send them that way now."

"Two things, Centurion," Lepidus suggested. "Feed them and let them clean up a little. That'll go a long way towards their healing. And it'll make them beholden to Rome. I can use that when I return them to the Isle of Rhodes."

"Yes, sir," the Centurion assured him. "I'll see to it personally."

Once the commander of the Tribune's bodyguard had left, Lepidus turned to watch a centipede-like line of men carry grain sacks and baskets out of the granary. When the last one left, a commander of the Athenian shield bearers raised a torch in salute.

"Burn it," Lepidus shouted. His anger at the Macedonians for the way they treated the prisoners from Rhodes still burned hot in his mind.

"Tribune Lepidus," a voice requested, "a moment of your time."

With the smell of the abused prisoners in his nose and on his mind, Lepidus spun to the speaker. His arm came up and his pointer finger poked at a scarred face.

"Optio Vibia, I apologize. You caught me at a bad moment," Lepidus emphasized. Then the Tribune noticed the blood splatter on Vibia's tunic. And the blood on the new but battered shield held by the Optio. "Where did you go after opening the side gate?"

"The Macedonians were holding the main gate and filtering their soldiers through," Vibia reported. "We cleared the defenders out of the way and closed the gates. But they got away."

"Who got away?" Lepidus asked.

"The Macedonian Captain and the war chest of King Philip," the Optio replied. Then he paused before saying. "Oarsman Kasia slipped out before we got armed. Said he was following Philip's war chest."

The Tribune seemed lost for a moment before speaking.

"During the planning for the raid, the war chest completely slipped my mind," Lepidus lied. He hadn't forgotten the chest of coins. What he forgot was the villa where the Macedonian officers were quartered. It sounded more noble to claim that money wasn't important than to admit the officer in charge of Chalcis had escaped because his quarters were ignored. "Thank you for the report."

A hint of daybreak touched the eastern sky, but smoke from the burning arsenal buildings hid the first rays. Vibia half turned to go when he about faced and saluted.

"Yes?" the Tribune inquired. "Something more?"

"Sir, before Oarsman Kasia left, he asked me to deliver a message to you. It makes no sense to me."

"I'll be the judge of that, tell me," Lepidus encouraged.

"Nightjars have soft feathers," Vibia related.

"Optio, get your people to the *Hawk of Peace*, they've done enough for one day," Marcus Lepidus directed. Then, once Vibia had gone, the Tribune replied to the smokey morning air with Scanlan's countersign. "But their feathers, Scanlan Kasia, make poor fletches."

Chapter 27 - Never Without A Blade

Scanlan raced from behind the government building, slipped by the Macedonia shield wall without being seen, and scurried out the main gate. Once outside of Chalcis, he slowed, searching for Captain Sopater and the war chest. Down the beach, a group of soldiers stood near a two-banker bireme. After spotting the Captain, and doing a quick calculation of oarsmen, Scanlan hid his smile and stumbled as if in a panicked rush.

A two-banker had benches for one hundred and twenty rowers. His count showed far less than the optimum number of soldiers to man the oars.

"Help. Please take me with you," the youth cried, dragging his feet as if too exhausted to lift his legs.

"Who are you?" a Lochías demanded. The Sergeant moved forward to block Scanlan.

"I was a temple boy for Dionysus," the youth confessed.

Two soldiers stepped forward, obviously drawn by the novelty of seeing a temple boy. Scanlan's heart sank. His outrageous claim might get him excluded from the crew.

But then one soldier leaned forward and asked, "Are you Fish?"

"Fish," Scanlan stated with no inflection because he had no knowledge of what Fish meant.

"Who is Fish?" the Lochías asked.

"Seven days ago, Priestesses of Dionysus were in town asking for a Fish," the second soldier answered. "No one could find him and the words from those questioned were Fish Don't."

"Fish Don't, what?" the Lochías demanded.

"Fish don't remain in captivity," Scanlan offered. "I escaped and hid. Then the raiders attacked and I ran. Look, I just want to get back to Crete. The men in my family are deep sea fishermen and not props for Priestesses."

"You can row?" the Lochías inquired.

"Yes, sir. I was born on a rowers bench and given an oar as my first toy," Scanlan bragged. "I've been pulling an oar since I was tall enough to reach the oarlock."

"Come with me," the Lochías instructed. After pushing through groups of soldiers, they reached Captain Sopater.

"What do you need, Sergeant Chronis?" the Captain asked.

"Sir, I've found an experienced rower," the Lochías reported.

"Can you navigate a bireme?" Sopater inquired. "And how many rowers do we need to operate the ship?"

Scanlan studied the two levels of oarlocks. He counted sixty on the Port side.

"You can power a two-banker with half the oarsmen," Scanlan guessed. He embellished the speculation by saying.

"We'll need thirty on each side. Let me seat them for the most efficient distribution."

"Sergeant, how many do we have?" Sopater asked.

Turning in a circle, the Lochías counted heads.

"Seventy soldiers," Sergeant Chronis reported. Then to Scanlan, he admitted. "Our oarsmen and navigator are trapped in the city. All we have are soldiers trained in war but not in rowing."

Scanlan looked to the main gate and watched it close. He only had a few moments. Soon, the Legion Marines would realize there were soldiers on the beach. They'd come out in force.

"We have to go," the youth instructed. "Everyone. Up the ramp one at a time. I'll direct you to a location."

Scanlan Kasia jogged up the ramp and stood with his fists on his hips, waiting for the Macedonian soldiers. Outwardly, he appeared as confident as an experienced skipper. Inside, the youth trembled. Any challenge to his knowledge would reveal his lack of command skills.

"You heard the navigator," Captain Sopater directed. "Up the ramp, now."

***

The bireme floated free and unarmed soldiers climbed up to the deck. Next, they stumbled over the stacks of armor, shields, and spears scattered across the deck to reach the short ladders down to the rowing positions. To staff the Engine section, Scanlan assigned the most massive men to the center. For the Bow and Stroke, he simply pointed to either end of the one hundred foot long vessel.

"Lieutenant Aetos. Sergeant Chronis. Call the stroke count," he ordered. "Stroke, all together stroke, stroke."

Rather than coach seventy reluctant soldiers in the art of rowing, Scanlan talked with File Leader Aetos and Rank Leader Chronis. Using their authority, he avoided hard questions from individuals.

If the ship had depended solely on the coordination of the rowers to guide the two-banker, they would have traveled in circles. But Scanlan manned the rear oar, keeping it heading north. And to his great joy, traversing the north Gulf of Euboean wasn't much more difficult than navigating Lake Maggiore where it spilled into the Ticino River.

"Stroke. Stroke. Pull together," Lieutenant Aetos and Sergeant Chronis chanted in unison.

Behind the bireme, smoke billowed into the air as the warehouses in Chalcis burned.

"It's all lost," Captain Sopater observed, watching flames leap higher than the defensive walls. "The siege engines, artillery, spears, and shields gone. Everything King Philip collected for the attack on Athens."

Beside the Captain, Scanlan adjusted the rear oar to take advantage of the currents of the gulf and the winds flowing along the watercourse. After Sopater's lament, the Insubri youth glanced at the war chest with the two guards.

"Not everything, Captain," Scanlan muttered.

"What did you say?" Sopater asked.

"The gulf is tricky," Scanlan told him, changing the comment. "We're getting a push from the southwest."

"That's good isn't it?" Sopater suggested.

"As long as we stay off the Starboard bank," Scanlan informed him.

He was tempted to wreck the bireme on the rocky shoreline and sink it. Being a good swimmer, Scanlan had no doubt he could survive and escape. Then later, he'd return and recover the war chest from the depths. He'd be rich. But that would end his quest to experience the world. Staying with his first impulse, he remained steady on the rear oar, maintaining a safe course.

Not long after he rejected the idea of the get rich quick scheme, three Macedonian warships appeared on the gulf. Not only did the five-bankers dwarf the bireme, between them the ships carried over eleven hundred men. It wasn't the number, but the likelihood that one oarsman or Marine was an expert diver who could retrieve the coins.

"Good call," Scanlan complimented himself on not wrecking the two-banker on the rocks.

***

Five days after the narrow escape from Chalcis; Being picked up by the trio of quinqueremes; And a sea journey of island hopping across the Aegean, the three warships approached two pillars of land. One or both might have been the tip of an island. Yet a color change in the sea hinted at something different. Bright blue marked the rippling water of the Aegean Sea. But ahead, the water transitioned to a darker blue-green, hinting at a greater depth.

"The Hellespont Strait," Captain Sopater told Scanlan. "It's a channel that divides Greece from Anatolia. On the other end, the strait connects to the Sea of Marmara."

Scanlan gawked at seeing a place he had only read about. He envisioned Xerxes I linking boats across the Hellespont to create a bridge for his Persian army to invade Greece. And he pictured the youthful Alexander the Great ferrying his Macedonian army across the Hellespont to invade Persia. Then the hull shuddered, and the keel drifted right, pulling Scanlan from the daydream. The warship had entered the strait.

"You're relieved. Thanks for the break but I'll take it from here," the second navigator announced. He accepted the Port side rear oar from Scanlan. "The Hellespont Strait is dangerous for ships."

The Starboard navigator explained, "Shifting currents and tricky shorelines require teamwork."

"And there are other dangers," the Port side navigator warned.

As the men on the rear oars guided the five-banker to the center of the watercourse, Scanlan noted the sides closing in as the strait narrowed. When it looked as if they would enter a box canyon, he saw the ribbon of water angle to the left and continue. From a feature in a wide sea, the Hellespont now resembled a winding river.

"Shields," ordered the warship's Captain. "Archers string your bows."

Despite not understanding the need for the instructions, Scanlan hoisted a spare shield and questioned.

"What's happening?"

"We're preparing for patrol boats from Abydos on the right and farther north from Sestos on the left," Lieutenant Aetos answered.

Before Scanlan could comment on the Macedonian officer's information, four patrol boats launched from a sand bar ahead. Each eighteen-rower boat had eight archers standing in the center between the oarsmen. A stone fort sat on a knoll above the beach.

"This is a squadron of three five-banker warships," Scanlan pointed out. "The rams could sink any of those patrol boats with just a nick from the edge of a fin."

The oarsmen in the patrol boats held water with their oars. Idling the length of an arrow's flight from the five-bankers, thirty-two archers began raining down shafts on the decks of the warships.

"This ship could sink them as easily as a man could kick over bean poles in a garden," Scanlan proposed from under the shield. Then he changed his mind. "On second thought, sinking the boats would be easier."

Rather than cruising to Starboard and ruining the day for the patrol boats, the five-bankers drifted left as they rowed deeper into the Hellespont. At the new range, many arrows fell short.

A moment later, four bolts, the length of a man's arm, splashed down too far from the five-bankers to be dangerous.

"Artillery from Abydos," Aetos identified the source as the fort above the beach. "If we go after the patrol boats, the bolt throwers will go after us."

"Why allow a danger to shipping like that to exist?" Scanlan asked.

"King Philip is working on the problem," the Lieutenant assured him. "But first he needs to capture the fort and the beach at Sestos."

The warships moved by the sandy point of Abydos and immediately angled across the strait. Five patrol boats launched from the opposite shore and archers began sending arrows at the five-bankers.

"Let me guess," Scanlan stated. "We're avoiding the bolt throwers from the fort at Sestos."

"You catch on fast for a temple boy," Sergeant Chronis complimented him. "Once we've taken the forts, sailing supplies to Anatolia for the invasion will be easier than rafting them across the Hellespont."

The fort at Sestos didn't waste bolts in a demonstration of their throwers. Evidently, they recognized the evasive maneuvers of the warships as an acknowledgement of their prowess.

***

With slow, energy saving strokes, the squadron moved beyond Sestos. Soon, all three warships were again in mid channel. The archers unstrung their bows and Scanlan put the shield back where he'd found it.

"It's always beautiful," the Lochías declared.

Following the direction of the Sergeant's gaze, Scanlan observed a field of bright yellow plants and green leaves. A hand would not span the large circular head of each flower. The carpet of flowers grew right up to the bank of the strait.

"Elecampane flowers," Chronis named the plant.

"They are beautiful," Scanlan agreed.

Just north of the flowers, the three warships cut half circles in the water and backstroked to the beach. Captain Sopater, Lieutenant Aetos, and Sergeant Chronis escorted the war chest down the ramp and up the hill from the shoreline. Scanlan, not having instructions to the contrary, followed the procession.

***

High on the left, the stone walls of a hill fort broke the natural lines of the slope. Combined with the steep grade, the walls presented an unscalable barrier. In a few places, Macedonian soldiers held shields overhead, protecting themselves as well as associates with hoes. On their knees, the diggers were attempting and failing at undermining the stone walls. The siege appeared to be at an impasse, except for one area. The wagon path into the fort had been blocked by a barrier of logs. Sestos militia threw spears over the barrier. Downslope, soldiers tossed spears up at the men behind the barricade. A mass of Macedonian soldiers had gathered on the road out of range from the spears.

***

The camp of the Macedonian army filled a flat area between hills. Mostly deserted as the occupants fought in the battle, the people in the encampment were wounded soldiers, craftsmen, or servants. Cutting between rows of tents and gear, the escorts and the soldiers carrying the chest of coins reached a compound of large tents.

"The King's pavilion," Chronis told the Insubri youth.

Noticing how few people moved about the compound, Scanlan inquired, "If it's not impolite to ask. Where's the King of Macedon?"

A servant lifted his arm and pointed at the zigzagging trail leading to the hillfort. Scanlan lifted his face and focused his eyes. Before he succeeded in locating the figure of a King, a surge by the group of soldiers on the dirt road happened.

***

Ten armored men with shields and spears charged ahead of the main group. As they rounded the final bend in the road, spears flew from above and a pair of shafts punched two of the attackers out of the forward line. The following mass of soldiers had to step around the dead or wounded. The jostling slowed the main body of soldiers. Ignoring what was happening behind them, the remaining eight warriors reached the log barrier. Placing a foot on the second log, they stood, extended their arms above the wall and threw their weapons at unseen defenders. Before they could drop back below the top of the barrier, two attackers were lifted into the sky by bolts as long as a man's arm. From the log wall, they were carried back and dropped into the mass of soldiers. Several warriors fell from the weight of the projected men. The added disruption further slowed the main body of attackers.

Scanlan realized why the artillery at Sestos hadn't launched at the three warships in the strait. They were saving their bolts for the infantry. Multiple shields presented little resistance to a bolt thrower. A single bolt launched at close range, as if a needle piercing cloth, stitched a pattern of death by suturing bodies.

The six forward attackers huddled at the base of the barrier. After glancing to the rear and realizing the disarray of the attacking force, they paused. Scanlan assumed the advance line would call off the attack and retreat. But one soldier with a long crest plume of blue and blond horsehair trailing from his helmet jumped up and drew his short sword. With the xiphos in one hand and the shield in the other, he began to climb the barrier.

Witnessing the heroic one-man attack, the remaining five of the original attackers drew their swords and scurried after him. A terrible shriek from the mass of soldiers in the rear carried to the base of the hill and certainly into the fort. Driven by the war cry, the mass of soldiers sprinted to the barrier. As if bugs scurrying over the carcass of a fallen bird, the Macedonian army swarmed the citadel of Sestos.

The fighting happened behind the walls, but the victor soon became apparent. Macedonian soldiers removed the holding posts and kicked the logs of the barricade down the hill. A roar came from the fort, which didn't seem to have anything to do with the timbers tumbling end over end, jumping, and twisting down the slope. Then a single scream silenced the choir of voices. The anguish ended when a body flew over the wall of the fort. Propelled by a bolt, the dead man, his back broken by the launch from a bolt thrower, soared out over the Hellespont before running out of momentum. Both the cadaver and the bolt plummeted through the air before splashing into the water. No sooner than the first appeared, then a second man bellowed in fear before he flew over the wall.

Across the strait, men in the higher sections in the citadel of Abydos watched in horror as body after body got launched.

***

As the inhumane drama played out, the soldier with the blue and blond crest plume strutted from the fort. His armor, shield, face, and arms were coated with blood. Yet, he moved gracefully, as if he'd spent the day watching others fight while he reclined.

Scanlan observed the man as he traveled the winding road from the fort to the camp.

"Who is the powerful warrior?" Scanlan inquired.

Chronis answered, "That, temple boy, is Philip V Antigonid, King of Macedonia."

Scanlan peered around the pavilion. Servants prepared bowls of soapy water for washing, drink for soothing the King's thirst, and food for the conqueror of Sestos. The ruler of Macedon had everything a King would want. Originally, Scanlan accompanied the war chest to perhaps take some of the coins, or at least to tell Tribune Lepidus where the coins were stored. But here he had an opportunity to be a real spy. If only he could find a way to make himself valuable to the King.

Philip walked into the pavilion, handed off his helmet and shield. When a servant reached for the bindings on his chest armor, the King stopped him.

"Sopater. What are you doing here?" Philip demanded. His eyes dropped to the war chest then rose to the Captain.

"Chalcis was overrun," Sopater informed the King.

"What of my artillery? My siege engines? The spears and shields for my recruits?"

"All lost, my lord to the Athenians and Romans," Sopater revealed. "I tried to fight them but failed."

Philip held out a hand to stop the Captain. Folding all but two fingers on his left hand, the King moved close and placed the fingertips over the Captain's lips.

"Hush," he whispered. "The time for regret is long past."

In a smooth, practiced motion, Philip of Macedon drew his xiphos and plunged the blade into Sopater's chest. A twist must have found the man's heart as he dropped almost immediately to the floor.

"Get this garbage out of my tent," Philip said in disgust. He walked to the war chest, placed a loving hand on the leather and peered at the Lieutenant from Chalcis.

"Aetos, what happened?" Philip inquired, still holding the short sword.

"We tried to warn the Captain about the lax discipline," Aetos lied. "When the garrison and detachment were overrun, Sergeant Chronis and I organized a fighting retreat and protected the war chest."

Philip stared at Chronis for a moment before asking, "Well?"

"Just as the Lieutenant said, my King," the Sergeant assured him. "We saved the war chest and barely escaped with our lives."

"Here clean this," Philip ordered a servant. "Do it now. A King of Macedon can never be without a blade."

Chapter 28 - City By The Strait

Philip downed a chalice of rich red wine. With his initial thirst sated, he allowed a servant to unhook his torso armor. Bodyguards came in and removed the body of Captain Sopater. Another servant kneeled and removed the greaves from the King's shins.

"Are we sure it's all lost?" Philip inquired with resignation. "I had planned to use the equipment for the attack on Athens. Now I guess, I'll have to restock."

"The fires were so hot that the flames topped the walls of Chalcis, my lord," Aetos offered. "I'm afraid it all burned or was taken by the Athenians."

From the fort, a victim's scream continued from over the wall and all the way down to the water. The onager catapult, unlike the bolt thrower, didn't kill when it launched the militiaman. Philip shook his head and exhaled in frustration.

"Those loads are ruining the frames of the throwers and the continuous use of the onagers are weakening the arms. Such a loss. Maybe we can collect artillery after I accept the surrender from Abydos."

Inside the King's statement was an historic event. Yet no one in the pavilion commented on the relevance of crossing the Hellespont with an army. Scanlan raised both arms, twisted at the waist, and scanned the pavilion.

"Is no one writing this down?" the youth inquired, his mannerisms revealing exasperation.

"What are you talking about?" Sergeant Chronis demanded.

"We know a little about Philip II of Macedon," Scanlan told the Lochías. "In comparison to King Philip II, we know much more about his son. His history, his personality, his sayings, his tactics of diplomacy, and especially about the conquests of King Alexander, known as the Great. Why?"

"Well, it's," Chronis started to reply, but couldn't find the words.

"We know about King Alexander because he was the most successful campaigner the world has ever known," Aetos insisted. "And he was Macedonian."

"That he was, I read it in scrolls," Scanlan agreed. "King Alexander spread the Macedonian Greek style across the world. But the question Lieutenant, how do we know so much about the King?"

Philip held out his chalice and allowed a servant to fill the vessel.

"Your use of rhetoric is excellent," the King granted before taking a large gulp of wine. "The answer as to why we knew about Alexander is cleverly hidden in your reply."

"Sir, I can remove the lad," Chronis offered, thinking Scanlan's talking bothered the King.

"No, Sergeant, I'm curious where he's taking this argument," Philip stated. With a smile, the King urged. "Tell them how we know so much about King Alexander."

"The Great King traveled with scribes who recorded his actions and sayings," Scanlan answered. "From Corinth to India, his record of accomplishments filled scrolls that documented the conquests, the organization, and his mercy towards conquered people."

"What conclusion do you draw from that?" Philip asked.

"You, King Philip V of Macedon, are participating in and creating significant events," Scanlan informed him. "Yet, you have no one recording them for posterity."

"You think the King of Macedon should have a scribe?" Philip proclaimed. "The idea is absurd."

"As you wish, lord King," Scanlan acknowledged, bowing before the force of the King's words. Then he focused his eyes on Philip's and counter argued. "However, when Xerxes I crossed the Hellespont to reach Greece, scribes recorded the engineering and the event. And when King Alexander crossed the Hellespont to reach Asia, he hired scribes to record the event. Will your crossing of the Hellespont be any less momentous?"

Philip walked outside his pavilion and looked up at the hillfort. After studying the stonework and the flow of Macedonian soldiers into and out of the citadel, he turned to Scanlan.

"I should have you launched over the wall for arguing with me," Philip told Scanlan. "But I'm curious enough to test your premise. Write about my conquest of Sestos. If your words please me, I'll make you my scribe."

"And if my words don't please you, sir?" Scanlan inquired.

"For a short period, you'll do what every man dreams of," Philip promised. "You'll fly. Or at least until your body flutters down into the strait."

Another scream from the fort acted as a dramatic accent to Philip's words. A moment later, a broken body sailed over the wall before splashing into the strait.

"I'll need ink, a pen, and parchment," Scanlan requested. "And a table where I can work."

***

General Chrysogonus strolled in, accepted a glass of wine and a chair near the King. Once the leaders were settled, a long string of Macedonian Captains trekked through the pavilion. Each reported wounded or dead from their sixty-four-man group and delivered spoils to their King. Philip honored them and their shield bearers with words recognizing their heroics. And he shared a glass of wine with every Captain. Finally, Philip V Antigonid returned a lot of the plunder for distribution to his soldiers. The Captains left knowing their leadership was recognized by their King and the sacrifices of their soldiers were understood.

"Scanlan, you worthless waste of goatskin parchment," Philip called out when the last Captain left the pavilion. He slurped from another glass of wine. "Where are you hiding?"

"Here my King," the youth answered from the table behind Philip. "Are you ready to hear of your attack on Sestos?"

"I was there. And I just heard from my Captains about the assault," Philip insisted. "Why would I need to hear your report?"

"Because, lord, no one outside this pavilion and the camp is aware of your personal bravery."

"My personal bravery. My personal bravery," Philip repeated. He took a long pull of his wine and directed. "Out with it. Tell me of my personal bravery."

Scanlan held up a large piece of parchment and read from it.

"An exploration of the bravery of the heir to the Antigonid Dynasty, the ruler of all lands touching the Aegean Sea, and the King of Macedon, Philip V. On this day, when faced with an insurmountable citadel, King Philip chose to attack rather than cower. Logs the size of a large man's waist blocked the entrance to the fort. And a multitude of spearmen guarded the entrance. Despite the barrier and the misguided loyalty of the defenders, King Philip charged ahead of his army. Emboldened by the courage of the King, his soldiers raced after him. When he climbed the barricade, pulled his sword, and leaped over the logs, the shield bearers lost sight of Philip. Not until they topped the logs did they find him surrounded by dead bodies and trembling militiamen. Thus, the world witnessed the bravery of Philip V of Macedon."

Scanlan rolled the document, walked over to a brazier, and held the goatskin parchment next to the flame.

"I realize my weak words didn't do you justice, King Philip," Scanlan announced. No one could see the dampness in his folded left hand, nor realize the plan of escape. With a flaming roll of parchment, he could hold off the guards and servants momentarily. And being an excellent swimmer, the

Insubri youth knew freedom existed down the hill and out into the deep water. Finishing his lament, Scanlan stated. "As I await my fate, the offensive words will burn."

The pavilion grew very still and tension built until Philip burped.

"Ruler of all lands touching the Aegean Sea," he exclaimed. "That is a great idea. You're now the scribe to the King of Macedon."

Scanlan moved the parchment away from the flame and asked, "Should I pack for the crossing, my lord?"

"My army just fought a battle," Philip said with a yawn. "They've earned a rest."

"Tomorrow then?" Scanlan inquired.

"We'll wait here at least ten days or until my barges arrive," Philip corrected him. "Go look around Sestos and see how I treat the citizens of a conquered city."

From the hill, another scream announced the launch of a militiaman. Based on the executions throughout the afternoon, Scanlan could only imagine the horrors he'd find in the town of Sestos.

***

Early the next morning, Scanlan followed a wagon trail away from the citadel. Under the trees north of the Macedonian camp, he enjoyed the play of light through the branches and the solitude.

A six-man patrol coming from the direction of Sestos slowed, preparing to question the lone traveler. But the sight of a King's messenger case slung over the Insubri's shoulder satisfied their curiosity. The patrol leader waved him onward, assuming the youth carried royal dispatches. In reality, the satchel contained ink, pens, and blank pieces of parchment. The shield bearers resumed their pace without stopping.

The ease of his passage let Scanlan know the power of displaying the King's symbol. With the sixteen triangular shaped rays of the Vergina Sun embossed on the leather, few Macedonians would dare obstruct his movements.

Patting the side of the satchel, Scanlan announced to the empty trail, "Make way for the King's courier."

What the King's scribe didn't see were the two men hiding just ahead in the woods.

***

Scanlan Kasia had been tutored by a Cretan Archer. Even in his relaxed state on a peaceful trail through deep woods, his senses picked up on the snapping branches and scraping of dead leaves under rapidly advancing feet.

Animals rarely charged unless they were protecting their young. Maternal attacks could happen abruptly, but usually with warning noises. The best defense involved getting away from their young. In the case of a sick beast, birds and forest critters scattered, providing a forewarning to the presence of illogical behavior and allowing a moment to get away. The sounds of approaching predators weren't generated by a mama bear or an ill beast.

The most dangerous animal of them all attacked without warning. And the best defense against a sudden attack by men wasn't to run, or to try and fight, at first. To prevent injury during the initial assault required the victim to avoid getting cut or wounded by a spear, blade, or club.

Scanlan took a half step to the right and jumped out of the line of attack. Rolling on his shoulders, the youth came up with a sica in his hand and the King's satchel held forward as a shield.

Two men sprinted forward and stumbled while attempting to follow Scanlan's lateral maneuver. To add to their confusion, the youth continued to circle until he faced south, the way he'd come from and the way the patrol had gone.

"We're going to gut you, Macedonian scum," one sneered as he swung a knife in Scanlan's direction. But his feet slipped out from under him and he slammed into the trail.

The second assailant stopped, hooked his forearm under his partner's upper arm, and helped him to his feet. They pivoted towards the youth. The men held short swords and wore the tunics of Sestos militiamen.

"You would cut a lad from Crete?" Scanlan asked, thickening his accent to mimic a southern Greek islander. His inflection confused them, giving Scanlan a moment to address the pair. "You'd serve your people better by taking a swim before the storm."

Rays of sunlight from a clear sky penetrated the branches, creating streaks of light on the trail.

"What storm?" the second militiaman demanded.

"King Philip will cross the strait in a few days," Scanlan whispered, as if telling a secret. "You need to swim to Abydos and warn them about the attack."

"But first, we're going to gut you," the first repeated his earlier threat.

"At least you're consistent," Scanlan offered before backing away and whistling. Reminiscent of a hawk's cry, the shrill sound lasted for two heartbeats. Next, he yelled. "You'll not have King Philip's satchel. Only by lifting it off my dead shoulder will you have this case."

He danced from side to side, slashing the air with the curved sica knife.

"You'll not have King Philip's satchel. Only by lifting it off my dead shoulder will you have this case," Scanlan shouted, so his words carried far down the trail.

The militiamen spread apart and moved forward.

"You'll not have King Philip's satchel. Only by lifting it off my dead shoulder will you have this case," Scanlan said again.

This time, the assailants realized he wasn't addressing them. One turned to look down the trail.

"Run. It's the Macedonian patrol," he alerted his partner.

As the pair ran for the woods, Scanlan, still slicing the air with his blade, chased them to the edge of the trail.

"Under penalty of death, do not challenge the authority of King Philip," he shouted after the militiamen.

The six Macedonians sprinted up and stopped.

"Are you cut?" the Sergeant asked. "Do you required aid?"

"The artillerymen in the fort missed those two," Scanlan asserted while pointing in the direction of the fleeing men. "I had them until you arrived. If you'd delayed, you could have taken their bodies."

"That'll teach them to challenge the authority of King Philip," a soldier mentioned.

In his heart, Scanlan was pleased that the patrol heard him say the phrase.

"We'll get them," the Sergeant assured Scanlan.

The six shield bearers charged into the woods. After pausing for a moment, Scanlan sheathed his blade and resumed his stroll through the woods. Around the base of the hillfort, the Insubri youth located the city by the strait.

***

Although they could easily be kicked down by armored men, the low walls stood as barriers to keep herd animals inside Sestos. Not only had the stockade walls survived, so had the buildings, streets, and covered meeting places in the city. Beyond the structures, citizens went about their business. Upon closer inspection, Scanlan noted the nervousness of the men, women, and children.

King Philip had invited him to see how the Macedonians treated a defeated people. The light display of merchandise revealed the low quantity of goods left in the town. Soldiers had taken most of the goods and probably many personal items as bounty. But the city continued and its people lived.

Scanlan located the docks on the far side of Sestos. As he stood mesmerized by the water of the Hellespont and the nearness of the distant shore, a merchant vessel rowed from the northeast and tied up at a pier.

"We're under a new King," a dockworker told the ship's skipper. "So far the tax hasn't gone up, but I bet it will."

"What new King?" the merchant Captain inquired.

"King Philip of Macedonia," the dock worker revealed.

"You'll not see us for a good while," the skipper announced. "We're based out of Athens. My business owners won't let me sail anywhere near a Macedonian port. They're afraid the ship and cargo will be impounded."

"Will you stay tonight and have dinner?"

"Maybe in the future," the merchant skipper told the dock worker. "Today, I need to top off our freshwater containers and get away from here."

"The well is unaffected," the dock worker assured him.

Scanlan found a spot on the pier, sat, pulled out a small piece of parchment, and a clay bottle of ink. With his legs dangling above the water, he wrote.

"My Dearest Tsolak of Fyli. Under today's full moon, I toured Sestos with my new patron. He'll be crossing the Hellespont in ten days or so. That will give me an opportunity to see Abydos. Give my regards to Marcus Lepidus and tell him I hope to see him soon. Sincerely, Scanlan Kasia."

He rolled the parchment and tied it up with a thin strip of leather. Then he wrote the philosopher's name on the outside and got up. Farther down the pier, he approached the merchant ship.

"Would you know Tsolak of Fyli?" Scanlan questioned the skipper.

"Tsolak the Stoic?" the skipper replied. "I know of him but I've never had an opportunity to sit and listen to the philosopher."

"Can I impose on you to deliver this missive to Tsolak when you reach Athens?" Scanlan requested.

"You don't appear to be a philosopher of stoicism," the Captain observed.

"I'm simply a humble student keeping in touch with my teacher," Scanlan said as he handed the skipper a pair of silver coins. "As you can tell by the coins, I haven't denounced physical things and the creature comforts purchased with money. I'm still working on releasing the physical world and embracing the reality of letting go of my ego and my control over anything."

"I didn't understand a thing you just said," the merchant admitted. "But there is little doubt that you are a student of stoicism. I'll deliver your letter."

"Thank you," Scanlan acknowledged.

He went back to where he left the Macedonian pouch. Being sure to hide the King's symbol from the skipper and the dock worker, Scanlan hiked back into the city of Sestos to continue his inspection.

Chapter 29 - Insult The Goddess Oizys

"An exploration of the temperament of moderation by the heir to the Antigonid Dynasty, the ruler of all lands touching the Aegean Sea, and the King of Macedon, Philip V. On this day, when faced with zealotry, King Philip chose a measured response. To that end, he dispatched Lieutenant Aetos across the Hellespont to parley with the magistrate of Abydos. While waiting for the resolution, Philip paced the floor of his pavilion speaking the wisdom of ancient philosophers. Yet at day's end, parts of Aetos arrived in a basket. And thus, King Philip's hand offered in friendship had been hacked off by men unworthy of the King's trust."

Philip raged. Not at the loss of a minor officer, but at the insolence of the rulers of Abydos.

"Cut down trees," he instructed. "If my barges don't arrive soon, I will strap logs together and raft my army across the Hellespont."

"Will you not pray on it, my King?" Scanlan inquired. He knew the Greeks, and especially the Romans, sacrificed to their gods before starting any major operation.

"Prayer? I'd need a priest for that," Philip slurred before downing half a chalice of wine. "But an excellent idea, scribe. Get me Lochías Chronis."

Although silent while waiting for the Sergeant, Philip's eyes bulged from anger and pent up fury. He drank to cool the fires of outrage.

***

The day grew old and the shadows long before the Lochías arrived.

"My lord, you sent for me," Chronis reported.

"I need a priest," Philip remarked.

"Yes, sir. There's a temple in Sestos," Chronis informed the King. "I can have him here before dark."

"Sergeant. I want a priest, no make that two Priests from Abydos," Philip instructed. "Take a five-banker across and as many shield bearers as you need. But bring me two priests from Abydos."

"Yes, my king," Chronis acknowledged.

He left, and Philip called for food.

"My lord," Scanlan inquired. "May I accompany Sergeant Chronis?"

"Go," Philip allowed.

The youth ran to catch up with the Rank Leader.

"Lochías Chronis, the King released me to go with you," Scanlan alerted the Sergeant.

"It's going to be a boring trip," Chronis commented. "There are temples outside the walls of Abydos. We'll snatch both priests from one and row back."

"That simple?" Scanlan asked.

"We're taking fifty shield bearers with us," Chronis explained. "Nothing about this is simple. But we'll accomplish the mission and be back before dawn."

***

After dark, the quadrireme slipped away from the beach. Rowing northeast, the five-banker slipped across the strait and almost immediately cut a half circle in the water.

The warship backstroked to a narrow beach and the shield bearers disembarked. Scanlan remained by the Rank Leader's side as they crept inland, seeking a path to the west.

"How will you find the temple in the dark," the youth whispered.

"Follow your nose," the Sergeant answered.

As much as Scanlan wanted to ask for more details, he held his tongue and marched with the column of soldiers.

***

Steps and shadows passed by like a dream in the night. Then deep into the march, the forest smells gave way to an ethereal aroma.

"Incense. The stink of temples," Chronis informed Scanlan while pulling him to a stop. "Wait here with the blocking force. If it the raid goes bad, get back to the five-banker."

"I want to be part of the raid," Scanlan argued.

"And I want to live," Chronis snapped back. "Getting the King's scribe killed won't be good for my health. Wait here."

When the Rank Leader slipped forward with the bulk of his soldiers, Scanlan thought about following. Maybe he could reach Abydos and warn the city.

"There you are," a voice whispered from the night shadows. "Chronis said to stay near the King's scribe."

Two shield bearers separated from the shadows and pulled Scanlan down with them. Any thought of slipping away ended with the arrival of the minders. They kneeled long enough for nocturnal creatures to emerge and begin hunting and feeding. Overhead, the moon climbed the sky, and the shadows shifted.

Scanlan heard rushed steps and muffled orders long before the raiders returned.

"Give me five shields on the trail with me," Chronis instructed. "The rest of you get back to the ship."

From Scanlan's location, it was difficult to make out the hostages from the line of soldiers. But when he sniffed incense on robes, he and his escorts fell into the march with the priests. Behind them, shields clashed and steel against steel rang out in the night.

They reached the beach and Scanlan got shoved between a wall of shields. Armed only with his curved sica, a small skinning knife, and his ink pen, Scanlan wisely ran up the ramp to the deck of the five-banker.

"We should get off this beach," a man warned.

"First Officer, if we leave the King's raiding party on the shore, we might as well row to Persia," the Captain advised.

Near the tree line, a Lochías commanded, "Let them through. Throw spears."

Men screamed in the dark as a flight of forty spears struck the temple guards, pursuing the raiders.

Then Chronis roared, "Board the ship. Captain, get us off this beach."

Shield bearers ran up the ramp and the First Officer shouted to the beach, "Get us wet."

The warship slipped from land, and the rowers climbed to the deck. Although Scanlan couldn't make out the hostages, mixed in with the smell of sweat and oiled armor, a whiff of incense drifted across the deck. Just as short as the trip across, the five-banker carved a half circle and backstroked to the beach at Sestos.

Scanlan waited for the shield bearers and hostages to leave before he glanced up at the sky. The first rays of a new day were showing in the east. As Chronis stated, there was nothing simple about the King's request. But the Rank Leader, as he promised, completed the mission before dawn.

***

The basket containing the body parts of Lieutenant Aetos sat outside the pavilion. Flies, maggots, and bugs crawled over and through the flesh and bones, creating a visual as disgusting as the stink. Every Macedonian, Thessalian, and infantryman from allies of the King walked by and got a view of the spectacle. Yet it wasn't just the body in the basket. On either side, the priests sat tied in chairs with a table filled with fruit, meat, and bowls of grain.

"My little drama is getting good reviews," Philip proposed when a couple of shield bearers stopped at the display. After examining the elements, they covered their mouths, jogged a few steps, halted, and heaved up their breakfast. Pleased with himself, the King of Macedon quipped. "Just wait for the heat of the day. Then things will really get ripe."

"My King," Scanlan requested, "why did you put the basket out for everyone to chance upon?"

"There's no chance to it, scribe. Every officer has been ordered to direct their soldiers to pass by my pavilion and see poor Aetos for themselves," Philip corrected. Seeing the confused expression on the youth's face, he explained. "The murder of Lieutenant Aetos was supposed to intimidate. Brutal but effective for the most part. Left to themselves, my infantrymen would discuss the horror until they all had nightmares about assaulting Abydos."

"But now they'll associate the smell of death with a single basket," Scanlan concluded. "It's that easy?"

"Don't overlook the priests," Philip remarked. "While the shield bearers smell death, they also see two priests from Abydos. The holy men represent an enemy to focus on. And with human villains in sight, the infantry can expand their stress from nervous to anger. Intimidated men are timid while angry men are fighters."

In a quick move, Philip dashed to the edge of the pavilion. The placement of the basket kept the stink away from the King's quarters.

"Scanlan go out there and refill the wine glasses of the priests," Philip directed.

"My lord," the youth agreed. Taking a pitcher of wine, he walked out of the pavilion. Five steps into the task, he smelled the rancid human flesh. At the priests, he told them. "I'm here to refill your glasses."

"What's your name lad?" the older one asked.

The other gazed at Scanlan as if trying to stare a hole in the youth's chest.

"Scanlan Kasia," Scanlan answered while pouring wine into one glass.

"Scanlan Kasia," the other addressed the youth. "I am Priest Pavlos and he is Priest Dimos. We are clerics of the Goddess Oizys."

"She who brings misery, anxiety, grief, depression, and misfortune," Dimos preached. "Without us to pacify the Goddess."

"Without our sacrifices to her," Pavlos warned, adding to the other's sentence. "The Goddess Oizys will unleash her blessings on this army."

Having no power to change the fate of the priests, Scanlan filled the second glass and walked back to the pavilion.

"What did they say?" Philip inquired, holding out his chalice for more wine.

"Priests Dimos and Pavlos are very good at theater," Scanlan informed the King. "Their speech passes your attention from one to the other as if your awareness was an egg to be thrown around."

"That's very disrespectable," Philip questioned. "Do you not understand the Gods?"

"I understand the Gods and Goddesses, my King," Scanlan said defending his education. "It's just my mentor, a Cretan Archer, didn't teach me fear of the gods."

Philip took a sip and asked, "What else did Priests Dimos and Pavlos have to say?"

"If you don't allow them to make sacrifices, the Goddess Oizys will bring misery, anxiety, grief, depression, and misfortune down on your army, sir."

"In that case, we should," Philip began a thought, but stopped. He changed the subject. "The wine is working. Look, see the wetness around the seats of the priests. They send me intimidation and I return the challenge with humiliation. Which scribe, I ask you, is more imposing?"

"The answer to that lord King," Scanlan told him. "Depends on the number of shield bearers in a man's army."

"How so?" Philip questioned.

"A man who gathers an army on the strength of his reputation is already intimidating," Scanlan advised. "To add humiliation to his arsenal of weapons, is almost boastful."

Philip sat in a chair, closed his eyes, and let a few chuckles escape his lips. When he dozed off, Scanlan went to his desk to consider what to write next.

***

Late in the afternoon, a group of Macedonian officers led by General Chrysogonus approached the King's tent. Alerted long before they arrived, Philip greeted them at the entrance.

"Is this what I think it is?" he bellowed. "Admiral Asterios, please tell me I'm correct."

"Twenty barges and ten triremes, my King," the Macedonian Admiral reported. "We can begin transporting men and equipment across at first light."

"Scanlan, did you get that?" Philip asked the youth. "Tomorrow, I make history. What do you think?"

"King Alexander used one hundred thirty-five triremes to cross the strait, my King," Scanlan replied. "And Xerxes I of Persia lashed together boats to build a bridge. Alexander burned his ships after crossing to show his commitment to the campaign. And a storm destroyed Xerxes bridge so the ruler had the water thrashed as punishment. How will you handle the crossing, lord?"

"Fourteen years ago on the Adriatic Sea, when the Roman Fleet came at me, I burned my fleet to save my army and rowers. This time, I'm keeping my five-bankers, three-bankers, and barges intact," Philip declared. "My army will have transportation both ways. I'll need the flexibility when I attack Pergamon next spring."

"The King of Macedonian remained unbending in his comment, nimble in his organization," Scanlan listed while making a note on a parchment, *"and flexible at all times to deal with any adversity."*

"And flexible at all times to deal with any adversity," Philip repeated. Then he invited the naval officers. "You'll feast with me tonight to celebrate."

They accepted because they had no choice. While servants filled glasses with wine, Philip eased over to Chrysogonus.

"General, I can't ever remember being this close to an enemy yet so far away," Philip admitted. "Station shield bearers on the beach and guard my vessels. If the militia from Abydos rows over to cause mischief, I want them to find mayhem."

"Yes, my King," the General stated.

The feasting and drinking, as Scanlan had discovered over the weeks, went on until near daybreak. At first light, the attendees splashed water on their faces, left the pavilion, and went to work transporting an army across the Hellespont.

***

Scanlan stood high on the embankment. From the altitude, he had a clear view of the far shoreline. A trireme towing two barges crossed the strait, angled left, and traveled north, staying just offshore. Sailors on the two barges threw lines to sailors on the beach. Once anchored, the trireme backstroked, and the barges were hauled to the shallows. The same thing happened up and down the Hellespont as Philip's army moved across one flatboat at a time.

Philip's trio of five-bankers watched the operation. If Abydos patrol boats decided to interfere, the smaller boats would be sunk. On shore with the supplies, shield bearers formed a barrier of shields against an attack as they unloaded.

Scanlan watched infantrymen carry the basket with the remains of Lieutenant Aetos. Behind the basket, a pair of shield bearers nudged Dimos and Pavlos, urging them to keep up. Despite their filthy robes, the clerics were unblemished and well fed. Scanlan had a bad feeling about the almost amicable treatment. They boarded a barge and waited as wagons were rolled onto the flatboat. Once loaded, the barge joined another in being towed across the Hellespont.

The historic crossing of the Macedonian army went smoothly even with the restrictions and insults directed at Dimos and Pavlos, the priests. No one understood the consequences of not being allowed to sacrifice to the Goddess Oizys, or who would receive her raw blessing of misery, anxiety, grief, depression, and misfortune.

Chapter 30 - An Enemy Army

The courier rode from the main gates of Abydos. On the walls behind him, militiamen, officers, and magistrates lined the ramparts. Picking his way between the stones and rocks the city's artillery had used to keep the Macedonian army away from the walls, the messenger arrived at the edge of the camp.

"I carry a message for King Philip," he announced.

"Wait right there lad," a soldier replied.

When the Macedonian didn't move, the courier questioned, "Aren't you going to tell the King there's a message for him?"

"You're the only entertainment this morning. Everyone knows you're here," the shield bearer told the messenger. "So you can bet the King knows, as well. You might as well dismount and save your horse."

From early in the morning to near midday, the soldier and the courier watched each other, neither speaking. On either side of the two men, shield bearers and hoplites ran drills, keeping their fighting skills sharp. Those on the walls of Abydos watched, never leaving their positions.

Before the sun reached the top of the sky, a rider came from King Philip's pavilion.

"Give me the message," Rank Leader Chronis instructed.

The courier handed over the message. When Chronis took it, the courier inquired, "Should I wait for a reply?"

Chronis shrugged and asked, "Should you?"

He rode back to the compound, leaving the confused courier standing with his horse and staring at the silent shield bearer.

***

King Philip unrolled the scroll, read the message from the Magistrate of Abydos, and tossed the missive to General Chrysogonus.

"He's as crisp as the father of a bride," Philip remarked.

The General read the message and handed it to Scanlan.

"Record that," Chrysogonus instructed.

Scanlan glanced at the words.

"Not very diplomatic are they, sir?" he remarked.

The youth placed the scroll on his desk beside a small and a large piece of parchment. He wanted to be prepared for the length of Philip's reply. Based on the note from Abydos, the response would be short.

King Philip, what are your intentions towards Abydos?
City Magistrate Kake

Philip paced the floor, thinking of ideas and discarding them with each lap of the pavilion. Finally, he stood still and pointed at Scanlan.

"Write this. Come with your top delegates, Magistrate Kake, and speak with the top envoy from Macedon."

Moments later, Rank Leader Chronis and scribe Scanlan Kasia left the pavilion and delivered the message to the courier.

On the walls of Abydos, after half a day of waiting, nerves were taut. The militia opened the gates just enough for the horse and rider to enter the city. Once he was through, they immediately slammed the gates closed.

"They're afraid of us, Rank Leader," the soldier commented.

"Not us," Chronis informed him. "They're afraid of King Philip."

"Same thing," the shield bearer boasted, showing his loyalty to Philip.

***

To facilitate the negotiations, servants constructed an open-sided tent. Then cooks built a fire, put a small pig on a skewer, and began roasting the pork. By late afternoon, Chrysogonus and Chronis trotted to the treaty tent and dismounted. Pulling his knife, the General sliced off two pieces of roast pig. He handed Rank Leader Chronis one slice. Holding the pork high above their mouths, in unison, they took bites and chewed contentedly. Next, they washed the meat down with wine. For those on the walls of the city, the consumption sent a clear message.

Philip had provided a tent, a table, chairs, wine, and a roasted pig. The tent and the food were ready, meaning the next step was up to Magistrate Kake.

When the gates opened, a column of cavalry appeared. The horsemen surrounded a military officer and a man in an extravagant robe.

The General and the Rank Leader spoke for a moment before Chrysogonus mounted and rode for the King's compound. Chronis remained at the treaty tent, waiting for the negotiators from Abydos.

***

When the principals separated from their cavalry escorts, the Macedonian Sergeant saluted and greeted the two dignitaries from the city.

"Gentlemen, welcome to the treaty tent. I am Rank Leader Chronis."

"I expected a person of higher status," the robed figure complained.

"Sir, we didn't know when you would arrive," Chronis explained.

"Well, we're here now," the militia staff officer declared.

"Sirs, if you would have a seat, we'll serve you refreshments until the Macedonian negotiator arrives," Chronis invited. He clapped his hands, and a servant poured wine and another brought a platter of roasted pork and rounds of fresh bread. The aromas caused the representatives mouths' to water. Once served, the Rank Leader informed them. "If you'll avail yourselves of the beverage and snacks, I'll signal for the Macedonian ambassador."

"Yes, yes. And hurry up," the robed figure insisted.

"Sirs, if I could have your names for the introductions," Chronis requested.

"I am Colonel Marios, commander of the city militia and this is the honorable Magistrate Kake," the military officer stated. "Now, where is the Macedonian delegation?"

"Sirs, I believe he's coming," Chronis assured him.

From the encampment, a low wagon pulled by a pair of gray mules traveled towards the treaty tent. At first, it was difficult to see what rode in the bed of the wagon. But as it drew closer, Colonel Marios and Magistrate Kake noted a pair of men seated in chairs with tables in front of them. Between the chairs rested a familiar basket. Before either Marios or Kake could react, the wagon pulled up beside the treaty tent and stopped.

"Gentlemen, may I present my File Leader," Chronis announced. "And the negotiator for Macedon, Lieutenant Aetos. He is escorted by Cleric Dimos and Cleric Pavlos from the Temple of Oizys."

A nasty aroma of Aetos' decaying corpse and the soiled robes of the priests floated over Marios and Kake. The delegates from Abydos leaped to their feet and fell back from the stink.

"What's the meaning of this?" Magistrate Kake challenged.

"Just a moment, sir. Allow me to check," Chronis proposed. He looked at the basket with the rotting corpse, then back to the Magistrate. "Sir, I'm afraid I have no answer. You see someone cut the Macedonian representative into pieces and he's unable to explain the situation."

Marios and Kake marched to their mounts on stiff legs. Obviously, they wanted to run from the scene, but dignity and decorum required them to walk to their horses.

As the calvary escorted them back to the city, Chronis instructed the servant, "Feed the priests and fill their wine glasses."

The gates of Abydos closed, and the city prepared for the first attack by the Macedonian shield bearers.

***

General Chrysogonus, in the King's pavilion, was of the same mind.

"We've ladders enough to breach two walls during the initial assault," the General reported. "Say the word King Philip, and we'll end their miserable lives."

"We have their dock and beach isolated," Philip mentioned. "The strait blockaded and the roads to the city closed. I think we'll wait and let the terror build."

"What terror?" Chrysogonus asked.

"I sent a dead man to negotiate with Magistrate Kake," Philip told him. "What message did that send?"

"That you aren't afraid a relief army will arrive to help them," the General offered.

"Exactly. A frightened man will do anything to survive and to get a peaceful night's sleep," Philip theorized before directing. "Run a few night attacks to keep them awake. But keep our men safe. I'll need them for the walls of Pergamon."

"Yes, my King," the General acknowledged before leaving the tent.

"What will you do with the priests, lord King?" Scanlan inquired.

"After they dig File Leader Aetos' grave, I'll release them to their temple," Philip answered. "Why do you ask?"

"I thought you might make an example of them in view of the city, sir," Scanlan answered.

"They served to stink up the treaty tent and to accompany the File Leader on his last assignment," Philip mentioned. "That's all I required of them. But tell me scribe, do you think they'll pray and sacrifice to the Goddess Oizys for my well-being?"

"That lord King, would depend on if they have the Roman's mania for cleanliness or a stoic's disregard for hygiene. People react differently after being tormented."

***

For the next few days, Files of shield bearers carried ladders to the walls in the dark and braced them against the stones. Next, they threw torches and rocks at the militiamen on the ramparts, yelled to wake the city, then took down their ladders and retreated. After each fake assault, lights showed militiamen flooding the area to stop the attack long after the Macedonians had gone.

At dawn of day five, an odd sight greeted the shield bearers. Ten armed and armored men with red cloaks, long spears, and large red shields appeared in two columns. A Legion staff officer, a combat officer, and a man with an unkept beard and a robe that could use a good washing walked between the lines of Legionaries. The strangers came from the strait and traveled directly to the King's compound.

"Romans," Philip said with recognition. "What are Roman's doing in the Aegean Sea?"

"Is there a restriction on who can sail the Aegean?" the staff officer inquired. "I'm Tribune Marcus Lepidus and I've been looking for King Philip."

"He's been right here," Philip responded with a thump on his chest. "I'm Philip and as you can tell from my greeting, I have not been looking for a Roman."

"We need to talk, King Philip of Macedon," Lepidus said, emphasizing the title.

"In that case, Tribune Lepidus, come into my tent so we can talk in comfort."

The Tribune and the King retreated into the pavilion. Selecting chairs, they faced off in a staring contest. Finally, Lepidus blew out a hard breath.

"Your actions of late are clearly a violation of the Treaty of Phoenice," the Tribune accused.

"Of late, I've been right here on the northern bank of the Hellespont," Philip uttered. "Before that, I was across the strait at the allied city of Sestos."

"I'm referring to your attacks on the shipping of Pergamon, the Isle of Rhodes, and Athens."

"Tribune, I barely have a fleet of warships," Philip protested. "How could I interfere with the shipping of my neighbors?"

"You've garrisoned almost every island in the Aegean Sea," Lepidus pointed out. "And now you have control of the Hellespont. Each port you control affects the shipping of goods by allies of Rome."

"So there it is," Philip announced. He got up and walked around the pavilion. "You're claiming a connection to the restrictions of the Treaty of Phoenice. But there is none. When I signed the agreement five years ago, the restrictions were to not attack territories of the Roman Republic. And to relinquish my holdings in Illyria and along the coast down through the Peloponnese. The regions mentioned are adjacent to the Ionian Sea and the Adriatic Sea. Tribune, today we are sitting on the far side of the Aegean Sea. An entirely different sea. See what I mean?"

"Philip, your actions are drawing you into another war with Rome," Lepidus warned.

"It's King Philip, Roman," he insisted. "As you've pointed out, I have no fleet to sink. But I have the Macedonian phalanxes, hoplites, loyal shield bearers, and Thessalian cavalry. My army says, I am the ruler of every city and region that touches the Aegean Sea."

"Pergamon, the Isle of Rhodes, and Athens are allies of Rome," Lepidus advised. "If you insist on molesting them, you will have to deal with the Legions of Rome."

"My capital, Pella, is two days sailing from the Hellespont," Philip told the Tribune. "How far away is your capital, Rome, from here?"

"You're tempting the Fate, King Philip," Lepidus noted as he stood.

"Or am I tempting Rome?" Philip challenged. "Why don't you come out with the truth. Rome covets Macedon's fertile farmland."

"No, King Philip, it's you who wants the farmland and resources of Rome's allies," Lepidus countered.

Philip glanced around before calling out, "Scanlan. Where are you, lad?"

***

Outside and away from the Tribune's protection detail, Scanlan talked to Tsolak of Fyli.

"Stoic. After he captures Abydos, Philip will march on Pergamon," Scanlan warned. "Tribune Lepidus needs to warn the city."

"He will, don't fret," Tsolak remarked. "Afterall, you sent the message, and the Tribune came to Abydos. For some reason, he trusts you."

Philip's voice came from inside the pavilion. "Scanlan. Where are you lad?"

"I have to go," Scanlan said.

"You can come with us," Tsolak proposed. "Next year we can see the plays of the Festival of Dionysus."

"I can't," Scanlan stated. "The greatest tragedy, comedy, and satire of my life are playing out right here, right now."

"From a theater seat, there is little chance of dying," Tsolak informed the youth. "This drama of yours is a deadly business."

Scanlan touched the hand of the Stoic before standing and racing into the pavilion. At the entrance, he collided with Tribune Marcus Lepidus.

As if the weight of the thin youth bent him forward, Lepidus said, "The Nightjar has soft feathers."

As if fending off the youth, Lepidus grabbed the lad's shoulders and pushed him back. Yet in the seemingly angry gesture, the Tribune hid a friendly squeeze of Scanlan's shoulders.

"Their feathers make poor fletches," Scanlan whispered as he stepped around the Legion officer.

Inside the pavilion, Philip was conferring with General Chrysogonus.

"Remember when we talked about no army coming to help Abydos," Philip remarked. "That's changed."

"What changed it?" Chrysogonus asked.

"The Romans have decided to interfere," Philip answered. "I don't want to get trapped between the Hellespont and the Legions. This siege has to end. We're taking Abydos in the morning."

***

The rousing of an enemy army at dawn was the second most terrifying thing in the world. At a distance, thousands of men slinging on armor, shields, and helmets blended together. From the walls of Abydos, the undulating mass of the army resembled a million ants crawling over the corpse of a dead animal. Not until squadrons of cavalry rode away from the camp and banners were unfurled and lifted into the air, did the army of Philip change from an unrecognizable carpet of activity to individual units of soldiers. Although the better defined Files of shield bearers and hoplites only served to increase the distress of the citizens, it didn't reach the supreme level of apprehension.

"The ladder porters will move to the front," Chronis described to Scanlan. "When the King gives the signal, shield bearers will shelter the porters all the way to the walls."

"What's the signal?" Scanlan inquired.

"You won't be able to miss it," the Rank Leader promised.

"I should ride to the King in case he has any final words before the assault," Scanlan suggested.

"You stay right here with me," Chronis stated. "The King is too busy for words."

Between the Macedonian army and the walls of the city, ahead of the ladder porters, shield bearers, and the heavily armored hoplites, Philip V Antigonid sat on his horse. When he kicked the animal in the flanks, he sent the mount racing across the front of his army. His soldiers responded to their King with a roar that echoed off the defensive walls and spilled over into the metropolis. It was then that the citizens of Abydos felt the most terrifying thing in the world. The rage of an enemy army outside their gates.

Chapter 31 - A King's Compassion

In a grove away from the battle zone at Abydos, Clerics Dimos and Pavlos lit a stack of aromatic wood. Once the flame burned at a steady rate, the two priests sprinkled herbs on the cedar wood sticks. As a cloud of pleasant smoke rose up through the trees in the grove, Dimos and Pavlos prayed.

"Goddess Oizys please accept our offering and bestow your blessings on the cruel culprit responsible for this battle."

Moments later, an invisible hand passed over Abydos. In its wake, an unhealthy dose of misery, anxiety, grief, depression, and misfortune smeared the Goddess' blessing over the area.

***

The rails of ladders ached over and slapped into the stones. As soon as the porters propped the ladders against the defensive wall, shield bearers began climbing. With their shields on their backs and spears clutched in one hand, the soldiers were almost defenseless. Helmets deflected arrowheads from archers and pebbles from slingers. But while the iron, bronze, or leather headgear resisted penetration, they offered little protection from boulders. As if giant pieces of hail, rocks rained down on the soldiers of Macedonia.

Some soldiers, when clobbered hard, lost balance and toppled off the side of their ladders. Others caught large rocks on their helmet, became disoriented, and tumbled backward onto the next climber. Both fell into the third which drew cheers from the defenders of Abydos.

At a fair distance, but still within an arrow's flight from the defensive wall, King Philip sat on his horse, ducking and dodging shafts as they whizzed by. Macedonian Kings might lead from the front, but they weren't suicidal. No one expected Philip to climb a ladder and face a barrage from the defenders of the city.

"We're taking too many loses," Philip observed.

"And making little progress," General Chrysogonus pointed out. "Orders, lord?"

"Withdraw the assault force," Philip instructed.

He turned his horse and trotted back to the camp. At the walls behind him, Macedonian shield bearers picked up their wounded, the porters lowered their ladders, and the assaulters raced away from the walls. From atop the ramparts, the loud celebration of the defenders sent a wave of depression over Philip's army.

***

King Philip stood outside his compound, saluting his returning soldiers. Between sips of wine, he exclaimed, "The walls were high and the defenders resolute. This we learned through the suffering of our wounded. But they learned nothing. Tomorrow, they will learn to fear us."

His speech, repeated over and over, lifted the spirits of his soldiers. By dark, the Files of shield bearers agreed. The militia of Abydos had learned nothing about the army of King Philip.

Later in the afternoon, a group of teamsters were herded into the King's pavilion. None had ever been inside the big tent. Even as they trembled in fear, curiosity caused them to peer around, looking for the opulence of a Macedonian King. To their disappointment, Philip required only a working tent with sturdy furnishings while on campaign.

"You teamsters have wagons," Philip remarked, which brought a chuckle from the nervous teamsters. "I need half of them."

"Yes, my King," one stated. "Take as many as you need."

"I'm not confiscating your property," he corrected. "I want the wagons stacked two or three high."

"For what purpose, lord?" another teamster inquired.

"See my engineer and he'll explain," Philip answered while waving them out of the pavilion. "Do what needs to be done but have it completed by dawn."

"How would you like me to record this meeting?" Scanlan inquired.

"Don't write it tonight," Philip told him. "Wait for morning to see it my idea works. I don't need a scroll stating how inept I am."

***

Sunrise found the Macedonian camp stirring and the soldiers dressing for combat. But on the day, wagons with other wagons stacked on top rolled ahead of the shield bearers and ladder porters. High up, archers and slingers occupied the upper wagon beds. Although not as high as the defensive walls of Abydos, the elevation made the defenders of the city targets for the arrows of the archers and pebbles of the slingers.

"Let the wagons pelt the defenders until they get in the habit of ducking," Philip directed. "Once the militia shows respect, we'll fake an assault on the walls."

"Sir, we have an advantage now," General Chrysogonus protested. "Why not take the walls and capture the city?"

"It's not much of an advantage even though the militia doesn't realize it, yet," Philip revealed. Then he expounded on the theory behind his hesitation. "Fear is a living thing. Easy to tamp down when it's just a sprout. But allow it to grow and fear can become a weight crushing down on a people's spirits or an army's motivation."

"You don't want the army to suffer another failed assault," the General acknowledged. "I'll pass the word not to press the assault all the way to the walls."

While they waited to begin the sham attack, the wagons pulled up online with the walls. Archers and slingers furiously launched projectiles. Soon, the defenders, while dodging the missiles, spent longer stints below the parapet than watching the approach.

King Philip, waving a sword overhead, kicked his stallion and raced across the forward ranks of his shield bearers. Despite the fake attack order, the soldiers roared their approval of the King.

The sound brought the less timid militiamen to their feet. Each collected a disproportionate number of arrows and pebbles. They dropped to their bellies and reported the advance of the Macedonian army. At that moment, the roots of terror took hold and the branches of fear grew heavy among the defenders.

After two fake assaults that came close to the walls but never placed the rails against the stone, the King dismissed the army.

Again, as he did the day before, Philip raced back and then waited for his soldiers to return to camp.

"The city militia will have nightmares of mighty shield bearers crawling into their beds tonight," he boasted.

Cheers greeted his exclamation as he repeated the speech for each File that marched by. The phrase would be recalled throughout the night, especially by guards on duty and their relief.

"Crawled into any militiaman's bed tonight?" a soldier would ask.

"As a mighty shield bearer for King Philip, I refuse to kiss and tell," the other soldiers would reply.

Philip's camp was confident. And even though they faced the defenders at the top of the ladders in the morning, the mood could be described as lighthearted. Unfortunately, after the first assault on Abydos at daybreak, the Goddess Oizys would end the cheerfulness.

***

File Leaders woke their Rank Leaders, and the Sergeants kicked their ranks of shield bearers out of their blankets. In moments, the camp came alive with soldiers strapping on armor, checking shields, the straightness of their spear shafts, and the edge of their blades.

"Grigoris, what happened to your spear shaft," the shield bearer's Rank Leader demanded.

He held the spear up to demonstrate the warp to the rest of the soldiers.

"It fell into a mud puddle last night," the shield bearer lied. "I pulled it out really fast but the damage was done."

"More like you fell asleep and didn't notice the water on your shaft," the Sergeant sneered. He took the bent spear and snapped it over his knee. "There, I've removed the bent part. Now, your shaft is perfect."

"But my spear is half the length it should be," Grigoris protested.

"Like the size of your half brain," the Rank Leader stated. "Get ready. I want you up the ladder first today."

"But I only have half a spear."

"Well, shield bearer Grigoris, that means you can climb faster," the Rank Leader informed him.

Grigoris whined while getting his gear on, but none of his rank mates paid any attention. As the resident problem in the file, he was constantly in trouble. When they marched out of camp, hands shoved Grigoris to the front.

"But I only have half a spear," he complained as they marched towards the walls of Abydos.

"The short shaft will help you climb faster," offered those behind him.

Dejected and sad, but knowing he had no choice, Grigoris marched to his fate.

***

King Philip sat on his mount, watching the wagons roll out ahead of his infantry.

"Today, General, we breach the walls or the walls will break my army," Philip remarked.

"I'm not sure that's totally true, lord King," Chrysogonus ventured. "Your men love you."

"We are Macedon," Philip reminded his General. "We love winners. And those walls are a test of my rule."

"In that case, sir, we should get on with conquering Abydos before they realize they only have two choices," Chrysogonus said, trying to bring a little levity to the King. "Fight us and lose or surrender to us and lose. It's that simple."

From the wagons, the archers and slingers thrashed the top of the wall. Their bombardment was so great, the defenders dared not show themselves. King Philip put heels to flanks and sent his stallion charging across the front of his shield bearers. With a roar, the infantrymen and porters bellowed their war cry and sprinted forward.

***

Shield bearer Grigoris ran at the head of his rank. At any moment, he expected to fall from an arrow, a slung pebble, or a thrown boulder. Beside him, the porters jammed the end rails into the dirt and shoved the tall ladder up and over. When the tips of the upper rails slammed into the defensive wall, hands grabbed Grigoris by the armor and pushed him to the first rung.

With his thoughts erased by anxiety, the soldier with the half shaft scrambled up the rungs. Faster than he expected, the shield bearer reached the top rung. Vaulting over the parapet, he landed with his legs spread and the pitifully short shaft held at an attack position. But no enemy was there to greet him.

Leaning over the wall, he called down to his Rank Leader.

"They're all gone," he yelled.

"You mean escaped in the night?" the Sergeant asked. "The whole town?"

"No, Rank Leader, they are all gone," Grigoris insisted.

***

A rank of shield bearers unbarred the main gate and pushed the doors open. King Philip and his scribe rode into Abydos. As soon as they were through the portal, Philip and Scanlan dismounted. After handing the reins to a groom, the two walked without escort down the main street.

"What a tragedy?" Philip uttered. He continued as they hiked down the street. "A senseless waste and an utter disregard for life."

Around them, the citizens of Abydos lay where they committed suicide or were slain by a zealot. Children looking surprised and their parents with horror frozen on their faces in death were stacked together. Merchants and militiamen, women and men, every person within the walls of Abydos had died a violent death.

"Why gods?" Philip seemed to pray. "Why this?"

Scanlan studied Philip's handsome but troubled face. In his mind, the scribe suffered a crisis of conscience. The Insubri youth had drawn a mental profile of a clever but cruel man. A competent ruler and an excellent General who cared only for his warriors. But now, in light of King Philip's contrition about the dead, Scanlan started to rethink his conclusion.

"Scanlan, see the metalworker sprawled beside his cold forge," Philip asserted. "I could have used his skills. As well as the talents of the other craftsmen from Abydos. And those strong bodies of the militiamen. They could have filled out my battle formation. Such a waste of flesh. Flesh, I could have used to further my conquest. May their souls, and those of the insane men who did this, rot in the lowest reaches of Hades. Come Scanlan, let's go find some wine, I need to get the taste of death off my tongue."

An exploration of the compassion of the heir to the Antigonid Dynasty, the ruler of all lands touching the Aegean Sea, and the King of Macedon, Philip V. On this day, when faced with the mass suicide of the citizens of Abydos, Philip offered prayers for the departed. As well, the King lamented the futures cut short by what must have been a gang of madmen. In the end, all he could do for the deceased was offer a toast to them for a peaceful afterlife.

Scanlan Kasia, scribe to the King of Macedon.

The End

Coming Soon:

***Provinces of Rome* series book #2**

Lies and Shadows

Coming later in 2025

Scanlan Kasia continues his work as the spy, code named Nightjar, in *Lies and Shadows*. With Rome declaring war on King Philip after the failed meeting with Tribune Marcus Lepidus, Scanlan takes on greater challenges and more responsibility in the Macedonian army. How deep undercover can a spy go before he turns a dark corner and joins the other side?

In *Lies and Shadows,* Scanlan's dubious loyalty to the Roman Legion gets tested. With every message passed to Tribune Lepidus and each face-to-face meeting with the stoic, Tsolak of Fyli, Scanlan stands a greater chance of being discovered. An unpleasant death is the consequence of exposure, while the rewards for success are a few coins from a Legion paymaster.

What started as a lark for an Insubri youth has become a game of avoiding the bright rays of truth while sticking to the deep shades of deception. As long as Nightjar remains obscure between light and shadow, he'll survive as a scribe to the Macedonian King and a Legion spy.

Come along with Scanlan as the great deception continues in book 2 of the *Provinces of Rome* series. Order your Kindle copy of *Lies and Shadows* today.

Author Notes:

Thank you for reading *Allies, Spies, and Conflicts*, book one in the *Provinces of Rome* series. It was a pleasure pouring over what little research I could find. Allow me to explain.

Information about the man, King Philip the Fifth of Macedon, was scarce. The battles he participated in, the foes he fought, and the areas he marched his army through, for those we have records. But personal facts about Philip V are few.

For instance, the mother of his son and successor Perseus, according to some historians, was Polycratia of Argos. But the mother or mothers of Philip's sons, Demetrius and Philip III Arrhidaeus, remain unknown. Of his Generals, we have Chrysogonus and Philokles but no others. For advisers at different times in his reign, history names Demetrius of Pharo, Aratus of Sicyon, and the mysterious Heracleides of Tarentum. The first two were historical figures and we know a lot about them. But what Philip's advisers accomplished or what specific influence they had on the King of Macedon remains pure conjecture.

Of course, for an historical adventure writer, the absence of facts allows for supposition, designing motivation through storytelling, and creativity within the confines of actual events. With all that stated, let's separate fiction from history.

Nightjar / Nighthawk

Both names describe medium sized nocturnal birds. Their soft plumage colored to resemble bark or leaves aids in hiding them from predators. The difference in designation comes down to location. In the Americas, the birds are known as Nighthawks while in Europe they are called Nightjars. Scanlan had to be Nightjar, as my books are Roman-centric.

Alexander the Great's General

In *Allies Spies and Conflicts*, Philip V, to further his argument, gives a derogatory description of Ptolemy's position in Alexander's army. This was my invention. In fact, Ptolemy was a trusted General, bodyguard for the King, and was at Alexander's bedside when the King died.

Battle Flags on Sails

The battle flags of Philip V of Macedonia and King Attalus I of Pergamon are not recorded. What has survived are images on coins from their era. On Philip's coin is a youth riding a prancing-stallion on one side and Philip's face on the other. For Attalus I, his coin shows the heads of two bulls facing each other, while on the other side of his coin, a helmeted head of the Goddess Athena. In the book, I used the imagery of the prancing-stallion and the facing-bulls on the sails to identify the flagships.

Battle of Chios

Prior to the sea battle, Philip V attacked and captured the Egyptian fleet on the Island of Somas. Shortly after capturing the Egyptian fleet, Philip island hopped to an adjacent island and besieged Chios Town. At least we believe the siege target was Chico Town on the island of Chios. Historian Polybius simply wrote, *"Philip had been digging away beneath the Chians' walls when the news came of the allied fleet's arrival."*

King Attalus I and his Pergamon Fleet, allies, and a fleet from the Island of Rhodes arrived and threatened Philip's supply lanes. Lifting the siege of Chios, Philip set his fleet in a battle formation and attacked the gathering fleets.

Historian Polybius also gave us an approximate size of the opposing fleets. At the Battle of Chios, Phillip V of Macedonia commanded fifty-three decked warships plus smaller ships against his opposition's sixty-five major warships and smaller vessels.

Polybius continued, *"…during the battle Attalus I of Pergamon, having become isolated from his fleet and pursued by Philip, was forced to run his three ships ashore, narrowly escaping by spreading various royal treasures on the decks of the grounded ships, causing his pursuers to abandon the pursuit in favor of plunder."* I absolutely loved this passage from the ancient historian and the opportunity to bring the scene to life in *Allies, Spies, and Conflicts*.

Admirals of Rhodes

Admiral Theophiliscus, commander of the first fleet from Rhodes, was wounded at Chios. He survived to deliver his final report to the Council of Rhodes before collapsing and dying. Admiral Cleonaeus commanded a second fleet that fought Philip V at Lade. There are no records that their fleets were designated by a Rose or a Sun. Both, however, were symbols of the Island of Rhodes.

Athens

The Pnyx was a hillside in central Athens, southwest of The Acropolis, where the Assembly of Athens met. At the time of *Allies, Spies, and Conflicts,* the Assembly may have moved to the larger Theater of Dionysus, south of the Acropolis. I used the Pnyx because I loved the idea of people crowded onto a hillside with a stonemason working on a wall while the Assembly held its meeting. According to historians, the safety wall at the Pnyx was never completed.

The Acropolis of Athens, featuring the Parthenon, a temple of the Goddess Athena, dominated the city of Athens. Of particular interest for this story, Athena was the Greek Goddess of Wisdom, War, and Crafts. I used the three traits to define the three fictional representatives sent to Rome. While we don't know the names of the Greeks who traveled to Rome and asked for help against Philip of Macedonia, we do know that the Roman Senate sent three officials to Greece: Proconsul Claudius Nero, Praetor Publius Sempronius Tuditanus, and Tribune Marcus Aemilius Lepidus.

Long Walls of Athens

In 200 B.C., the long walls of Athens that guarded the harbor and ran to encompass the city were still standing. In historical fiction novels, writers often put elements in their stories that sound good but are only era adjacent. I try not to resurrect artifacts that would have been gone by the time of my stories or use quotes from people not yet born. For instance, the Colossus of Rhodes fell in 226 B.C. Ambassador Aeson in *Allies, Spies, and Conflicts* would not have experienced the majestic statue in the harbor. In an earlier series, I managed to have fictional character Alerio Sisera from *Rome's Tribune*, book #14 in the *Clay Warrior Stories* series, pass under the giant statue of the Sun God Helios. As for Athens, the long walls existed in 200 B.C. They would stand until taken down by Roman General Sulla in 86 B.C.

The Dying Gaul

My tale of the Dying Gaul contains a few guesses. I did them to compress the story of Pergamon leader Attalus I Soter's defeat of the Gauls. The bronze statue in the public garden to commemorate the victory is historically accurate, although the statue has been lost to the ages. Today, a marble replica of The Dying Gaul is on display at the Capitoline Museum in Rome.

Alexander meets Diogenes

There are many versions of the meeting between the young King Alexander of Macedon and the stoic philosopher Diogenes of Sinope. I may have embellished it, but I'm a novelist, not a historian. *"Move aside, you're standing in my light,"* said to a warrior King was dangerous and served to dramatize Diogenes' disregard for authority, wealth, and correctness. And *"If I weren't Alexander, I'd be Diogenes,"* supposedly gives us an insight into Alexander's feelings about stoicism, or possibly a wish for a life free of responsibilities.

The Goddess Cybele

In 204 B.C., warning signs in the Republic showed the Gods were offended. They included meteor showers, failed harvests, famines, and snakes entering temples. The omens drove Rome to fear their imminent defeat. It was understandable, as Hannibal Barca campaigned throughout southern Italy, and defeat was a real possibility. The Senate consulted the Sibylline oracle books and the Oracle of Delphi.

Livy wrote, *"Whensoever a foreign enemy should bring war into the land of Italy, he may be driven out of Italy and conquered, if the Idaean Mother should be brought from Pessinus to Rome..."*

Pessinus was a part of Pergamon and King Attalus I Soter gladly assisted the Romans. He sent a black stone representing the Goddess Cybele and priests of her cult to Rome. This fulfilled the directions of the Oracles and pleased the Senate and citizens of the Republic. If nothing else, this act should have moved the Senate to defend Pergamon against Philip V of Macedonia. Yet it wasn't enough to secure Rome's help on the first vote.

I wrote of the arrival of the Goddess Cybele to Rome in *A Legion Archer* series, book #8 *The General's Tribune*.

Macedonian Dynasties

Philip II and his son Alexander the Great were from the Argead Dynasty. Philip V descended from the Antigonid Dynasty and was not related to Alexander the Great.

Although the ancient Macedonians didn't use surnames, in sections of this book, I inserted the dynasty name to separate and dispel any claim of Philip V being related to Philip II.

Sulpicius Galba

Sulpicius Galba attempted to get the Senate of Rome to declare war on Philip V of Macedonia but failed. Even a plea, done once Galba became Consul, was voted down. Not long after the measure was defeated, Galba called the Senate back into session and delivered a speech stating that Philip V was as dangerous as Greek King Pyrrhus and Carthaginian General Hannibal Barca. The threat of another invader attacking Italy convinced the Senate to declare war on Macedonia.

Three Roman Ambassadors

I combined Galba's speech about war against Philip with the appointment of Tribune Marcus Lepidus, Praetor Publius Tuditanus, and Pro-consul Claudius Nero. The three were sent to Greece on a goodwill tour to assure Rome's allies, especially Egypt, Pergamon, and Rhodes, that the Republic was strong after the war with Carthage.

The appointment of the three in the Senate and any scenes with the historical figures are fictional. Although Tribune Marcus Lepidus did meet with Philip V at the Siege of Abydos. Other than a few instances, we have limited knowledge of their travels. As a historical fiction writer, I am grateful for the lapse in the documentation.

The Peace of Phoenice

The First Macedonian War ended in 205 B.C. with the signing of the Treaty of Phoenice. In the document, Philip was forced to give up his holding on the west coast of Greece, from Illyrian to the Peloponnese. And to promise not to invade or be aggressive towards Rome.

The Death of Gaius Ampius

Consul Publius Aelius ordered Gaius Ampius, the commander of his auxiliary Legions, to move directly into Boii territory. While the Consul took his Legion forward on an easier route, Ampius' Legions discovered grain fields ready for the harvest. As the less disciplined auxiliary Legions began cutting grain, spearmen of the Boii Tribe attacked. Gaius Ampius was killed in the fighting and the survivors of his Legions retreated to the Consul's Legions. While Historian Livy gives a good accounting of the operation, I shortened the action to fit this story. Also, the Legions of Consul Publius Aelius marched on the Boii in the fall of 201 B.C., meaning I moved the date to fit the book.

Aristophanes

Greek playwright, 446 B.C. - 386 B.C., Aristophanes wrote forty plays but only eleven plays survived through the ages. In *Allies, Spies, and Conflicts*, Scanlan Kasia used the premise of Aristophanes' satire, *The Wasp*. He brought Senior Tribune Clario Moresina out of his physical and emotional shock by asking him if he was addicted to armor. This was the same argument used on the father in *The Wasp* when they questioned if the father was addicted to the courts.

Attack on Chalcis

Historian Livy wrote, *"On this information Pro-Consul Claudius Nero proceeded to Chalcis, and although he reached Sunium early enough to allow of his entering the strait of Euboean the same day, he kept his fleet at anchor till nightfall that his approach might not be observed."*

During the raid, Philip V of Macedonia's stores of grain, siege engines, artillery pieces, shield, and blades for his army were destroyed. One can only think that the loss of so much equipment hampered Philip's eventual attack on Athens.

There was no war chest in Chalcis. I created that to carry the story. Also, commander of the city's defenses was not executed by Philip V of Macedon. Sopater died during the attack by Romans and Athenians.

The Dardanelles Strait

Today, the strait that divides Europe from Asia and connects the Aegean Sea with the Sea of Marmara is called the Dardanelles Strait. In ancient times, the Greeks called the watercourse the Hellespont. Throughout history, the Hellespont has been the gateway from one region to the other. Of the many armies to cross the strait, two stand out. Xerxes I in 480 B.C. linked boats across the Dardanelles to create a bridge for his Persian army to invade Greece. Conversely, Alexander the Great in 334 B.C. crossed the Hellespont with his Macedonian army to invade Persia.

Abydos and Pergamon

In *Allies, Spies, and Conflicts*, we have the siege of Abydos (200 B.C.) before the attack on Pergamon. Historically, Philip V laid siege to Pergamon in (201 B.C.) For the sake of the story, I've moved events around to help compress time and help with continuity.

Abydos

Tribune Marcus Lepidus arrived at Abydos during the siege. The Tribune proposed that Philip's aggression against allies of Rome violated the Peace of Phoenice. Philip disagreed, and the two argued. After Lepidus departed, Philip continued the siege. And soon afterward, the history turned more horrible than fiction.

The siege of Abydos ended with most of the citizens committing suicide. I couldn't find a definitive answer as to why they feared being captured by the Macedonian King. But as I've stated before, missing motivations in ancient events are fodder for a historical fiction writer.

***

Thank you for reading *Allies, Spies, and Conflicts*. I love researching and writing what will be the Provinces of Rome series. If you enjoyed this book, consider leaving a written review on Amazon or Goodreads. Every review helps other readers find my books.

I welcome emails and your remarks. If you have comments, e-mail me.

E-mail: GalacticCouncilRealm@gmail.com

To get the latest information about my books, visit my website. There you can sign up for my monthly newsletter. In every newsletter, I start with an original article about ancient history before giving you updates on my books. Please note, I do not use AI to write any part of my newsletter or my books. Nor will I ever sell your e-mail address. So sign up at:

Website: www.JCliftonSlater.com

Other books by J. Clifton Slater

Provinces of Rome series, set during the 2nd Macedonian War

#1 Allies, Spies, and Conflicts
#2 Lies and Shadows

A Legion Archer series, set in the backdrop of the 2nd Punic War

#1 Journey from Exile
#2 Pity the Rebellious
#3 Heritage of Threat
#4 A Legion Legacy
#5 Authority of Rome
#6 Unlawful Kingdom
#7 From Dawn to Death
#8 The General's Tribune
#9 When War Gods Battle
#10 Salvation of Exile

Clay Warrior Stories series, set in the backdrop of the 1st Punic War

#1 Clay Legionary
#2 Spilled Blood

#3 Bloody Water
#4 Reluctant Siege
#5 Brutal Diplomacy
#6 Fortune Reigns
#7 Fatal Obligation
#8 Infinite Courage
#9 Deceptive Valor
#10 Neptune's Fury
#11 Unjust Sacrifice
#12 Muted Implications
#13 Death Caller
#14 Rome's Tribune
#15 Deranged Sovereignty
#16 Uncertain Honor
#17 Tribune's Oath
#18 Savage Birthright
#19 Abject Authority

Gygax Odyssey series, historical fantasy set in 607 B.C.
Historical novels inspired by stories passed down from Ernest Gary Gygax, the co-creator of the board game Dungeons & Dragons.
(Co-written with Luke Gygax)
#1 The Gygax Odyssey
#2 Wrath of the Cyclops

Printed in Dunstable, United Kingdom

69120515R00201